RUST

SUSANA K. MARSCH

ISBN:0-9987866-0-8
ISBN-13: 978-0-9987866-0-5

To Dad, Mom, Victor and Faduita

I would like to thank my dear family and all my friends who have supported me in this new venture, particularly Regina, whose insight and knowledge brought my characters to life, and Ana Maria Guardia, whose artistic instruction has inspired me for many years.

I would also like to thank Maureen Brady for her valuable revision and critique.

Table of Contents

CHAPTER ONE

The Funhouse

His name was Mike Monroe. He called me over as I ran out the door pale and trembling, while my house screeched behind me like a car crushed at a junkyard, and offered me coffee on his porch. The warmth of the cup steadied my nerves.

"Young man, ya don' know what ya've gotten yourself intah, do ya?" He said taking a sip, "It's been almost twenty yeahs and I can't forget it, I'm not surprised the house hasn't forgotten eithah."

"What happened here?" I asked.

"The realtah didn't tell ya?"

I shook my head.

He glanced at me and sighed. There was doubt in his eyes, as if he wasn't sure he should tell me. I'd seen him since I moved in and he'd always seemed nice, yet reserved. This was the first time we'd interacted beyond the occasional wave and "how aah ya?".

"Listen, kid, I'm gonna tell ya the whole story, just as she told me. Remembah, these are *her* words, not mine."

Mike Monroe took another sip and began. His husky old-man's voice broke through the lazy quiet of the summer afternoon. As I listened, the words became pictures, and the pictures became words on paper, thus portending the next story I was going to write and the woman that would shape it.

It wasn't so much the stench of blood that bothered her, but the taste in her mouth; metallic, reminiscent of rust on her long-forgotten bicycle. She hadn't used that bike since the fifth grade; when she had let it drop on the grass in the front yard, running straight for the house, unaware of the unsettling silence surrounding it.

She had run into the parlor trailing mud from her white sneakers, while the screen door had slammed behind her, making a loud thwack as it hit the door frame, followed by a quieter one as it bounced back and finally settled in place. Back then, she couldn't have possibly known what was happening in the living room. There'd been no indication of

1

anything wrong beforehand, no hint that her grandfather would be dying while she happily rode her bike up and down the street; but years later, she would remember it as the before-and-after moment of her life.

Now that moment seemed so far away, so unimportant, insignificant. Funny, how it had once been paramount in the shaping of her person, yet now seemed so puny she probably wouldn't even have thought of it, if not for that metallic taste in her mouth; the taste of a rusty bicycle, the taste of blood.

The smell remained in her nostrils as she stood in the parlor, the same screen door closing noisily behind her. Everything seemed as it should be, but there was something wrong, something eerie about the place. She felt as if the house and her whole life had been violated, yet everything seemed in order.

She cautiously started up the stairs, the sensation of lingering violence growing stronger with each step.

She dared not speak, lest she rip apart the ghostly silence that suffocated the house and bring more violence into being with the sound of her voice. It seemed as if this unnatural silence had created a vacuum somewhere deep in the walls and sucked away all comfort and safety, which normally defined this home.

As she opened the door to her brother's room, her memory jumped back to the day so long ago when she had run in with muddy shoes, expecting to find a smiling mother and the much promised afternoon snack of milk and cake.

It had not been so then, and somehow, now, she knew that she would not find her brother asleep. He was on his bed, yes, but his face was turned toward the door, his eyes wide open in terror and blood spilled down the side of the bed from his gutted body.

She staggered back, and trembling, moved down the hall to her parents' bedroom. The door was slightly ajar. She pushed it open as the reek of blood hit her full on. They were on the bed; their bodies hacked, blood creating pools on the carpet and splattered on the walls. There was so much of it. It seemed to eat into the plaster. It poisoned the air and defiled all relics of happiness, family, childhood and innocence.

The house was silent, it was an eerie quiet, and yet, deep inside, she knew she was alone in that big, dead house. She knew 'they' were gone. Only a few hours before, the house had been empty, but even with her father at work and her mother and brother at the park, there had been life pulsing through it. Now, it was full of death, and she was alone in that tomb.

She could stay there no longer, not among the destruction of all that she held dear. Woozy and faint, she ran down the stairs. She passed the living room where she had found her family that day far in the past, kneeling beside the couch and sobbing as her beloved grandfather had taken his last breath. She flew out the door, death clinging to her, and despair leaving a wake of malodorous rupture in the night air.

"What became of her?" I asked. He finished his cup and set it down on the window-ledge behind him.

"I dunno. I remembah she said she ran to her boyfriend's. Some guy lived not so fah away. The police came and went y'know, but never found nothin'. They watched for weeks an' knocked on our doahs for months, but nothin'. They never did catch who did this. All I saw was the doah gapin' open. I called the police, y'know."

He looked up at the house across the street. It stood, gloomy and dark, at the end of the lane, surrounded by the thick, tall trees of the forest. I followed his gaze; I knew there was something wrong about this house, the darkness within it was different—it was heavy. And the old man was right, there was a metallic taste to the air inside.

"Anna," he said out of the blue and I froze at the sound, "her name was Anna, boy's name was Tommy, Beth an' Paul were the parents. Last name Jenkins. I saw her y'know, the day she left with nothin' but a suitcase. Just walked out the doah. I was standin' right heah', tendin' the roses when she walked by an' I talked to her, called her ovah, y'know. Her face was all sad an' pale an' her eyes were sunken as she said goodbye. Said she'd go stay with her boyfriend for a while an' then an aunt up in Maine. That's all I know. But y'see, I was lookin' right in her eyes an' when I told her I'd pray for her an' her family, I saw a glint, like a spark light up from way inside, an' I swear there was somethin' evil about that look, an' it gave me the chills. 'Twas ninety degrees out heah an' I was cold as ice. I watched her walk down this street an' I remembah thinkin' to m'self: that girl had somethin' to do with it all."

"Nobody heard anything? Screams, anything like that?" I asked, trying to maintain my composure. 'Anna' was the word that rang out through the house at night.

"Now you're stahtin' to sound like the cops did back then. Nah, it was Memorial Day weeken' an' the Dawsons an' Connors were already gone for the holiday. My wife (God rest her soul) was deaf, so thankfully she didn't know nothin' of what went on. I was workin' the late shift for the Big Dig back then an' it was gettin' to be our busiest time. Aftah all, buddy, this is Boston, there's only two seasons: wintah' an' construction. I was turnin' onto our street when I saw someone duckin' into a yahd, but thought nothin' of it till I got to the Jenkins house and saw the doah wide open. It was past midnight, so I called the cops. Anna told me latah she hid behind a hedge cuz she thought it was them comin' back for her."

I asked him a few more questions about the investigation, but he knew next to nothing. He said the police had kept a tight lid on the whole thing and that the papers didn't really cover the murders much. Politics had been the order of the day back then. He remembered they had asked him what the family was like and whether he thought the girl could've done it.

"I said no way, sweet girl like Anna, nevah. But that was befoah she said goodbye, befoah I saw that evil in her eyes."

Apparently, the police couldn't find any convincing evidence, and no motive was clear.

We talked for a while longer. He was a big man and I could tell he'd been quite muscle-bound back in the day, your typical construction worker. Now he was gray-haired and had a musty smell about him.

He told me how this was once a quiet street where most people knew each other; Anytown, USA really. They kept their doors unlocked and their yards clean. They waved and talked and had coffee together. Dinner parties almost every week. He said it used to be all friendly and whatnot. He told me the family was nice, quiet, and nothing suspicious ever went on there. They weren't noisy or disrespectful, they were good people, he said with a shake of his head; good people.

I asked him to tell me again what had made him think that the daughter had had something to do with it. I couldn't really say the name, the house said it too often. He shook his head and said,

"Just a feelin' y'know. Like a hunch. Somethin' about her eyes that day she said goodbye. They scared me shitless. Then lotsa pieces stahted fallin' into place, y'know, details that you only think of aftahwahds. I told the cops, but they said it wasn't enough."

He described how Anna always seemed more detached and distant than the rest of her family. How she was often cold and mean to her much younger brother. Little things she did and said—he couldn't really remember now—but it had seemed right back then. Seemed right still.

There was a stark contrast between the Anna in his story and the Anna now. He said that just as Anna had told him her grandfather's death was the before-and-after moment in her life, for him there was a "befoah and aftah 'The Look'".

"Have you heard from her, did she ever come back?" I asked.

"All I can tell you is what I've already told ya, kid," he nodded towards the house, "there's been people movin' in for a while an' then they leave. Just up an' leave, y'know. The last time 'twas a couple a yeahs ago, a young family about your age with small kids. They weren' heah' two months when they just up an' got in their cah' one night. Left the doah wide open an' everythin'."

He looked up at the house and shook his head again, "Yeah, somethin' ain' right about that house, just like somethin' wasn' right about that girl. I can only hope her aunt in Maine is still alive. "

I looked up and down the street and realized for the first time that none of the houses looked inviting. Yes, the stoops were clean and flowers bloomed in the sunshine, but there seemed to be invisible dark clouds hanging over them, like miasma.

Could this horrible incident be permeating the walls of the other houses on this street too, staining their lives with grief and fear? The old man said that no one locked their doors before. Now they go on with their daily lives, but always looking behind, jumping at shadows, unable to separate themselves from the carnage that happened next door.

I wish I'd known the extent of the damage before I'd bought the Jenkins house for a song. This was not something that can be painted over.

I walked back to the house and smelled the rust scent as I climbed the stairs. It was always there, like a trail leading from the front door to the parlor and up the stairs to the small hallway. There were two bedrooms on the left and the master bedroom on the right. The bathroom was at the end of the hall. The master bedroom had a bathroom of its own.

When I bought the house, I figured once I was finished renovating, the smell of rust would be gone. I even told the workmen to look for anything rusty and let me know what could be done about it. They didn't find anything, and now the house is done, with brand new doors and freshly plastered walls, but the scent remains.

I went to the master bedroom—my bedroom—and gulped. My bed was ruffled and the closet doors were opened wide. Things and clothes were strewn about the room, and I took deep breaths in an effort to calm myself down. This was new, the house had never done this before, it had never touched my things. I stood in the doorway trying to decide whether to walk in and clean up or sit down at my desk and write. I closed my eyes, but the images of murdered parents were still on my mind, and the mess in my bedroom was not distraction enough to remove them. I couldn't help but imagine blood splattered over my newly painted walls and it made my skin crawl. Mike Monroe's account was all too vivid, and I shook, not just from fear, but from the need to write it down. The words still rang out in my head and, in spite of the impression they'd caused, I held onto them, lest they should curl up in the back of my mind and torment me in my dreams. I knew that once I wrote, once Mike's account was visible on paper, the images it formed would not be so horrifying anymore. Once they were out of my system I might be able to relax. *Maybe you can even get this published, Johnny-Boy, cross over into another genre.*

I went into one of the small bedrooms, which I had turned into an office, and sat down at my desk. It faced the window that looked out on my backyard. The yard itself turned seamlessly into the woods. I don't know why, but I always thought of Rivendell, The Last Homely House, as if the backyard was the final outpost looking out into The Unknown. When I first bought the house I even toyed with the idea of putting up a lamppost at the farthest end (my very own tribute to Narnia), but now I wasn't even sure I could live here much longer. It wasn't really homey at all.

I wrote and the evening crept up around me, the light from my monitor eerily casting blue shadows on my bookcases. I rubbed my eyes and stretched. I was done with my draft and now it was time to clean up the mess in my bedroom. I went in, opened the window and began putting things away. On my bed, a big plastic box laid on its side, its contents spilled out like guts. I knew that box, it was full of my grandfather's things, and I had taken it from my parents' house as they'd cleared everything when they'd moved to Maryland a couple of years ago. It had sat unopened in my old cubby-hole apartment and I had brought it with me to this house.

I felt a pang of sadness as I put everything back into the box. His blue wool scarf, a couple of books, his reading glasses, and finally, a notebook that had "Adams Family History" handwritten on its cover. I was about to open it when a strange, cold breeze blew through it, its pages flapping from beginning to end, and I thought I heard the breeze whisper my name. My heart jumped and I quickly stuffed the notebook in the box, closed the lid and shoved it way into the back of the closet. *You're losing your mind, Johnny-Boy*, I thought, and yet, I had this strange feeling that notebook was some kind of harbinger, and I was right on the verge of unearthing something frightening. I felt I was in a different dimension, like the stuff around me wasn't real, like I was in some kind of dream, just about to discover its meaning, when my stomach grumbled and the spell was broken.

I took a deep breath and looked around. I had put away everything. Right, time to get something to eat. I looked out into the black hole the woods became every night, trying to decide whether to make myself a sandwich or go out, when I noticed I couldn't hear the crickets chirping from the open window.

It was coming, I knew it by now. Everything went quiet moments before, as if it needed to draw a deep breath and suck in all that existed.

"ANNA!" the house screamed, the sound coming from inside its very walls. It was louder every time; what had begun as an almost imperceptible whisper when I moved in had turned into a harrowing scream.

I grabbed my wallet and went to the small diner a couple of blocks away. I was becoming a regular there, and as I nibbled on the sandwich the waitress brought me, I thought about what was going on in my house. Doors would be slamming and lights would be flickering. It seemed that whatever remained in its walls drew its power from light and sound. Then the screams, blood-curdling 'aaarghs' and pleas of "no, wait" and finally the horrible rumbling, as if the house caved in on itself. Then nothing after that, not even the creaking of wood or the settling of the foundation. Moments later it would all be normal: the sounds of the forest coming in from the open windows, the hum of the refrigerator as it started up, even the lightbulbs would shine brighter.

As I paid the check, it occurred to me I could've had the exact same meal at home. I could've eaten outside on my deck looking out at the woods with a nice cold beer and it would've been much cheaper too. I decided it was time to put an end to this business.

When I first saw the house I imagined myself living here, a yet non-existent wife by my side, little juniors at our feet. But now, I couldn't wait to get away from it. At thirty-two, my career had just taken a turn for the best—I was becoming successful as a writer, and I finally had the means to own a home. Peaceville wasn't the swankiest neighborhood in the Boston area, but it was close to the city without the posh suburban feel. All in all, the house was exactly what I was looking for and I considered myself lucky to have found it in my price range. It had everything within walking distance, but the woods behind it gave the isolated feel I was looking for.

Why don't you just leave, Johnny-Boy, just pack up and call it a day, I thought, and immediately stopped the fantasy. I couldn't leave. There was no way I would ever sell it above what I had paid, however cheap it had been. My grandfather had left me a pretty good inheritance, but I had spent most of it on my education and career, on the house and furniture and, while my best friend, Mark, the Engineer, had taken care of the renovation at a discount, I had given a good down payment, to lower the mortgage. It had been an excellent deal at the time.

My financial situation wasn't dire, but I couldn't afford another place without selling this one, especially not at a loss. I'd thought about asking my parents for money, but they seemed to be finally enjoying themselves after retirement, and I didn't want to seem like a whiny kid who quit at the slightest obstacle. Asking my sister was out of the question; she's been telling me for the past few years how she hoped my artistic profession would pull us both out of poverty someday. She joked, but somehow, I felt there was truth behind it. And besides, the house was perfect for me; I just hadn't counted on it being haunted.

The problems started a couple of weeks after I moved in; around Memorial Day, now that I think of it. At first it was only a feeling of dread, whispers, creaks, drafts; but now, on some nights, it turned into a real house of horrors. It had to stop. I decided on my walk back I would find out what really happened and see if that would put the house to rest. My sister loves ghost stories and has always told me that hauntings stopped when the mystery of ghosts' deaths was solved or whatever they had left undone was finished, so I figured I needed to find the killer and solve the murders to bring some closure.

I had plenty of clues from my conversation with Mike Monroe. I would look for this Anna Jenkins in Maine. A Google search would be a good start, I thought, as the house loomed before me, as dark and uninviting as I had left it.

Always terrified of ghosts and things that go bump in the night, I looked up at the house and realized I was literally living my worst nightmare. I tugged up my jeans and made my way to the front door. I was certain I'd lost some weight since all this had started, and now, as I trembled and opened the door, all the courage and resolve I'd felt on my walk was slowly fading in the face of the sinister darkness. I took a deep breath and stepped in.

I ran up to my office, turning on the lights as I went. I always turned on every light in the house even though by now I knew it did no good; when the voices started, the house always went dark. But still I felt better. It was emasculating, but I felt safer.

"Johnny-Boy, you're such a wuss" I said to myself, "you're such a lily-livered, pansy-ass wuss."

Everyone calls me Jack. My grandfather was the only person who ever called me Johnny-Boy, and, since I can remember, he's always been my own Talking Cricket. His is the voice of reason in my head and it always calls me Johnny-Boy.

"Look at you, Johnny-Boy, talking to yourself and afraid of the dark like a little girl. It's time to man up," I said, "it's time to take your house back."

So I sat at my desk and googled Anna Jenkins. Not surprisingly, the first link that came up was to the Peaceville Daily News. It was a digital transcript of the short article published after the unsolved Jenkins murders in Peaceville. It contained pretty much the same information as Mike Monroe's account, except that there was no mention of anybody hiding out in the bushes. There was even a quote from Mike himself on finding the bodies. It also stated the police were still searching for the murder weapon and that no suspects had turned up.

The next couple of links lead to Facebook or Twitter accounts, but there was no way of knowing which was the Anna Jenkins I was looking for. I knew she was a teenager in the nineties, since Mike had mentioned working on the Big Dig project, so she must be about my age now. None of the ladies on these accounts fell within my age range.

I scrolled further down and came across a link to the Osprey Cove Memorial Library. It led me to the Events page for 2013 which announced a lunch commemorating fifteen years since the death of the beloved librarian, Jennifer Jenkins, in December 1998. It also included a digital transcript of the original obituary and, as I read it, I froze.

"Ms. Jennifer Jenkins of Osprey Cove, Maine, passed away on Christmas Eve. She fell down the stairs of her home, fatally breaking her neck. She was found by her niece and only surviving relative, Anna

Jenkins. After a thorough investigation, detective Babcock of the Osprey Cove Police Department declared the death an accident."

It was nothing more than a few cold lines, but it was enough to confirm Mike's theory: this girl was a modern-day Lizzie Borden—she left a trail of suspicion behind her, but never enough evidence to convict. I also wondered who'd written this morbid obituary, it seemed too detached to come from a loving relative.

I had my first clue. I searched for the Osprey Cove Police Department website and found the contact numbers. I would call the non-emergency line and ask for a detective Babcock. I looked at my watch and saw it was close to ten at night, surely there was no reason to bother anyone there now. I figured I could live through one more night of the house's shenanigans, and try to contact the detective tomorrow.

I leaned back in my chair and closed my eyes for a moment. I was suddenly exhausted and, even though I'm young, I felt ancient. A little embarrassed at myself, I decided to call it a night.

"Johnny-Boy," I said, "look at yourself; ya just turned thirty-two and you're already going to bed like a seventy-year-old man. What's next? Frequenting the early-bird special at the diner?" *Wacka wacka.*

I sighed. *I need to get out more*, I told myself as I headed to my bedroom.

I brushed my teeth and began undressing for bed. I had gotten one leg out of my jeans when the world went quiet again, so I looked up. There was blood dripping from the walls. It wasn't really dripping, more like being splattered from the inside out. More and more stains were appearing rapidly as the lights flickered. I felt cold and began to shake. When my breath turned to mist, I inexplicably began to laugh. It was a strange hysterical laugh at first, like a 'heeheehee', and as I realized how ridiculous I sounded, I threw my head back and guffawed, both at my inanity and at the absurdity of the situation. There I was, bare-chested and one leg still in my jeans, laughing my head off; a lone man in the Last Homely House.

"Really?" I said loudly, "Could you be any more clichéd? Blood on the walls and cold spots are so last century! It's all been done before!" and quoting *South Park*, I yelled, "Simpsons did it! Simpsons did it!" in a screeching, childish voice.

Then, I felt as if someone put their mouth to my ear and heard a strange distorted whisper, like the voice of a man, a woman and child all in one. "Keep you safe" it said. My heart stopped. I lifted the covers on my bed and dove in head-first like Superman, although in mid-change; the leg in my jeans a frightened Clark Kent and my bare leg a pathetic Man of Steel.

I pulled the pillow over my head and lay still for a long while. I was scared shitless. I had gone from ancient to childlike in a matter of moments, as if my life had happened in reverse—the old man exhausted after a long life, then the young man with a big mouth and a big bravado and finally the small child, helplessly hiding under the covers.

CHAPTER TWO

The Manly Man

I was in a smoldering desert and the air was so heavy I couldn't breathe. I had been walking for months, years even, and no matter how long, I couldn't get out of this never-ending wasteland. Sand dunes seemed to go on forever and the heat created a nebula that kept getting denser and closing in around me. I was trapped in this airless heat. I had walked long enough; I was exhausted. My legs failed me and I fell face down. The sand burned my cheek and got in my nose and mouth. I was suffocating slowly and could no longer move. *This is it*, I thought, *I'm dying*.

Then, Alice Cooper's voice came softly through the dense cloud of heat that surrounded me. I couldn't place the song at first but realized it was "Welcome to My Nightmare" as it got louder and louder. I gasped for breath and inhaled heat; sand slowly morphed into fabric. I opened my eyes and was surrounded by a blue silky film. I rolled onto my back and pushed the covers away from me. I breathed cool, refreshing air. I was sweating. My jeans were still half-on and I recalled the night before. I had fallen asleep under the covers and nearly suffocated from the heat beneath. *Stupid, Johnny-Boy, stupid.*

I rolled onto my side and turned the stereo off. "Welcome to My Nightmare" had ended and some singer I didn't recognize was beginning her dying-cat wails. I looked at my iPod, wondering why the fuck this was on it, and remembered that my ex-girlfriend had transferred some of her music to it. I suppose that musical style suited her—she too had wailed like a dying cat during our last conversation. I sat on my bed and rubbed my eyes. I finally finished pulling my jeans off and looked around. Everything seemed normal and quiet. There were no blood spots on my walls and no disembodied voices whispered in my ear.

I showered while mentally berating myself for my wussy behavior. There was no way I was going to get anywhere by diving under the covers every time the house decided to act up. I am a Man, I am a Man's Man, and I was not going to run scared over a little haunting.

"Last night will never happen again, Johnny-Boy" I said to myself as I pulled on a fresh pair of jeans and my Metallica wife-beater. Wife-beaters were manly, Metallica was manly, I was manly.

I flexed my muscles in front of the mirror and went to get some breakfast. But first things first; I grabbed my iPod off its dock and plugged it into my MacBook. I looked for the playlist titled "Megan" and permanently deleted everything in it. I smiled contentedly and went to get some grub.

The familiar scent of rust surrounded me as soon as I left my little office. It was always like this, as if it led the way to the murdered family. I wondered if Mike Monroe had smelled it too when he first called the police. I found it hard to imagine he hadn't—it was too strong to be imperceptible, and, by his account, Anna Jenkins certainly had.

I made myself a big manly breakfast of eggs and bacon and ate it outside on my deck. It was a beautiful day, and a soft cool breeze was blowing through the woods and into my little backyard. It lifted fallen leaves off the ground and made them dance to a ghostly midsummer's tune of crickets and cicadas. Birds were chirping in the trees and all seemed right with the world. I turned and looked up at the house. I fancied I saw a gray storm cloud above, as if the sun could never really break through and shine its warm healing light upon it. The windows seemed dark despite the bright morning and the sound of the breeze blowing in through the back door made a soft whispering "whooooo".

I sipped my coffee and looked at my watch. It was already nine in the morning. I would wait another half-hour or so before calling the Osprey Cove Police Department. I leaned back in my chair and closed my eyes. This was how life should be, calm, quiet, easy. No murders and no hauntings.

The breeze picked up and whirled dead leaves around me. I opened my eyes, and, amidst the flying leaves and dirt, I thought I saw a little boy. It was only for an instant, and as the wind blew the leaves away, I thought I heard the soft sound of a child's giggle. My stomach sank to my feet and I clamped the plastic armrests of my chair with sweaty hands. My heart beat so fast I could hear it in my ears. I quickly got up, grabbed my wallet and keys and almost ran out of the house. I got to my car and sat there for a minute. It was going to be a hot day and the car was already getting stuffy. I had to think. Where could I go? Should I just drive up to Osprey Cove, waltz into the police department and ask for Detective Babcock?

I pictured that scenario for a moment: young guy walks in, asks for a detective and tells him he thinks Anna Jenkins murdered her family and that his house is haunted. *No way,* I shook my head, *he'd have me in handcuffs in no time.* Best to give him a call and see what happens.

I reached for my phone and realized I'd left it in the house. *Shit.* I could've killed myself; now I had to go back into The Funhouse. That's what I called it now: The Funhouse; not Home, not My House, but, The Funhouse.

I climbed out of the car and made my way towards the front door. That's when the screaming started. Sitting in the car I hadn't noticed the world had gone quiet, and now the show had begun. I didn't want to go inside, so I simply sat down on my stoop and hoped that the goings-on wouldn't drain my phone's battery.

I heard the screams and what sounded like groans coming from inside the foundations themselves. I thought that I almost felt the house pulsing, as if what went on inside was trying to get out. The screaming continued, and the pleas, and what sounded like furniture moving around. *My* furniture.

That was it. I'd had enough. The house could mess with me, but it had better leave my stuff alone. Moving day had been a bitch and I wasn't about to clean up something else's mess. I stood up and pounded on the door.

"Stop it! Stop it right now!" I yelled. I sounded exactly like my father.

And like the teenage me, the house didn't care. It went on screaming and moaning, until it suddenly stopped with that earth-wrenching groan. Then, nothing. I stood for a moment, waiting for the familiar feeling that everything was back to normal and reached for the door. It opened without me touching it.

"Thank you."

I gave the door a nod and went inside. My heart began to pound; that burst of outrage and momentary sarcasm I had begun to use as a shield against my paralyzing fear placated.

The place was a disaster area. It looked as if a tornado, a hurricane and galactic explosion had all happened at the same time. Stuff had been thrown off shelves, chairs were broken and scattered everywhere, the couches were all upended and the dining room table was split in half. Inexplicably, the couch cushions were ragged and stuck to the ceiling.

"WHAT THE FUCK? I've had enough! I'm leaving now and when I come back this place had better be spotless! You hear me?" Now I sounded exactly like my mother.

"AND WHERE THE FUCK IS MY PHONE?"

Just then it rang. I looked for it in the rubble and found it in the kitchen beneath an overturned pot. The caller ID read "John Adams's iPhone". Great, my phone called itself now. I grabbed it and walked back out into the sunshine.

Mike Monroe was standing on his front lawn, staring.

"Hiya, Mike!" I gave him a nonchalant wave.

"How aah ya!" he answered in equal manner.

The Funhouse was grumbling loudly behind me, yet we both acted as if nothing was amiss.

"Termites, ya know," I nodded towards the house, "gotta call the exterminator."

"You got a guy?" he asked.

"Sure, I hear a guy up in Maine might like the job. He's a specialist in vermin that cause people to have fatal domestic accidents."

He lifted his eyebrows for a moment, in understanding I think, then he bowed his head and sighed. He shook his head and walked over to his mailbox.

"Give 'em hell, kid!" he called as I climbed in my car; the indignation, bravado and indifference gone the moment I closed the door.

CHAPTER THREE

Meet Pluto Babcock

I called the Osprey Cove Police Department and asked for Detective Babcock. After a brief conversation he agreed to meet me in person later. The drive up to Maine was uneventful and I got to Osprey Cove a little past lunchtime.

"Hi, I'm Detective Pluto Babcock, how may I help?" he extended his hand and I shook it.

"I'm Jack, how're you?"

We were standing in the Police Department and I thought 'Pluto' suited him well. Detective Babcock was short, fat and bald, just like a dwarf planet. He looked to be in his late sixties and was dressed in khakis and a white Polo shirt that was stained under the arms. He looked at me expectantly.

"Did you mind much when they demoted Pluto? Y'know, the planet?"

It was all I could think of to say, and the words came out of my mouth before I could stop them.

"Is this what you came here for? Look, kid, I got a ton of shit to do today. It's my last day on the job, so if you got anything useful, out with it." He frowned at me.

I stood, like the idiot I am, not saying anything.

"All right, have a nice day."

He turned on his heel and was about to walk away when I found my voice.

"Wait! I'm sorry, I didn't mean that," I called, "it's just... I don't know how to begin."

"You here to report a crime?"

"Well, yes...and no." I said, looking down at my shoes.

I hadn't felt this small and shy since I was a kid. All that manliness I'd felt this morning was gone in front of this man, however short he was. We stood there a while longer. Him looking up annoyed at me, and me looking down at him, rocking on my heels like a little boy.

"I've never talked to a detective before," I said, "and I don't know how to say this without getting into trouble."

"Did *you* commit a crime?"

"No, it's just that," I took a deep breath, "I think Anna Jenkins killed her family."

He lifted his eyebrows and led me to his desk. It was devoid of personal items and there were boxes all around it, as if he'd been packing everything up.

"State your name please?" he said, fishing around in a box and taking out a pad.

"Jack—um, John Adams."

"*John Adams?*" There was an almost imperceptible smirk on his face.

"Yah," I rolled my eyes, "like the Son of Liberty."

"How's that workin' for ya?" He was trying hard not to laugh now and I just sighed; this was my lot in life.

"Not very well, to tell the truth. Every history teacher I ever had made me write a report on the man. Got to the point where I just handed in the same report with a different date. I prefer 'Jack' though, it's the lesser evil."

"How so?"

"'Jack Adams' makes me sound like a pirate."

He threw his head back and laughed. It was a hearty, thick laugh and I couldn't help but join in.

"You could always go by Johnny," he said when we had calmed down. He was red like a tomato and wiping tears off his face.   *That's you, Johnny-Boy, a barrel of laughs.*

"Nah," I sighed, "'Johnny Adams' sounds like an old doo-wop crooner. I prefer pirate any day."

He nodded in agreement.

"I can't complain though," I went on, "my parents didn't name me 'Pluto'."

"Touché, kid. So, tell me about Anna Jenkins."

Maybe the banter and laughter had closed some sort of gap between us, but I was no longer apprehensive about telling him everything, my conversation with Mike Monroe, the Internet search, and the Osprey Cove Memorial Library announcement. He listened closely and only lifted his eyebrows when I spoke of the goings-on in my house. It was the hardest part to get to, I wasn't sure how he'd take it. I half expected him to handcuff me when I told him about the screams and the blood spots and what had happened today.

"Couch cushions were stuck to the ceiling?" He asked, "Is that even possible?"

"I hadn't thought so till this morning."

"Huh," he wrote something down, "you didn't happen to get a picture of that?"

"No, I didn't have my phone. It had to call itself so I could find it."

I could see another fit of laughter coming on. Apparently, I'm a natural comedian. He managed to control himself and only coughed a little before speaking.

"Listen, I believe you. Not so sure about this "Funhouse", but I believe Anna Jenkins is no innocent victim. Jenny Jenkins's death was ruled an accident but I've always thought there was something funny about it. But let's not talk here." He squinted his eyes and looked slowly around. I thought only people in Film Noir did that.

"Are you going back to Massachusetts or can you stay around here?"

"I've no idea. I just left the house as it was and drove up."

"Okay, I'm going to give you this address, it's a diner, meet me there at six p.m. Meantime, there's a pretty good, affordable motel nearby if you think you might want to spend the night."

He handed me a small post-it and lowered his voice,

"I suggest you stick around, there's something you gotta see."

Jeezus, Johnny-Boy, looks like you just walked into an episode of Dragnet.

I walked out into the hot summer day and looked around. When my stomach grumbled I decided to search for a place to eat.

Osprey Cove is a small summer beach town. The police department is located inside the William Cooper Community Center, on Shore Road. I walked past the small Fire House and waved to the firemen sitting out on lawn chairs, in front of the only fire engine that could fit in the garage. It was almost too big for it, but I noticed it had all the fixin's including the ladder. I supposed the town only needed one, and extra care had been taken to make sure it was the best they could afford.

Shore Road seemed to be the main commercial strip, and I walked past several businesses; clothing stores, souvenirs, grocers and cafes. Clearly all were mom-and-pop shops, down to the small store that read 'Millman's Hardware'. There was a laundromat straight out of 1950 and next to it a small house with a sign that read 'Osprey Cove Physicians'. Not a single chain store in sight and I wondered what this town lived on.

The town reminded me a lot of Rockport, Massachusetts, only on a much smaller scale, if that's even possible. The shops were all small houses with storefronts built in typical old-fashioned New England style, but I got a sense of newness, as if the town had only just been settled. The houses and stores were all well-painted, the streets were clean and nothing was out of place. This town definitely lived off summer tourism and was more than willing to cater to their every whim.

The place was beautiful, but I imagined how silent and sleepy it must get in the winter. Some of these shops, particularly those that sold souvenirs, no doubt closed when the season ended and all that was left were the locals. They probably all knew each other and had known Anna and her aunt. Did *they* think the aunt's death was an accident?

I came to a small park that marked the end of the street. It had a perfect, white gazebo and a brick building stood behind it. At three stories high, it was the biggest building I'd seen so far, and, 'Osprey Cove Town Hall' was engraved in stone above the door.

The pavement veered off towards the right and the street became Beach Street. I walked down it, hoping it would lead me to the beach. It was a narrow two lane road with a wide sidewalk on either side where people in bathings suits strolled. Here was a small residential area with beautiful houses and perfectly manicured lawns. In truth, the whole town seemed to be perfectly manicured.

I wondered what Detective Babcock investigated here; *minor crimes, Johnny-Boy, nothing more* . No wonder they had been quick to rule Jennifer Jenkins's death an accident. I found it hard to imagine people living here could be murderers. Then again, no one had thought so in Peaceville either.

The houses came to an end and the road cut through a small channel of water, like a natural bridge. Ahead, the narrow street opened into a peninsula and I supposed the open ocean beyond. Soon, I got to another row of small commercial buildings. Here were the tourist restaurants, all with outdoor patios with chairs and tables, some even had decks and terraces. I glanced at the menus and saw that they all served fish and seafood, mainly lobster; I wasn't surprised, this was New England, but at twenty-five dollars a lunch dish, I passed. I was certain there had to be a restaurant that catered to the local residents, and since this looked like the tourist hub, no way I was going to find it here.

Further along, I came to a Public Parking sign that pointed to my right. I peeked around a corner and saw the parking lot behind the buildings. It was by no means full, but this was a weekday and most of the weekend tourists were probably still at work.

At the end of the strip, the landscape opened up to the sea, and, there were two rows of benches under a giant rectangular awning. Next to it, was a similar structure, only with rows of Adirondack chairs instead. Beyond it was the beach. 'Peregrine Falcon Beach' was engraved on the stone cairns which signaled the entrance, and next to it there was a sign that said, "No Dogs Allowed May 1 to September 30".

The beach was beautiful, with fine sand and very few pebbles, a rarity in the New England landscape. It led to a tiny, rocky peninsula to the right with a white lighthouse atop, and was separated by a wide opening that fed into the channel; the restaurants and the beach jutted out into the clear blue sea. To my left, the rest of the town was dotted with swanky looking houses and possibly bed-and-breakfasts. I wondered if those were the summer residences.

I was getting hungrier and thirsty, and while I liked the sun, the heat was making me crabby. I retraced my steps and walked around the Osprey Cove Common with its flawless gazebo, past the town hall, onto Main Street and into the first decent-looking, non-expensive sandwich shop I saw.

I was finishing my lunch when my phone rang; people turned to look as the James Bond ringtone went off. I quickly grabbed it and answered, my cheeks burning.

"Dude, what's up?" Mark Andersson and I had lived twenty minutes away from each other all our lives and never met until our sophomore year in college. He was now a very close friend and I was glad to hear from him.

"Nothin' much (*apart from living in a haunted house*). 'Sup with you?" I answered.

"You wanna hang out tonight, grab some drinks?"

"Can't tonight. I'm in Maine and I'm not sure what time I'll get back." I looked at my watch, it was still a while before my meeting with Detective Babcock and I suddenly felt lonely.

"What the fuck's in Maine?" he asked. I wished I'd asked Mark or Apollo to come along.

"Research." I said.

"Well, just let me know if you up for it later."

"Yeah, will do."

We were about to hang up when I suddenly said, "Dude, how about you and Apollo come by tomorrow night for a few beers? We could sit out on the deck, maybe put something on the grill?"

"Sounds good! I'll tell him. Later!"

I looked at my phone as it blinked 'call ended'. I felt a little better. Maybe it was time to share the Horror Show with someone. Of course, with my luck nothing would happen. It hadn't occurred to me that perhaps the house only acted up when I was alone...

I dismissed the thought quickly since Mike Monroe had said entire families had lived there and weird stuff still happened.

I paid the check and walked out. Mark and I were close and I could trust him, and Apollo was a really good guy. He and Mark had grown up together and were like brothers (their fathers had been close since college and they had always lived on the same street). Apollo had become a close friend of mine too. I wasn't sure how either of them would take it, but I could almost bet Apollo would be less freaked. He was artistic and seemed open to stuff out of the ordinary, more so than the square, mathematical, engineer Mark.

The prospect of having company brightened me up a little. They'd been to the house sure, but that was before the shenanigans had started and I hadn't mentioned it to them, perhaps out of fear or embarrassment. But now it was time to finish this, and if I didn't have to do it alone, the better.

I walked down Shore Road towards the Police Department where I had left my car. I was deep in thought and didn't realize that I'd walked right past the community center. I stopped, I was standing in front of a sign that read "Goshawk Walkway Entrance" *(this town loves birds of prey, Johnny-Boy).*

There was a little paved path leading down to the ocean-front and I decided to follow it. The path led around a winding walkway with seaside cliffs and rocks on one side, and one enormous hotel on the other. It was a very ritzy-looking inn that reminded me of the one in Woodstock, Vermont, where my parents had renewed their vows before moving south, and I thought there was no way I could ever afford to pay even one night there. This hotel looked like it targeted the uber-rich and I suspected it accounted for most of the town's wealth and employment. It reminded me of hotels straight out of old movies, with chaise lounges on the vast lawn all painted in the color palette of the hotel, royal blue and white. If I had to describe this town in one color, I would say white,

white as a dove. There was nothing out of place and the hotel didn't have the old cozy feel of the typical New England bed-and-breakfasts.

I came to a little side street and decided to get back to my car. I wanted to get out of the sun and rest a little before meeting Babcock again. I turned around and realized I had walked farther away from the lighthouse, which meant I was now where I had seen the houses from the beach. I decided to walk up the street and try to find my way back without retracing my steps. It would give me a better feel for the town, and the leafy trees seemed to invite me to indulge in the coolness of their shades.

I huffed and panted as I climbed the steep street, looking around at the fancy mansions and expensive summer homes. Some were built in the Victorian style, but somehow, I got the feeling they were much newer, as if trying to recapture the halcyon days of long ago.

Apparently, I had picked the one street that led up a hill.   *Jeezus, Johnny-Boy, you gotta get your ass to the gym.*

I was back on Shore Road and walking towards the police department, when a cold breeze suddenly blew around me, giving me goosebumps. I paused, and rubbing my arms, realized I was standing in front of a small burial ground. The sign at the entrance read "Falcon Grove Cemetery, 1786". There was something ominous about the place, as if the cold breeze had come from it. I wondered if Jennifer Jenkins was buried here. A chill went up my spine; I sped up and made my way back to my car, and drove over to the motel Babcock had mentioned.

It was just outside Osprey Cove, and yep, it was called Eagle's Nest Motel; it was across the street from The Owl and Pellet tavern (established 1785). The price was a little high for my taste, but I figured one night away from the Funhouse was worth it.

I wondered if everything had calmed down over there. I wondered how I was going to get everything cleaned up before Mark and Apollo came.

Meh, I shrugged, it might help my case, and besides, they'd never care how the place looked anyway. Apollo wasn't the tidiest cat around and I'd even seen Mark's underwear draped across floor lamps before.

I registered and went to my room, which was small and smelled slightly dank. At least it didn't smell of rust. I climbed on the bed and turned on the TV.

I gasped when I realized *Poltergeist* was on. I changed the channel, but on this one, it was *The Others*, the next was playing *It*, the one after, *The*

Shining. My heart beat faster when I realized every channel was transmitting a horror movie, each one scarier than the last. When I got to *Nightmare on Elm Street* , I turned the TV off.   *It's not Halloween yet, what the hell's going on, Johnny-Boy?*

I closed my eyes and was drifting on that strange sea of black and color that lies between the dream state and the waking mind, when I was jolted out of it by the sound of a slamming door in the hallway outside.

"C'mon, Anna! Baby, don't be like that!" Someone said, as footsteps padded away.

CHAPTER FOUR

The House of Usher

I met Detective Babcock at the diner he had suggested, oddly called Moose Crossing Diner. He was already there and waved as I went to the booth he had chosen. It was your typical New England eatery, with thick wooden tables and booths, paper placemats and lots of pictures on the walls. The place looked homey, and I liked it.

Pluto Babcock made a motion to stand as I approached, but his huge belly impeded it and instead bumped the table. His water glass turned over and, with the loud clank of crockery, spilled its contents on the wooden surface and down onto the seat across from him.

"Aw, jeez, look at that, kid. I'm sorry." He said, dabbing the water with the teeniest, wettest napkin in the world.

"Nancy!" he called as I looked around the other tables for more napkins.

Babcock had managed to slide out of the booth without further incident and was slowly standing up. He offered me his hand and I shook it. The waitress appeared out of nowhere and wiped up the mess.

She was a middle-aged woman with a remarkable body and I noticed Babcock checking out her behind as she leaned over to wipe the seat. I smiled conspiratorially as our eyes met. He raised his eyebrows up and down in quick succession and winked. I burst out laughing and he snickered.

"Did you guys enjoy that?" Nancy said as she finished up, rolling her eyes at Babcock and walking away.

"Thank you, darlin'!" he called after her and slowly, but noisily, slid back into the booth. I sat down and picked up the menu.

"Listen kid, I called you here because we can't talk about this at the station." He lowered his voice, in that you-can't-trust-anyone tone he'd had this morning.

"Officially, Jenny Jenkins's death is an accident, though I know it ain't. I'm sure of it, but there was nothing I could do at the time, there wasn't even reasonable doubt. Anna Jenkins had an alibi, and there was no motive. Jenny Jenkins didn't have a lot of money left, I mean, she was

24

a librarian, it's not like they're rollin' in dough, and while the family had once been pretty well off, I suspected some of her inheritance had dwindled. But still, somethin' never sat right with me. I grew up with Jenny, she was one of my closest friends, and it's always bothered me that I couldn't bring her justice."

"Okay," I said, "but did you have anything on Anna Jenkins? Do you know where she is?"

"No. She went away to college and never came back. See, that was one of the pieces that didn't fit: Jenny died on Christmas Eve when Anna was a college freshman. She had supposedly just arrived to visit her aunt when she found the body. She was already out of the house right? Even if she'd hated her aunt, why kill her? She was already old enough to be on her own, and from what Jenny told me, her parents had had a pretty sizable estate, so she didn't want for money."

"Then maybe she didn't kill her aunt?" I said. "Maybe it really was an accident."

Though if that was true, then I'd hit a dead end.

"Nah, it's not right. Jenny was in the process of restoring the upstairs. The house has a guest bedroom downstairs and she had already moved into it, since the work was taking far too long. The workmen were on vacation and the heat had been turned off in the second story. There was no reason for her to have been upstairs, especially because her knees were so bad she needed a cane. She wasn't expecting to move back upstairs once the work was done, but she liked to keep her house well maintained. She'd made sure anything she needed had been already brought down. Hell, I'd helped her do it. There was nothing up there that warranted her to climb the stairs."

"So you think Anna lured her upstairs and then pushed her?"

"That's my guess, and as you can see, it's not a lot to go on."

"But it could've been anything, you know, it could've been a legitimate accident." I closed my eyes and shook my head, "Did anyone else suspect that it wasn't an accident?"

"No, but really, at the PD there's only five of us full time, don't need anymore; and during the summer we use reserves, they're mostly college kids patrolling as a summer job. The Chief back then was on the fence— he didn't want to think his best friend's daughter had been murdered, yet he couldn't really believe she'd gone upstairs for no reason—but we couldn't find any evidence against Anna. He retired soon after when he was diagnosed with Alzheimer's. The town doctors, Michael and Susan Lansbury were away for the holidays and did not perform the autopsy."

He took out a handkerchief and wiped his forehead.

"If anybody could have proven me right, it was them; they loved Jenny as much as me, and I'm sure they would have been meticulous in their report. The autopsy was performed by some quack in Portland, named Murphy, and he reported her injuries were consistent with falling down the stairs. I've always believed Anna and her alibi, David Saunders, had paid him off, or had something on him, because his report was extremely expedited and way too concise. When the Lansburys came home, they intended to speak to him, but he'd been in a horrible car wreck and was in a coma for the next two years. If he found anything suspicious, he took it to the grave. Anna had Jenny cremated, and the Lansburys only just made it to the funeral. There was no other choice, we had to close the case and rule it an accident. Nobody else believed it was murder; you gotta give 'er that, she really staged it right."

Nancy was back to take our orders. Babcock ordered the steak tips and I opted for the surf n'turf. He suggested I try a Spotted Harrier; I must have made a strange face, because he chuckled and explained that was the local brew. I assented and he ordered two. We watched Nancy's swaying backside as she sashayed to the kitchen.

"I thought it was an accident at first, but when I interviewed Anna, somethin' didn't seem right. She was crying much like a grieving niece; but it seemed like she was acting. And that obituary; you read it, right? Anna wrote it and insisted on publishing it as is. It seemed cold and distant and much too morbid, as if she hadn't cared for Jenny at all, and instead, had delighted in the details of her death. Also, Jenny's cane was nowhere to be found; it was an old, very distinctive cane, a sort of heirloom, I believe. If she'd fallen, it should've been near the body, or on the stairs, but to this day, the cane is gone. I've looked and looked for compelling evidence against Anna, but it's been useless."

He scratched his nose, looked around and leaned forward, beckoning me closer,

"Listen kid, no one knows this but me. Jenny had her own suspicions about Anna's role in her family's death, and she had meant to tell me something about it, but what with the holidays, we never got around to talkin'."

"What kind of suspicions?" I raised the beer Nancy had set before me, toasted with Babcock, and took a sip. It was delicious, cool and flavorful, just like a beer should be. The engraving on the beer glass read 'Osprey Cove Brewing Company' and I wondered if it was available in Massachusetts.

As we ate, Pluto Babcock told me a little about Anna Jenkins.

Anna had been a strange child. She was very selfish and, even though she hardly ever cried, she would go into a tantrum if her things weren't 'just so'. Apparently, she had been a nightmare in pre-school and kindergarten, kicking and hitting her peers, sometimes for no reason at all. She never liked to share and she acted like she was entitled to everything. She was extremely intelligent and the school counselor suggested she skip a grade when she started elementary school.

"Jenny said she'd gotten better in grade school, y'know, less violent and more amiable. As if she'd learned how to behave towards others. Mind you, I never met Anna until she moved in with Jenny. But anyway, Jenny told me that at home she was no different from how she had been at school before. As if there was a real Anna and a fake one."

He scraped his fork with his teeth as he took another bite of his steak tips and went on,

"I remember telling her that that was normal, that we all had a sort of 'friend persona' and a 'family persona', but she said the contrast between the two was greater in Anna than in anyone else. It was like, outside her house, she had learned to be what people wanted her to be, but at home she put on a different show. At home, it was the real show."

The surf n'turf was pretty tasty and I just listened, making assenting motions with my head. He told me about how they never had any pets, and how strange that had seemed to him since Paul had always loved animals, ("growing up, kid, their house had always been like a zoo, with different pets throughout the years; they'd even had a pet goat once"). Babcock didn't know why, but Jenny had cut off almost all relationship with her brother's family when her own healthy dog had suddenly died, and when he'd asked her why, she wouldn't explain, just shrugged it off. Anna was in middle school when Tommy was born, and because of the baby, Jenny began visiting them again.

"Did Jenny think Anna had done something to her dog?"

I was beginning to get a mental picture of the girl, and it wasn't pretty. I'd heard about sociopaths and psychopaths but didn't think I'd ever encountered one. Of course I'm no psychologist, but *Criminal Minds* could be a very enlightening show.

"She implied it," he shrugged, "but nothing more. Paul, Jenny and I used to be great friends growing up and she used to tell me everything, but around the time Anna was a small child, Jenny became more and more reserved. As if she wanted to keep that part of her life quiet. She only spoke openly about Anna's childhood after the murders."

He looked down at his plate and pushed the remaining food around on it.

"In hindsight, I think she was giving me clues about her niece, warning me."

The diner door opened and closed, and the waitress led someone to a table. Babcock glanced at the door, leaned back nonchalantly, and took a sip of beer.

"Well, Johnny-Boy, it's been a long time since you paid your ol' Uncle Pluto a visit! How ya been, kid? Got a girlfriend?" he said loudly, as the man who had come in sat down at the table across from us, his back to me.

I was taken aback by Babcock's coincidental use of my old nickname. I thought it had been retired when my grandfather died and it was both welcome and sad to hear it spoken aloud again. I looked Babcock right in the eyes and saw a strange seriousness beneath the mirth he was trying to project. I was compelled to play along.

"Aw Uncle, ya know me, I've always got a girl. How's Auntie?"

"Gettin' older every day," he gestured for the check and went on, "listen, we better get on, your Auntie's blueberry cobbler is waiting."

We paid the check and, as we were walking out, Babcock "accidentally" bumped into the newcomer. The man turned around and surveyed Babcock intently. He was about my age, maybe a couple of years older, with black hair, square jaw and cleft chin. *Pornstar,* I thought as I looked from him to Babcock.

"My apologies, Saunders, it seems my body had a senior moment." Babcock joked.

He was smiling at the man, but his face showed no amusement, and there was a coldness to his gaze that startled me. He certainly didn't look at me like that. The man just nodded and went back to his menu.

We stood on the sidewalk and Babcock motioned for me to follow him. We walked down the street past a few businesses and around the corner to what looked like a small residential area.

"That guy in there," he said suddenly, "don't forget him, kid. His name is David Saunders and he was Anna Jenkins's boyfriend when she lived here with Jenny. He was also Anna's alibi the night Jenny died. I've always believed he was in on it."

"If she really was murdered," I mumbled. I felt deflated, nothing that Babcock had said confirmed that Anna was a killer, so maybe I was going to have to start all over.

He stopped and turned to look at me. His gaze was so intense I felt like a small child again. I wondered if he had this effect on everyone. It must come pretty handy in his line of work to intimidate others so subtly and so easily.

"I told ya I had somethin' to show you. Maybe this'll change your mind."

We walked further on and, I suppose in an attempt to break the awkward silence, he explained a little about the town.

Osprey Cove was established in the early part of the eighteenth century and, as of the latest census, was home to a mere nine-hundred people year round, but that number swelled to a staggering (or so he thought) ten-thousand during the summer. The main industries were fishing, lumbering and tourism, although lumbering had declined during the twentieth century and eco-tourism was on a rise due to Osprey Cove's thick and dark forests.

I'd seen lots of camping and RV sites on the way, and many of these had signs out front offering bird-watching tours, zip-lines and hiking trails. My first impression had been that Mark and Apollo, who loved camping, would love this place, and I'd wondered whether they'd even heard of it.

Babcock continued saying that there was a bit of farmland further inland and most of the permanent residents owned their own businesses or worked in these industries. Some people commuted to bigger localities nearby, such as Brunswick and Portland.

I mentioned the town seemed to be quite affluent and he assented, explaining that The Gyrfalcon, the big hotel I'd seen, accounted for the big boom in the economy. The hotel was established in the early part of the twentieth century and was still running smoothly. He said that it's one of the preferred lodgings for the super elite; gentry, aristocrats and the hereditary rich stayed there every summer. Osprey Cove's relative unknownness made it especially attractive to members of these circles. They could easily vacation in privacy and discretion.

"Lobsterin' and boat buildin' were once the town's biggest industries, and it is how most of our ancestors made their fortunes, but we owe most of our current economy to tourism. You should check out the marina and shipyard, which have been in use since the town began. There is a lot of heritage here too, and most houses are as old as the town itself. We are proud people, us 'Ossies', as we call ourselves, and we take pride in our town."

We came up to a house at the end of a dead-end street. It was atop a small hill and seemed to lord over the rest of the area. It was a big Victorian with a front porch and dark, empty windows; but like all houses in this town, it was in perfect condition, no peeling paint, no sign of rot, nothing to suggest it wasn't lived in. The front yard was mown and well tended, but something about it seemed unnatural, as if there hadn't been a gardener near it for years. Unlike the houses I'd seen, this one felt like the real deal, not some new knock-off.

The wind howled from the ocean at the back of the house. The place had a sinister countenance; the breaking of the waves nearby and the setting sun behind it only added to its eeriness. I felt dread as we approached it and a strange sense of familiarity as well. This is how my own house had looked when the realtor, who had made a small effort in fixing it up before putting it on the market, had shown it to me.

"This is Jenny Jenkins's house. It's one of the oldest houses in town, built in 1799—I know this because our own family home was built the same year—and has been passed down from Jenkins to Jenkins, since its construction. She and her brother Paul grew up here. When Paul married Beth, they moved to Massachusetts, while Jenny remained here. She never married and after their mother passed away, her father moved in with Paul and they didn't see each other much. Jenny mostly went down to Massachusetts to visit them during the holidays, but Paul and Beth hardly ever came up. It always struck me as strange, and when I asked her about it, she'd blame Paul and Beth's work schedule. But I always felt as if something had come between brother and sister."

We stood in front of the house and I looked over at Babcock as he spoke. I thought I saw his eyes fill with tears, but it could just have been the orange and yellow rays as the sun set over the horizon. The house was in silhouette now and its grimness was almost tangible as it fell into darkness. Babcock sniffed and told me about how, after Tommy was born, Jenny seldom went to Massachusetts, but instead took care of her nephew during school vacations. The boy would spend weeks and even months with his aunt, only seeing his parents on weekends.

"Ya see kid, there was somethin' goin' on there. Why would Jenny only take one child in? She never said outright, but I suspected there may have been some abusing of the brother. Not sexually, I don't think, but physically and mentally. It was as if Beth and Paul were trying to keep him safe by sending him away."

The hairs rose at the back of my neck. It's what the garbled voices had said the night before, "Keep you safe".

"Did you know Tommy?" I asked, trying to maintain my composure.

"Yeah, quite well. He was a cute kid, very gentle and kind. He used to call me 'Uncle Pluto' and he and Jenny would often come by the station for a talk, or a walk, or dinner. He never talked about his sister, though. He would just clam up if she was mentioned."

"That's odd," I said.

"Yeah, it was, and I wish I'd been more observant. I may have been able to help in some way. As a small town detective you don't often see much of the evils in the world, even though you know they exist."

He lowered his head, as if paying homage to the boy's memory.

The sun had set completely now and we were still standing in front of the house, its dark, lonely appearance daring us to come closer.

"C'mon, kid," he said as he walked towards the front door.

He opened it and stepped into what looked like a big foyer. The lights came on as he flipped a switch by the door. I had a strange feeling about this house, it was perfectly well kept, but it seemed as if no one had lived in it for years. It reminded me the demo houses in the gated communities I visited with my parents when they were house-hunting in Maryland: completely devoid of life and emotion.

We were under a threshold that opened into the living room. The ceiling was very high and had some beautiful cornices. It had wood-paneled walls which gave the place a sense of wealth and elegance different from that of the town itself. The town felt almost like an
amusement park, everything built in order to entertain, but the house seemed like it was meant to be lived in. It was as if the house had been built first and the town developed around it. The house was old, but it had been taken care of over the years. Everything was clean and in its place, and I sensed that the threshold we were standing under, was actually the threshold to the past.

"This is the living room, the dining room is that way towards the back of the house, and the kitchen is through there."

He pointed to an open archway and then a swinging door. To the left were the stairs, they were wide and steep and led to a wide landing which from here looked almost like a parlor, and it veered off to the right and narrowed. I couldn't see too well from down here, but I imagined the upstairs had open hallways that looked down onto the small space surrounding the stairs. I could definitely imagine someone falling down these imposing stairs and dying instantly. I was becoming more and more convinced about Jenny's death being an accident, regardless of what Babcock thought. I understood that it must've been hard for him to lose a lifelong friend so suddenly and so senselessly.

"There's a guest bedroom with a bathroom, next to the kitchen. That's the room I told you Jenny was occupying. To our left, there is a small sitting room, sort of like a closed-in porch. Upstairs there are six bedrooms and four bathrooms. There's also a narrow staircase that leads to a small studio, which opens up to a widow's walk overlooking the ocean out back. The house has a big yard that leads to a set of cliffs. Beneath is a small, pebble beach with hidden, jutting rocks on either side that make it private. When we were kids, we used to spend hours playing hide-n'-seek in this house. Jenny's parents would grill and barbecue in the backyard every weekend in the summers."

We moved towards the stairs. They were very deteriorated and I wondered how it was that the rest of the house was in perfect condition and not these rickety, old stairs that would probably crumble if so much as a mouse stepped on them.

"Does anyone live here?" I asked, "Did anyone buy it after Jenny's death?"

"Jenny had left the house to Tommy and never changed her will after he died; although Rick Larson, our childhood friend and lawyer, said she had, but the new will has never been found. He said they had an appointment after the holidays to make the new one legal and binding, but he didn't have a copy of it, just the empty template. He and I tried looking for it, but nothing. He managed to persuade the court to name me as executor until the new will was found. He's away for the summer now, visiting his grandkids; I don't know when he'll be back (he usually stays there the whole season), otherwise he'd be here with us now, telling you all this in legalese. No one has lived in the house since her death. I've often felt the emptiness she left behind. When Rick and I went over the old will, it struck me as sad that such a good family would be wiped out so easily and so suddenly, with only friends left to take care of their affairs."

"Sounds like what happened at my house."

"Yes," he answered, "this place used to be so homey and welcoming, and now it just looms; like the House of Usher."

I looked around and realized that Babcock was right, the place was in perfect condition (save for the stairs) but it wasn't homey at all. It was empty of any feeling of welcoming or joy or anything. Something dark lurked here, like the imaginary storm clouds over the Funhouse.

"Have you ever thought of selling it?" I turned to look at him.

"Never," he answered, "it's always belonged to Jenny's family and I just can't let it go."

"Are you gonna fix up the stairs?"

"Can't."

I was about to ask him what he meant when the house suddenly groaned. The lights died and we heard the distinct noise of footsteps around us. I felt as if the walls were bending down towards us and then away, like a heartbeat. Then, I heard the sound of hurried feet in the kitchen followed by a dull thud on the floor. I looked around, trying to find some sort of light source and thought I saw a flickering light moving towards us from the living room.

"Hang in there, kid. This doesn't take long." Babcock whispered beside me.

I was trembling. I had decided I was done being scared with what went on in my house, but this was shaking my confidence. At the Funhouse, the happenings were violent, almost as if the house itself was being ravaged; but here, there was a calm spookiness which unnerved me.

The flickering light moved past us and up the stairs. Beneath it, I thought I saw the decayed steps repaired, as if the stairs were regenerating under the strange light. Once the light was gone, there was the sound of wood breaking and the smell of rot. The light disappeared when it reached the top floor and as we looked up, we heard more footsteps, what sounded like furniture being dragged, and then one long blood-curdling scream.

The parlor lit up once more, and the strange, dreadful tranquility was gone. I felt my phone vibrate in my back pocket as it restarted itself. I looked at Babcock. The low light of the ceiling lamp overhead cast eerie shadows on his face.

"Do you believe me now? Jenny's death was no accident," he said, and his voice rang out over the silent, gloomy house, "You were about to ask why I couldn't fix it up. Simple, it won't let me. That's also why Rick and I have never found the new will, or Jenny's cane. If I try to change something, say, repaint the front door, the moment I turn around it would go back to the color it had been before."

I looked around, everything seemed tidy and placid and it made my skin crawl. Babcock pointed to the rickety stairs.

"The one thing that hasn't stayed the same are those goddamn stairs. They have been rotting for years. You have no idea how many times I've repaired those steps, only to find them rotted immediately after. Nothing in this house can be changed, therefore, it can't be lived in. Believe me, kid, I've tried."

"But that doesn't necessarily mean she was murdered." I said, still playing the Devil's Advocate, even though I myself was beginning to think that no accidental death could cause such strange occurrences.

"I didn't get around to telling you this back at the diner, but, remember I said Anna had just arrived to visit her aunt for the holidays?"

I nodded.

"Well, there was no indication that Jenny was expecting any company, let alone an overnight guest. The upstairs was still closed off, and there was nothing to suggest Anna would be sleeping on the couch. Also, Jenny was going to spend Christmas Eve with my family, she'd even dropped off her presents that morning, we were going to open them at midnight. She had gone home to change and finish her Christmas dish. She never mentioned Anna coming home."

I pondered that for a second and told him that maybe Anna had wanted to surprise her aunt. Babcock shook his head and said they didn't have that kind of relationship. He said that Jenny's sudden need to restore the house was like a cleansing after Anna moved out. She had admitted she'd needed to clean everything of Anna's presence, he said. I raised my eyebrows in wonder.

"What about the furniture," I asked, "you said nothing could be changed. Is the furniture still the same?"

"Yep, and it can't be moved. The couch feels like it's bolted to the floor, so do the chairs and the tables. It's like trying to lift the sword from the stone. Shit, everything is exactly the way it was when I came in that night. And," he went on, "the house hasn't been connected to the electric grid since Jenny died, yet, you can still turn on the lights, the fridge runs and so do all the appliances. The creepiest thing is the TV; it only transmits what was on back then. It's as if time here stood still the night she died."

We went back out into the remnants of twilight. The house was shrouded in darkness which seemed to extend past the front yard and onto the street. I wondered if what happened here had affected the neighbors the way the murders in Peaceville had.

"They fought a lot," Babcock broke our pensive silence as we walked down the street towards town, "and Jenny couldn't stand that Saunders. Rich punk is what he was. Still is. Little shit joined the PD after college. I don't know why, he could've just gone somewhere else and been a pain in someone else's ass."

"D'you think he knows where Anna is?" I asked.

"Absolutely, I bet he keeps tabs on her and updates her on what goes on around here. I've caught him a couple of times coming up to the house, supposedly out for a jog; but he don't fool me, he's watching the place."

"What for?"

"Dunno," he shrugged, "maybe he just wants to make sure no one finds anything incriminating. He was Anna's alibi, after all. Said he'd picked her up at the bus station in Portland and drove her to her aunt's. Then she found the body as she walked in. Bullshit."

We walked back to my car in silence and Babcock pulled a small book out of his inner jacket pocket.

"*Innocent, Evil,*" he said, handing me the book, "this was Jenny's final gift to me, it was under our Christmas tree when she died. There was only one edition, it was never a hit, but you should read it, you might understand what I mean."

I took it with both hands and looked at the cover. It was old and it seemed to be a first edition.

"It's been great to meet ya, kid. Hopefully we can put this all to rest," he smiled as I climbed in the driver's seat.

I looked up at him and nodded. He was a good man and I suddenly felt overwhelming respect of him. I was glad I'd come, it really was time to put this all to rest.

On the drive back to the Eagle's Nest, I saw a different side of the town. Osprey Cove seemed to be divided in two parts, one where the locals lived and the other where the summer residents vacationed. I passed the marina and shipyard with signs that advertised whale watching tours, tall ship adventures and fishing expeditions.

I decided to walk around the marina a little and look at the boats. Out on the pier, the lighthouse jutted out to my left, but there were no lights in between, just tall cliffs, which I supposed were the same ones that Babcock said Jenny's house overlooked. Here lived the locals, and Jenny Jenkins's house, as well as the Moose Crossing Diner belonged to this part. Goshawk Walkway led to the summer resident part of town, which I now referred to as Imitation Row. The houses on the locals' side were not as luxurious as the others, but they were far from poor.

I now understood what Babcock had said about people's ancestors having made fortunes; the houses were old, but very well kept, and though I'm sure some were living beyond their means, I got the feeling that the houses they occupied had belonged to their parents, and their parents' parents and so on and they weren't willing to let them go. I understood Babcock's sentimentality towards Jenny's house better, he was an 'Ossie', born and raised; and 'Ossies' respected their past.

I flopped down on the hotel bed and looked up at the ceiling. It was painted light gray and there was a big crack that ran down the middle, like a lightning bolt through a stormy sky.

"Two haunted houses, two different murders and one girl between them. What've you stumbled upon, Johnny-Boy?" I asked the ceiling and opened Babcock's book. There was a handwritten dedication on the title page, "Plu, this is Anna to a T. Let's hope…(illegible). I wish you all happiness, love and abundance for many, many years to come. Merry Christmas! Love, Jenny"

I closed my eyes and took a deep breath. An overwhelming sadness came over me just then, Jenny Jenkins had left her best friend a clue to her death, whether she knew it or not; but what really got to me was that her last words to Pluto Babcock had been the best of wishes, not a cry for help, nor a plea for her life.

Babcock was right, Jenny Jenkins's house had convinced me.

I dreamed of the book. It happened often. Sometimes, I couldn't get stories out of my mind and they would come to me in dreams, so I knew I was dreaming when I looked in the mirror and saw a strange man, brown-haired with a square jaw. I could almost see myself in him, his features were similar, but I knew I wasn't him, or rather, I knew he wasn't me.

The man lowered his head and let out a sigh, heavy with sadness and resignation.

"What do we do?" He whispered to the blond woman next to him. She was nursing a baby, and while she was aglow with love for the new child, worry peeked out of her eyes. There was more than that, there was fear too.

"What *can* we do?" her hushed voice broke as silent tears streamed down her face.

"We've always known she was odd," he said, "we've always known something wasn't right, but I just never thought she could…Oh God, how I wish Dad were here."

"Are you sure you saw her?" she asked.

"Yes," he said, meeting her eyes with such a certainty that his wife couldn't hold his gaze, and instead looked down at their son, "she was trying to suffocate him in the crib. She said the baby was cold and crying, and that she was just putting a blanket over him, but that's not true, he slept soundly throughout. And I heard her, too; "Sayonara, Tommy" I will never forget those words, nor the sound of her voice. She was going to kill him."

His wife broke down in tears and hugged the baby to her breast. He looked down at the book in his hand.   *Innocent, Evil* , the words swimming and spinning in his brain, their meaning taking hold of his heart and changing his life forever.

"We watch her," he said in a broken voice, through broken dreams, "we watch her like a hawk. She must never be alone with him. We hunker down, together, you and me, and we keep him safe, and when he's old enough, we let him go, we get him as far away from her as possible. My sister will help. I only hope our daughter doesn't kill us first."

He was about to put his arms around his crying wife, whose sobs were so soft and quiet, almost as if she was fighting to keep them inside, when they heard a cold voice behind the door. He bid her enter, and the door opened to reveal a young girl in a pristine, 1920s pink dress and ginger, braided buns atop her head. There was an ugly, hateful look in her eyes when she saw the baby clutched by her mother's arms. She was about to say something when I gasped myself awake.

The lamp was still on and I looked up at the lightning crack on the ceiling. The book lay face down on my chest, open wide to the last page I'd read. The image in my dream had been that of Marla Henson, the author's cold, neat, unnerving child character, but, even though my mind had given her someone else's likeness for lack of a visual reference, I knew the girl in my dream was Anna Jenkins, and she had tried at least once to kill her baby brother.

CHAPTER FIVE

The Horror Show

I got home a little after noon. The house stood silent and grim, as always. I took a deep breath as I turned the key in the lock, not knowing what I would find.

The Funhouse was immaculate. Like seriously spotless. My neat-freak grandmother couldn't have done a better job of cleaning up. I felt a strange sense of disappointment when I realized I had no proof of the hauntings now that I'd decided to tell Mark and Apollo.

I walked around the parlor running my fingers over the chairs and walls and coming up empty of dust. In the kitchen, everything had been put away and possibly sanitized, even the dishes I'd left uncleaned from yesterday's breakfast. I went into the dining room and my heart skipped a beat. The table was there. Yesterday, it had been split in half and now there was no trace of any kind of damage, in fact, it looked like it had been polished too. I rushed into the living room and saw the couches had been set upright and reupholstered, but the cushions weren't there. I looked up, they were still stuck to the ceiling.

"So, you couldn't get those down, huh?"

I made a mental note to snap a picture for Babcock later, when a breath of cold air crept up my shoulder. My skin crawled and my breath hitched. I stood for a moment, my fingers shakily drumming on the side of my thighs. *Shake it off, Johnny-Boy. At least you've still got your evidence.*

I went upstairs and everything was in perfect order. I hadn't seen whether much damage had been done the day before anyway. I went into my office and plugged my phone since the battery was dead. The last message it had relayed to me before conking out was that Mark and Apollo would be by around six this evening. I turned to my laptop. It woke up as soon as I sat down.

I screamed. Loud and high-pitched, like a little girl. The scream seemed to go on forever as my brain took in and analyzed what my eyes saw: the word "Sorry" meandering across the computer screen in diverse fonts and colors, like a 1990s screensaver. I gasped and clutched my chest the way my father did whenever he walked too fast. This place was going to give me a heart attack.

I rushed into my bedroom, hopped onto my perfectly well-made bed and put the pillow over my eyes. I didn't want to know more. I just wanted to lie still and wait for my friends to get here.

"Aw, shit," I said sitting up. I'd forgotten to buy the burger patties. Apollo was bringing the beer and chips, while Mark the hot dogs and bread.

My heart skipped a beat. Grandpa's notebook was on my nightstand, the one called "Adams Family History". I was certain I'd put it back in the box, and I was certain I'd shoved the box back in the closet. I gulped and looked at it for a moment, unsure whether go to the supermarket or to open it, but my friends would be by soon and I had to hurry. The notebook could wait. I got up and, dragging my feet, made my way out of the rust-scented house.

I was on the deck getting the grill ready, when Mark and Apollo came around the house. They had Apollo's dog, Jude, with them, who gave a little friendly bark as they climbed the wooden stairs that led up to the deck and greeted me warmly. Mark gave me a quick 'bro-hug' and said, "I gotta take a dump" before going in the house. Apollo, tall and forever smiling, shrugged and asked how I was doing, while I bent down to pat Jude.

We leaned on the railing, chatted and drank beers straight from bottles, while Jude ran gleefully around in the yard. Apollo's presence always seemed to put me at ease, as if his cheerfulness and carefree attitude was contagious. I tended to be a bit of a natural worrier, Mark was a skeptic with a little bit of cynic thrown in, and Apollo was, well, in short, a free spirit.

"Dude, what's up with your housecleaning superpowers?" Mark said as he walked out, sliding the screen door behind him.

And that was my cue. I just let it all out. Told them everything that had happened—the whispers, the screams, the lights, yesterday's mess, the creepy message on my computer and the indelible scent of rust. I left out my trip to Maine and the conversations with Mike Monroe and Babcock. I don't know why I did that, but it seemed right at the time. When I was done, they looked at me in silence, Mark with his mouth slightly open and Apollo with an expression I can only describe as nonplussed.

Suddenly, Mark burst out laughing.

"No way, man, you're so pulling our chain!" he said cheerfully.

I motioned them to follow me, and as we made our way towards my office, Mark rationally explained everything that had happened. He said the lights could be due to some power surges from the grid and that I should get surge protectors, the whispers were probably drafts, the creaks and groans just the house settling, the blood stains possibly leaks and I should take care of that quickly, that my mind was playing tricks on me when I heard the voices, hysteria he called it, you know, you're already scared, blah, blah, blah. As if I hadn't thought of all that myself.

We went through the living room; I pointed at the stuck cushions and Apollo opened his eyes wide, but Mark was in his Mark-Explains-It-All mode and didn't see or hear anything beyond what he thought and said, so Apollo and I just walked silently along. As we climbed the stairs, I noticed Apollo scrunch his face when the smell of rust hit us, but Mark still talked on, oblivious to it.

I showed them the message on the computer.

"Oh, c'mon dude, seriously, just admit it, you're so pranking us," exclaimed Mark, "or someone is pranking you. You probably got hacked, and someone is trying to scare you or something. This has an easy fix you know."

He sat down at my computer and a few moments later, the screensaver blared the words "JACK ADAMS SMELLS LIKE ASS" in bright, bold letters. He looked up triumphant, when Apollo pointed to the screen.

"How do you explain that then?" he said.

The message Mark had written was dissolving and merging into different words: "KEEP YOU SAFE". The hairs rose at the back of my neck and I noticed Mark's hands begin to tremble.

Then, the computer went black and the world went quiet.

The Horror Show went on for quite a while. I mean, the guys got the works. The screaming, the groaning, the flickering lights, and I swear, this time even the house shook. Mark screamed as books fell off the shelves and slid across the room. Then, as the violence escalated, blood dripped down the walls and eerily formed the same words my computer had shown us just moments before, "KEEP YOU SAFE".

When it all died down with that gut-wrenching groan, I looked at my friends and almost burst out laughing. They stood like statues, pale as death. I could almost hear their hearts beating in the deathly silence that followed.

"Wh-wh-wha-at?" Mark stammered.

Apollo, ashen under his natural tan, shakily lifted his hand to his head and pushed his blond hair back from his face. Then he walked to the doorway, leaned against it and slid down until he was sitting. He sat like that, head lowered, for a few moments, while I sat crosslegged on the floor and Mark re-occupied my desk chair.

"Jack, start from the beginning," Apollo looked at me, his deep voice breaking the stunned silence, "and this time, tell us everything."

His gaze was full of fire, something like rage and excitement at the same time, but without a trace of fear. I guess you could call that courage. I'd never seen him look like that before, and it scared me a little, not to mention how he'd known I'd held some things back. I saw a part of Apollo that seldom showed but lay beneath his natural, calm optimism.

"Not here," I said, "let's go back out to the deck. I'm actually getting really hungry."

Mark turned to me with an expression of disbelief, while Apollo broke out into his usual beaming smile.

"Yeah, a burger sounds good," he said.

We went back downstairs, (Mark yelping a little when he noticed the cushions on the ceiling) and stepped outside. Jude was nowhere to be seen and, for a brief moment, I thought he might have run off into the woods. We went down to the yard and called his name. As I neared the underside of the deck, which had a door to the basement, I heard soft whimpers. I went under the darkened structure and found the little beagle cowering in the corner, his head on the floor and his paws over his eyes.

"Aw, Jude-o, it's ok," I whispered and slowly put my fingers under his nose, "it's over boy, it's all right."

I stroked his head and coaxed him forward, then picked him up and walked back out into the sunshine.

I fired up the grill, while Apollo lovingly comforted his little dog. Mark was silent, opening beers. I think he meant to get hammered. He was still white as a sheet and his hands trembled so much that he had trouble keeping the bottle-opener steady. I could tell the wheels in his brain were turning a mile a minute, trying to rationalize everything he had just seen. This was typical Mark; he used to say he wasn't sure he believed in God, but he definitely believed in Physics. Everything had a rational explanation; there were no ghosts, no spirits, no psychics, none of that "esoteric mystical crap" as he termed it. And now, in just a few minutes, his rational mind had been put through the wringer.

"I know how you feel. I've been scared shitless for weeks. It's a lot to take in and I'm still not used to it," I said.

"No, you don't know how it feels."

I nodded. I supposed it must be hard for a guy who found an explanation for everything to realize some things cannot be explained. As a writer, this was more normal to me; not everything had to be explainable, things just happened because they happened. A character could lead you down a path you never even thought existed. In books, dragons were real, magic was normal and anything could happen. To Mark, a haunting was something beyond what his mind allowed him to believe, and now, he had to wrap his head around it. If ghosts were real, what else could exist?

I looked at Apollo, who, having consoled Jude, had gone in to wash his hands and was stepping back out onto the deck. He was the opposite of Mark in many ways. Apollo was spiritual and meditated often. He was creative and imaginative and loved art and literature. Most importantly, he had grown up with his formidable Aunt Tallulah. She was his father's sister, and her New Age spirituality had paved a path of enlightenment and tolerance in his teenage years. Apollo was as open-minded as Mark was rational, and to me, it was a wonder they'd stayed best friends all these years.

Apollo helped me with the patties and hot dogs, while Mark, still trembling, finished with the beers and began getting out the condiments. We ate standing by the grill, while I told them everything I knew about the Jenkinses, here and in Maine. Mark ate less than usual, which was strange, since the guy seemed to have a black hole in his stomach. He could eat forever and not gain an ounce, but today, he only ate one burger and one hot dog.

"If we were in Mexico," Apollo spoke when I was done, "I'd tell you to look for hidden gold."

Mark and I looked at him, nonplussed. Apollo was half Mexican, and he explained that the country's folklore claimed that wherever there was a haunting, there was hidden gold. He said this superstition dated all the way back to the Spanish Conquest, but grew in fervor during and after the Mexican Revolution, when people hid their gold, valuables and women, so the Revolutionaries that often ravaged a place would never find them. They said that the dead always came back to guard it. He said that some haciendas even had false walls, that, when taken down, had revealed tiny, secret rooms.

We had by then pulled up the plastic chairs and were sitting in a circle with beers in our hands, while Jude lay sleeping in the middle. A cold breeze blew in from the woods and hovered around us. In the fading summer light, I saw a little boy squat and pat Jude's head. The dog immediately woke up and barked. The sound seemed to break the enchantment and the cold dissipated, taking the little boy with it.

"You all saw that, right?" I whispered.

One glance told me they had. Mark had a crazed look on his face, and Apollo had blanched. He set his dog on his lap and we sat quiet for what seemed like hours. We were all deep in thought—at least I was—when Mark broke the silence.

"You might be on to something," he said, turning to Apollo. "There's gotta be a reason for all this, right? However unreasonable this whole situation is, I have to believe there's a reason for it."

We looked at him expectantly,

"So, what if, there *is* gold hidden in this house?"

I pondered that for a second.

"Nah," I said, "this was the nineties, nobody hid gold anymore, and besides, from what Babcock said, Anna inherited everything."

"Then why haunt this place? Why not move on?" Apollo asked, rubbing the beagle behind the ears.

"The violence maybe?" I turned to Apollo.

"I don't think so. If everyone that died by violence stayed in this physical world because of it, we'd all be living with ghosts every minute," he took a sip of his beer, "hell, I'd be talking to my dad and my brother right now."

Apollo's father and twin brother had died in a horrible car accident when he was a kid. I'd forgotten that and felt a little embarrassed. I've never experienced anything so devastating in my life; I mean, my parents are still alive, so is my sister, and my grandparents had died peacefully at ripe old ages.

"But look," Mark said, "there's gotta be something to all this. What about those messages? It's the same thing over and over, "keep you safe" right? What if that's what's going on? What if that's the reason? What if they want to show us what happened, to keep you safe from her?"

He was getting excited now that his mind was beginning to make some sort of sense of all this.

"But we *know* what happened, and we *know* who did it," Apollo adjusted himself in his chair, "it's obvious Anna Jenkins did it. I don't think it has anything to do with keeping Jack safe, I think it has to do with the one person they *couldn't* keep safe, the brother. Maybe that's the whole idea, to point out the motive. The violence gets recreated every time."

Mark and I looked at each other and waited, since Apollo looked like he wanted to go on,

"There's gotta be more though, some way to prove it all. Why go through all this trouble? There's already people like Mike Monroe and Babcock who believe Anna is guilty, and if these people were in danger of her retaliation (it's not like they've kept quiet all these years) stuff would be going on in their houses too, right?"

We sat silent for a while longer. Jude left Apollo's lap and went around the grill looking for any pieces of meat that might've fallen on the deck.

"But see here," Mark said shaking his finger like an angry dad, "maybe there *is* something hidden in this house. The murder weapon was never recovered, right? And you said the house in Maine is also haunted, so maybe there's something there too."

"Yeah, but the haunting there is different. It's like *The Dollhouse Murders*." I patted Jude as he shuffled by my chair.

"The what?"

"*The Dollhouse Murders*. This girl's book my sister had growing up," They chuckled, but I rolled my eyes and went on, "she and her friends used to talk about it all the time, and one day, the curiosity got to me, so I took it from her room and read it. 'Twas pretty good, actually."

Truthfully, the book had given me nightmares for weeks, but I wasn't about to admit that; and it had been the first and only ghost story I'd ever read. In fact, I'd never finished it. I'd caved and shamefully asked my sister to tell me the ending.

"Oh-kay..." Mark said trying to hold back the laughter, while Apollo failed.

"It's about a girl who gets clues from the ghost of her great-grandma about who murdered her. The ghost does this by playing out the murders in an old dollhouse made to be a replica of the actual house they lived in."

"That sounds pretty cool." Apollo stopped laughing while Mark gave him an icy stare. Mark was not much of a reader, like Apollo and me.

I explained the eerie calmness that came over the house, and how nothing deteriorated but the stairs, and about how impossible it was to change something.

"It's as if *that* house is trying to show what really happened, y'know, how Jenny Jenkins died. Babcock doesn't believe her death was an accident. And as far as I know, there aren't any cryptic messages there, only the light that shimmers up the stairs, almost like beckoning us to follow. Besides, I think Jenny Jenkins believed Anna was going to kill her."

"Why?"

"She started telling Babcock about Anna after the murders here, but gave him her final clue the Christmas she died. Her present to Babcock was a book called *Innocent, Evil* by some guy named Wheatcroft (I don't think he ever wrote anything else). Babcock lent it to me yesterday, and I began reading it last night. It's about a mother who starts believing that her perfect, well-mannered daughter has committed murder. Jenny left a hand-written note to Babcock saying that it described Anna to perfection."

"Send it my way when your done with it, will ya?" Apollo smiled.

"Is there a movie?" Mark asked. We shrugged, but a quick Google search told us there wasn't, in fact, the author had died shortly before the book had been published in 1922. Wheatcroft had been a Maine local and the publisher a small-town company that had folded more than half a century ago. *Innocent, Evil* had been his only novel.

Marks scrunched up his face, and said he just might read it, *if* he had time. Apollo and I rolled our eyes. Mark would do anything to get out of reading a book. He loved stories, though, as long as they were told to him, or watched by him, and he often got so excited he couldn't wait to know how they ended. He'd even begged us to tell him how they destroy the One Ring as we'd walked out of the movie theater when *The Fellowship of the Ring* first came out.

"Anyway, I think we should visit Osprey Cove and take a look at that house," he added.

"Yeah," Apollo looked at me, "I have a feeling there's something there that we need to find. Maybe there's a clue to Anna's whereabouts or something."

We decided to visit Osprey Cove the following weekend. I agreed I'd let Babcock know.

They didn't stay much longer that night, I think the fright had left them exhausted, like it left me all the time. I was surprised how it still got to me. I mean, I could be all sarcastic and macho afterwards, but that was just my way of dealing with my fear. Though every time it started, I got scared out of my mind. I can only imagine what it must have been for them. This had probably been the scariest manifestation so far, and their first. They'd each offered me their couch, in case things got too heavy, but I refused. Oddly enough, now that I had somewhere else to go, I felt like I didn't want to leave the house. With or without the Horror Show, this was still my house.

I took out Babcock's business card, texted him the picture I'd taken of the couch cushions and threw myself down on my bed. I lay looking up at the ceiling, wondering how we could find Anna Jenkins. Babcock had mentioned that Saunders guy probably knew where she was. My phone rang.

"Hello?" I said, wiped out.

"So, I guess it *is* possible for cushions to be stuck to the ceiling, huh?" Babcock joked on the other line.

"Yeah, when I got home the house was spotless, I mean, like sterile. Anything that was broken looked brand new, except those cushions."

"Wow." He was a heavy breather on the phone. Actually...he was a heavy breather in person too.

"Also, my computer apologized for the mess."

He broke into a hearty laugh.

I told him all that had happened with Mark and Apollo, and he agreed to meet us when we came up. He also thought there was something to those messages, and he said he believed that keeping Tommy safe had always been the family's intention.

"Say, Detective," I rolled over on my side, "do you know anything about where Anna went to college? Is there anyway you can get the info out of Saunders?"

"Call me Pluto, kid. I only know she went out west somewhere, and no, I can't get the info out of Saunders. Believe me, I've been trying for years, the guy just won't say. Claims he doesn't know, but his mouth says something while his eyes say the opposite, you get me?"

"Yeah," I sighed, "it was worth the try though."

We said goodnight and hung up.

I rolled over onto my other side and saw the clock on my nightstand blinking 12:00. Setting the clocks on my electronics had lately become an exercise in futility.

I wiggled out of my jeans, and reached for Grandpa's notebook. It looked like a family tree of sorts. I hadn't known that he'd been interested in genealogy. I opened it to the first entry; Grandpa would never have won a penmanship contest, not in a million years. His handwriting looked like monkeys had trampled over chicken-scratch. I managed to make out some tidbits about Albert (or Alfred) Adams, who'd been born in 1717, and had been chased by a moose (or mouse, or goose; maybe in mongoose) when he was ten, before I started to nod off and decided to call it a night.

CHAPTER SIX

The Blast from The Past

Nothing much happened for the next few days; I slept, I ate and I worked. The House showed me how much it loved me at least twice a day, so I'd begun to spend my work hours away. I tried the diner I went to, but it got too busy and too noisy, so then I tried the park, but still couldn't find a place where I could work pleasantly. Peaceville Centre was not much different and I was running out of places to go.

I needed a quiet place where I could submerge myself in the story I was writing, and not worry about people bumping into me, loud parties, dogs, joggers, and what have you. When I was a kid, I used to spend much of my free time in the school library. I've always been a bit of a loner, and more importantly, a writer. The school library was the only place outside my home where I could sit and write without anybody bothering me.

Johnny-Boy, like Apollo would say: you've got farts in the brain, I told myself when I realized what an idiot I'd been. I'd gotten so used to living in the digital age with all sorts of information on Google, thousands of songs on my iPod, books galore on my Kindle, Google Earth, Hulu Plus, Netflix, etc., that I'd completely forgotten about one place—the library! I didn't even know if Peaceville had a library, but, like the child of the times I am, I took out my phone and looked it up.

The Peaceville Free Library was only a few minutes from my house, and I spent the next two days there, happily typing away. No one bothered me, no one shouted, no one cared what I was up to as long as I behaved. It was writer's heaven! Every few hours I got up and went to a different section. It was good to get away from the house, the murders, Anna Jenkins and everything that was happening around me, and just write. My father had once said that I wrote my life away, and at the Peaceville Free Library, I was happy to do so.

I was working in the genealogy section when I stretched and looked up at the ceiling. There was a crack like a lightning bolt across it and I was reminded of the Eagle's Nest Motel. I started thinking about Anna

Jenkins and suddenly realized that I was at the perfect place to find her, at least a past version of her.

I asked Doris, the librarian, for help in finding yearbooks from the 1990s. Doris was an older, heavyset woman, very pleasant in her manner and quite motherly. She pointed to my laptop and told me they had all been digitized and were available online. I shifted it so she could bring up the website.

"There are two high schools in Peaceville," she said, "are you looking for someone in particular?"

I told her I was looking for someone who had lived at my address during the 1990s. She told me I'd have to look for the yearbooks from Peaceville North High School. She left and said she'd be around in case I needed anything else.

I thanked her and sat down. I knew that Anna Jenkins's family had been murdered in 1996, and that she'd been a college freshman when Jenny Jenkins died in December 1998, which meant that she was class of 1998 and finished her high school in Maine. That meant she'd started high school in Peaceville in 1994. So I had only to look through the yearbooks for '94 through '96. I figured it wouldn't take me long.

As I scrolled through the first yearbook, I hit a snag, only the senior class portraits were present. If all yearbooks were like that, then I'd have to look for her in Maine.

I sighed and stretched. I went to look for Doris, and asked her if they had any middle school yearbooks archived for 1993 and 1994. She looked at me a bit suspiciously and told me no, those were at the school itself. I thanked her, grabbed my stuff and left.

I was hungry and thought about going home. I was disappointed, I wanted to at least get a look at Anna Jenkins and try to find her on social media, but it was useless.

I walked home with my head down, said hi to Mike who was out on his lawn, and went inside the Funhouse. I had just walked in the door when everything went silent again. I sighed, pulled up one of the chairs in the parlor, closed my eyes and waited for the Horror Show to be over. I may have seemed cool as a cucumber, but inside, my stomach felt like a cannonball, tight and heavy; my heart was pounding out of my chest and my muscles were trembling so bad they ached. I fought the urge to run out screaming, and told myself that it would all be over soon. This happened more than once a day, and I still couldn't get used to it. I was still afraid.

As the house grumbled for the finale, I breathed deep and calmed myself down. When I felt sure my knees would not buckle, I walked into my living room, stood under the cushions on the ceiling, and, like I'd done every day since, clung to them and let my weight hang. Nothing happened. I felt like a child hanging from the monkey bars in the playground. In truth, the cushions were a lot sturdier than the playground equipment we'd had growing up. I'd been trying to get them off the ceiling for days now, but they never budged.

I shrugged and got myself some dinner. I ate on my deck and watched the moths twitching by the light of the outdoor lamps. I heard a child's giggle and looked up to see the same little boy run into the house. I heard footsteps running up the stairs and doors slamming inside.

"Hey Mark, wassup?" I'd dialed his number and was relieved when I heard his voice.

"Eh, not much," he said, "how's the Horror Show?"

"Aw, multiple daily screenings I'm afraid. Listen, we still on for this weekend?"

"Yeah," he sounded edgy, as if he wasn't sure he wanted to go, "Apollo wants to leave Jude with his mom, so we'll be there about nine-ish Saturday."

"Sounds good," I paused, "listen, it's okay if you don't want to go, I'll be fine. You don't have to do this, you know."

"Dude, I don't understand any of this, but there's no way I'm leaving you to handle this alone. Hell, you should've come to us sooner."

"Yeah," I said, "wish I had."

We chatted for a while longer about work and life and whatever, as if nothing was out of the ordinary. When we hung up, I went inside and turned on the TV. I watched "Renegade" on Hulu. It was one of my favorite shows growing up and, watching it now, it was terrible, but I loved it. *It's so cheesy, it's awesome*, I laughed out loud, *Johnny-Boy, you had the worst taste in TV back then.*

I remember I used to dream about riding across the country on a motorcycle, and now, I wished I'd bought a Harley instead of this house.

The next afternoon I was in the library, typing away at my story when I felt someone plop down into a seat in front of me. I was on a roll, writing the most exciting part, when the newcomer cleared their throat—I supposed in order to get my attention —but I ignored them. When they did it again, louder, I sighed and looked up.

A short stubby woman was sitting in front of me. She was about my age, maybe older, and upon closer inspection, had somewhat of a resemblance to Doris the Librarian.

"May I help you?" I asked annoyed.

"I hear you were looking through high school yearbooks yesterday. My Aunt Doris told me, she thought I might know you from way back when."

She had a high squeaky voice. It wasn't pleasant to my ears, but I had to admit, she had a nice smile.

"Yeah," I said.

"Were you looking for someone in particular? I grew up here, so I might be able to help. I'm still in touch with a lot of people from school."

I watched her intently, not wondering if she *could* help me—I'm sure she could, she must've known about the murders—but wondering if she *would*. I decided to take a chance, what could I lose? At worst, I could say I had been Anna's pen-pal or something back then.

"Yeah," I cleared my throat, "I wonder if you know Anna Jenkins, and how I may contact her?"

Her smile faded instantly. She looked down at the table and twitched her fingers. I waited. I didn't want to encourage her, lest she ask for too much information.

"Yeah, I knew her," she mumbled, "her family died, you know."

I looked at her blankly, hoping she'd go on.

"She made my life miserable."

It figured; plain-looking, chubby girl like that was sure to have been bullied. As a victim of school bullying myself, I recognized my brethren instantly and knew how to get them to open up.

"Yeah, Matthew Russell was the most popular guy at my school, and he pushed me around every day of my life. What did Anna do to you?" I asked.

"Well, she called me names, made fun of my clothes, my family, you know, the same thing she did to girls who weren't 'up to her level'."

"Is that all?" I leaned closer, I knew there was more to that. I could see it in her eyes. I hadn't thought of Matt Russell in years, but I could tell Anna Jenkins still haunted this woman.

"She dated the boy I liked," she looked down at her hands, "his name was Dave Murphy and he was gorgeous."

I smiled. Her voice was like nails on chalkboard.

"I'm Jack," I extended my hand, "nice to meet you."

"I'm Kathy," she shook it.

I asked her to tell me more about Anna Jenkins, and she was more than willing to get a lot of stuff off her chest. It seems Anna was no angel in school. She wasn't very popular nor well-liked by the student body in general, but got excellent grades, which gave her a good reputation with the teachers. They held her in high regard, so she often got away with subtle bullying but, to those she deemed inferior, she was the Devil incarnate. This fit with the mental picture I already had of her, and I couldn't imagine how hard it must have been for this girl and many others. I'd finished *Innocent, Evil* a couple of days before (I'd even lent it to Apollo), and totally understood why Jenny had said it described Anna perfectly. Like Marla, Anna was the perfect child to adults, but was a monster to kids. And even though the adults knew she had flaws, they chalked it up to children being children, and she had made sure that no one could fault her for more. But concerning her peers—especially her little brother—when push came to shove, Anna was a snake in the grass just waiting to strike.

Kathy had a lot to say about Anna Jenkins and time dragged on. I wasn't getting any useful information about her whereabouts now, nor about the murders, so I just flat out asked.

"I don't know. I heard she went up to Maine to live with her aunt, and then, well, I didn't really want to keep in touch," she went on, "all I heard was that the cops couldn't find who killed her family and she was all broken up about it."

I began packing up my stuff to take my leave.

"You know, she could've just left Dave Murphy alone after she left, but I know that's why he went to college in Maine." I raised my eyebrows.

"What do you mean?"

"Yeah, we had just finished our sophomore year when her parents died, but Dave was a senior. He was gonna go to college somewhere in the Midwest, but suddenly changed his mind and enrolled in a community college up in Maine. I think it was to be with her. I don't know much about him now, I mean, he didn't even know I existed back then, but I'm sure he followed Anna to Maine."

I told her it was great meeting her and that I'd enjoyed our conversation, but that I had dinner plans and needed to go. I walked out into the sunshine and almost bumped into Mike Monroe walking in.

"Hiya, Mike," I said cheerfully.

53

"How aah ya, kid?" He smiled, "You're lookin' cheeahful. Life must be bettah, huh."

"Sure is," I said, then, almost as an afterthought I went on, "listen, do you remember if a Dave Murphy was Anna Jenkins's boyfriend?"

"Dunno, kid. Don' think I evah heard his name," he said, "still lookin' into that? Did you find anythin' interestin' up in Maine?"

"Sure did," I waved as I walked down the library steps, "have a good one!"

As I walked home, I thought about what Kathy had said; David Murphy was Anna Jenkins's boyfriend in Peaceville. He had gone to college in Maine, the year she moved in with Jenny. David Saunders was Anna's boyfriend in Maine when Jenny died. It was quite a coincidence that she would have two boyfriends named David...Both around the same time...Both involved with her when her family members died...

Johnny-Boy, you are an idiot, I slapped my forehead, *you should've looked up David Murphy in the yearbook!*

"Dammit!" I said out loud. A cat meowed from a nearby fence.

It was too late to go back to the library; Doris would be closing soon and I didn't want to bump into Kathy again, so I kept walking home.

I needed to see if Murphy and Saunders were one and the same; I sat in my office and looked up the webpage Doris had used the day before. It loaded easily and I entered the parameters of the yearbooks I was looking for.

I'd just typed 'David Murphy' in the search box when the house went quiet again.

"No, no, no, no, wait, wait," I said to the walls, "please wait. It's important!"

I was desperate for the page to finish loading before the computer went dark. Yearbook portraits were just appearing when the screen went blank and I was plunged into utter and complete darkness. I trembled. Outside, the sun still shone in the long New England evening, but in here, I couldn't see a thing despite the light from the open blinds. It was as if a barrier was stopping all light from coming through. I stuck my hand out towards the window and almost screamed when I couldn't even see my fingers in front of me.

I heard noises behind me and I was scared to turn around. They sounded like footsteps coming up the stairs, and the hairs rose at the back of my neck. For one brief moment, I thought someone had broken into my house, but the footsteps sounded hollow, as if coming to me from another space and another time. They weren't real footsteps, and that's what scared me most.

My chair swung around and I found myself in a child's bedroom, facing a bed. There was a strange bluish light in the room and the wallpaper had little images of dinosaurs; there were Hot Wheels strewn on the floor. In the bed, there was a small lump tucked beneath Spiderman covers. I tried to look away, but felt as if something was blocking my muscles, I couldn't move, and I imagined this is what being paraplegic must feel like. I couldn't shut my eyes either, so I was forced to look at the little blond head laying on the Spidey pillow and I knew what was about to happen.

The doorknob turned slowly and I heard a little voice whisper, "Mommy?"

It broke my heart and tears leapt from my eyes. I was certain it wasn't Beth Jenkins behind that door and I knew that these were Tommy's last moments of life. The door creaked open; I screamed.

"NO! NO! I DON'T WANT TO SEE THIS! NO!" I yelled to no avail.

I saw the glimmer of metal as some kind of blade swung down onto the bed. The little boy screamed as blood and guts exploded from his little body, splattering my face and my clothes. It was in my mouth and the taste of rusty metal almost made me vomit. It was on my eyebrows and I felt it drip from my hair. I still couldn't move and I saw a tall thin figure approach the broken body and spit on it. The eerie light shone on the ghostly, smiling face of a teenage girl. I'd found what I'd been looking for; I now knew what Anna Jenkins looked like. She looked in my direction and smirked. Then, cocking her head, walked over to where I was sitting. She loomed over me and was bending down as if to whisper something in my ear, when I heard a deep booming voice from the door.

"STOP!"

The word seemed to create sunlight and, as Anna turned in its direction, it swallowed the images before me, blinding me with one final flash.

When my eyes adjusted I saw Apollo walking over to me while someone hovered in the doorway behind him. I was shaking and tears streamed down my face. The dinosaur wallpaper was gone and I was back in my own little office. I rubbed my face and ruffled my hair as if trying to wash the blood off me, when I felt Apollo's hands on my shoulders.

"Jack," he said, "it's okay. It's all right."

I mumbled something about blood and he assured me there was nothing there. The other person had come up next to me and I realized it was Mike Monroe, looking down at me the way my father used to when I'd woken up from a nightmare as a child.

"It's all right, kid" he said in his heavy Boston accent, "it's all ovah."

Mike shakily pulled up the other chair and Apollo sat down on the floor. They were both pale and their cheeks were sunken, and I could only imagine what I must look like. I put my face in my hands and sobbed like a little boy.

We sat like that for a while longer, until my tears died down and Apollo broke the silence.

"C'mon, Jack," he said, patting my shoulder, "let's go. You're staying at my place tonight. We can pick up Mark tomorrow morning and go see this Babcock."

"I know what she looks like now," was all I could say.

"Yeah," Mike said, "'twas definitely her. An' she had help."

I turned to him, confounded.

"She was with a guy," Apollo explained, "they both had some kind of small blade, like camping axes. I couldn't see the weapons too well."

"David Murphy," I said, and swung my desk chair around.

I clicked the spacebar on my computer and moved my fingers around the trackpad, but the screen remained dark. Then I pressed the power button and nothing. I had plugged it in when I'd sat down, but the indicator light was dead.

"Aw shit, kid," said Mike, "I hope ya didn' lose anythin' impoahtant."

I shook my head. Everything was saved on the thumb-drive I always carried with me, and luckily, I'd backed up the entire hard-drive to an external drive the night before. My computer was my life and my living, I never took any chances with it, and for once, I was grateful for my paranoia.

We walked out into the evening sunshine and the warmth felt good on my skin. I hadn't realized how cold I was, it had felt like winter in there. I locked the front door and walked over to Apollo's car. We shook Mike's hand and he told us to call on him for any reason, at any time. He gave us his phone number and, as I looked into his eyes, I could almost swear I saw my own grandfather peeking back at me. This was a seriously nice guy and I felt lucky to have him as a neighbor. He had behaved like a real man in there, they both had; neither had mocked, nor joked, nor judged me for being so afraid. Standing in the street with them, I felt comfortable in their company, and I knew that some barrier between us had crumbled. I now had one more person to turn to.

We got in the car and Jude gave me a little doggie kiss. Apollo explained how he had made plans with his mother for dinner and had decided to drop Jude off that night, instead of in the morning. He said he had been driving to his childhood home in Lexington when he suddenly decided to stop by my place and ask if I wanted to come along; just out of the blue, he said, the idea just hit him.

Apollo was getting out of the car, while Mike was walking in his own door, when the Horror Show started. They heard the house rumbling like thunder, he said, and went in when they saw two dark figures walk through the front door. They thought someone was breaking in.

"We saw them reach the upstairs landing," he went on, "and as we ran up, we heard you scream. The guy was standing by the door to the small bedroom, and he didn't do anything when Mike and I looked inside. I thought she was going to murder you, so I yelled to stop it. That's when they vanished."

"Thank you," I said.

I tried to remember if I had thanked Mike before we left, but my brain was going a mile a minute and my thoughts felt fuzzy.

"You did," he said, as if reading my mind, "you thanked him when you shook his hand."

We arrived at his mother's house and what had started out as a lonely and horrible evening, suddenly became one of the most pleasant ones I'd had in years.

Apollo's mother Lupe, and his aunt Tallulah, are two of the nicest ladies I've ever met, and I wished my parents hadn't moved to Maryland before I'd met them—they would've gotten along really well. Their house was homey, just like a house should be, and I realized how much I missed the feeling.

After dinner, Apollo sat down at his piano and regaled us with his amazing talent, while I sat quietly on the couch and thought about what had happened tonight.

"Why'd it have to be Tommy's murder?" I said aloud, and Apollo stopped, "Why not the parents? Why did the house have to show me the murder of a little boy?"

I suddenly felt enraged and tears sprung to my eyes, as if I had been unjustly treated. I felt like I'd been tortured. I'd had to endure the death of a defenseless creature while being helpless to do anything about it. His little "mommy?" whisper still resonated in my head.

"I don't know," Apollo said, "maybe because he was the first to die?"

"She spit on him, you know."

"That's fucked up."

We were silent for a while longer, listening to the sound of crockery and women's voices in the kitchen.

"I don't understand any more than you do," he said, "but I agree with Mark, there's a reason to all this. I don't think ghosts just haunt us for the heck of it. There's more."

"Maybe they're asking you for help," we looked up to see Tallulah leaning against the doorway, "maybe they're grieving and need your help to move on."

She had a heavy British accent, and her voice, melodious and kind, rang out through the living room like bells.

"And, Jack," Tallulah moved into the room, "everything you experience in your past leads you to your present. It becomes a part of you and makes you who you are. There is a reason for everything, even witnessing the murder of a little boy. Don't worry if you don't understand now, the meaning will be revealed when the time is right."

She yawned.

"I'm an old woman," she said as she walked out and bid us goodnight.

I asked Apollo if he had mentioned anything to her about the Funhouse, and he denied it.

"She's like that," he said, "the supernatural doesn't faze her at all. She has no trouble believing in ghosts and spirits, and I think we should talk to her when we get back from Maine. She might be able to help us out."

I nodded.

Tallulah was in her seventies but didn't look a day over sixty. She was tall and graceful and held herself like royalty. She was a force of nature and I had no doubt any input she might have would be valuable. If anything, she could probably kick Anna Jenkins's ass just by looking at her.

CHAPTER SEVEN

Away We Go to Osprey Cove

I spent the night on Apollo's futon, but didn't get much rest at all. Over and over, I dreamed of Anna's satisfied face as she spit on her own brother's body. I just couldn't get the image out of my head. How could she do something so horrible? And the guy that was with her, what role did he play?

We should've looked up David Murphy on Apollo's computer, but we were too tired to think about investigating further. If that's what we could call investigating. I felt as if we had all the information at our fingertips, yet had nothing concrete to put Anna Jenkins in prison, save that horrible scene from yesterday. It's not like we could go to the cops and tell them I'd seen her kill her brother.

Dawn was coming in through the window of Apollo's spare bedroom, which he had turned into a small music and books studio. The room was incredible. The walls were covered with bookshelves practically overflowing, and I knew there was a state-of-the-art music system in the closet surrounded by shelves upon shelves of CDs. I remember how the move into his place had been a bitch too. Apollo is the only person I know who has ever rivaled me when it came to book ownership.

There were several electric guitars resting on their stands, and, as the dawning light seeped in through the window and shone on their strings, I felt as if an idea was dawning inside me. As if we'd missed something. But I just couldn't place it. I looked up at the posters on the ceiling and tried to drag that thought out of the back of my mind, but my hold on it just kept slipping. I sighed and closed my eyes.

I must have dozed off, because when I opened my eyes, the light in the room had gotten brighter and I heard Apollo moving around.

"Hey, man" he said, as I walked into the living room, "you all right?"

"Yeah,"

He lived on the North Shore, in a two bedroom apartment overlooking the beach. The view from his living room and balcony was amazing; the morning sun shone on the water, and I could hear the sound of waves breaking and seagulls cawing, even through the closed sliding-door. He was in the kitchen making coffee, already dressed and showered.

"Want some?" He offered and I nodded, "Couldn't sleep well, you?"

"No," I answered, "I couldn't stop thinking about what I saw, and I have the feeling we're missing something important, but I can't think what."

He nodded and poured me a cup. We stood in the kitchen sipping the warm coffee.

"I finished the book, you know," he said after a few moments, "it got in my head too, I dreamed all night about the Hensons. How do you even begin to live with someone like that?"

"I dunno," I whispered, and we went back to our coffee. The apartment felt strangely quiet without Jude. After a few minutes, he offered to lend me some clothes. I looked at the microwave clock and thought about how great it was that it showed the correct time, instead of blinking the default. It was seven-thirty.

"We should have some breakfast too, before we head out," he said smiling.

I could tell he was getting excited about a day trip and I've always admired that about him; the guy was always up for something new, and he always found the bright side to the darkest situations.

I showered and felt oddly clean, as if the water hadn't just washed my body, but also cleaned my mind and soul. As if it had washed away all that had happened yesterday at the Funhouse. I was glad I'd accepted Apollo's offer of clothes—I wasn't sure I could wear what I'd worn without feeling the grime of the ghost blood that had been spilt on me.

Apollo's jeans were only slightly long on my legs, but other than that, they fit well enough. Apollo is the tallest at six foot four, I'm in the middle at six feet and Mark is the shortest at five foot ten. We often tease him about his "dwarfish" stature and call him such names as 'Gimli', 'Frodo' and 'Leprechaun'. We really have quite an arsenal of names for him.

I smiled as I put socks on. It felt good to think about something other than Anna Jenkins.

We picked Mark up in Salem. It's always struck me as funny how such a skeptic like him could live in the witch capital of the world. Don't get me wrong, I love Salem and Halloween there is one giant costume party, but I just hadn't imagined Mark living there until it had actually happened.

We told Mark all about the night before and he listened attentively, no longer willing to explain everything away. He just sat and listened, nodding occasionally. I think this situation was getting too much for him, and I feared it would change him forever. After all, his world view had been altered radically in a few minutes already, how much more could he take?

I looked at Apollo and I knew that he at least was going to be all right. He was calmly looking out the window. We were in his car, but I'd offered to drive since I was the reason we were going anyway, and he'd agreed. He must have been very tired, otherwise he would've insisted on driving.

He leaned forward and turned on 60's on 6 on his satellite radio. I smiled thankfully; he knows I'm a sucker for Oldies and I felt the gesture as some sort of get-well-soon card. Like a balm to soothe all that was happening. Apollo, Mark and myself were all about the Heavy Metal (it was what had brought Mark and me together in the beginning), but Oldies were my everything's-going-to-be-all-right music. It was what my parents played in their car and at home. I remember my mom used to sing "And I Love Her" to me at bedtime, only she'd sing "you" instead of "her" as she tucked me in. Oldies was the music of my childhood and now, it was like comfort food for me. Whenever I listened to The Beatles, or Tommy James, or the Grass Roots, I felt that everything was going to be okay.

Mark was silent in the backseat and, through the rearview mirror, I saw his face obscured by his longish, full, brown hair and copious beard as his head slumped on his shoulders, either deep in thought or fast asleep. Mark had a wild, bearish look to him and I've often thought that's what Mowgli might've looked like if he'd grown up with Baloo.

Apollo was still looking out the window when "Cool Jerk" came on. I was instantly transported back to the hundreds of times I'd watched *Home Alone 2* growing up and began singing the song. Apollo joined in and Mark followed. We sang at the top of our lungs, Apollo and Mark moving their arms up and down like Kevin McCallister's inflatable clown in the hotel tub. Then, in unison, we raised our right arms and quoted Uncle Frank's famous line in the movie.

It was such a spontaneous moment that we exploded into laughter; Apollo's thunderous roar drowning out Mark's own straight up no-nonsense ha-ha-ha and my slightly dopey yuk-yuk.

The grimness vanished, as if whatever spell the Funhouse had put on us had been broken by that one song and that one collective memory we'd never actually shared together.

"So," Mark said as the song ended, "the other night I had date with the most boring girl. I mean, she was smokin' hot y'know, but even the sex was boring; she just laid there...Oooh, there's a Mickey D's coming up, I'm starving."

Apollo and I looked at each other and smiled, our boy was back. Good ol' douchey Mark was back! The Funhouse could dish out whatever it wanted, I could take it, Apollo could take it, and Mark, maybe lagging a little behind, could also take it.

We were ready.

CHAPTER EIGHT

The Death of Pie

We met Pluto Babcock outside the Moose Crossing Diner. As I was about to introduce the guys, he held up his hand.

"Never mind that for now, my wife will have my ass if I don't bring all of you for lunch at our house."

He motioned us to follow him. I looked at the guys and shrugged.

We walked in silence as he led us down the street to his house. Like everything in Osprey Cove, the house was well taken care of and I got the feeling they hired someone to tend the yard for them. It was a big one-story ranch surrounded by a huge yard with shrubs groomed to perfection. There was a path leading from the driveway to the front door with flowers on both sides. I liked the house, it felt like a home.

"I would've thought you'd have one of those old Victorian houses. I remember you said your house had been built the same year as Jenny's."

"That was our family home, only it burned down when I was a kid. Grandpa claimed some furniture spontaneously combusted, but I believe he left a lit cigar lying around. Oh well, at least no one was hurt. This isn't the house I grew up in; my cousin Joe was an architect (he passed away last year) and he built this for us as a wedding present."

He opened the door.

"Come in, come in, boys," I heard a cheerful woman say as Babcock ushered us in, "I'm Amelia. It's so good to meet you all!"

She was a chubby woman with blond hair that flipped up at her shoulders, a lovely voice and a warm smile. She was wiping her hands on a dish rag as we approached.

"I'm Jack," I said, offering her my hand, "this is Mark, and this is Apollo."

They both shook hands with her as Babcock slapped me on the back.

"Oh my," she said, "you boys sure are tall and handsome! Come on out to the back yard, lunch is all ready."

She led the way, waddling like a goose. In fact, the woman was a lot like a goose; short, with stubby legs and a big behind. She wasn't sexy like Nancy the Waitress, but she wasn't graceless like Kathy the

63

Librarian's Niece. *Motherly, Johnny-Boy, that's the word you're looking for.*

"I think we just met Mother Goose," Apollo whispered beside me; I chuckled softly.

The Babcocks had set up a table in the middle of their enormous backyard. It was one of those white iron tables with squiggly decorations on the legs. We had a very pleasant lunch of salad and sandwiches while Amelia talked about Jenny Jenkins. She told us what a sweet woman she had been, tranquil and affectionate, and about how she couldn't understand why no decent man worth his salt had ever snatched her up.

"She was very good looking too, and when I first met her, I thought she looked like a doll. Maybe it was the fact she was a librarian, right Pluto? Maybe that's what put men off?"

Babcock shrugged.

"I guess in those days there was no such thing as a sexy librarian," Amelia went on, "I never did understand it, and you know what? That Anna, her niece? She was nowhere near as good looking as Jenny had been in her prime."

I nodded grimly as the memory of Anna Jenkins over her brother's body flashed through my mind. I remembered every feature of her face, and in that moment, I would never had said that Anna was pretty at all.

We finished our food and Amelia got up and collected the plates with such authority and efficiency that we barely knew what had happened. Mark banged himself on the table as he tried to stand and help her; Apollo and I helplessly watched her clear everything while she insisted we not lift a finger. Babcock looked at me intently as she walked inside.

"What's up, kid?" His tone was serious, "Did something happen?"

"Yeah," I nodded, "how much does Amelia know about what's going on?"

Babcock assured us Amelia knew everything, including the reason we were here and that we were free to talk about anything at all in her presence.

She came back with a pie in her hands and a photo album under her arm. Babcock took it from her as she set the pie on the table. She cut the pie and handed us each a plate, giving me an extra big slice ("you're skin and bones, Jack") while Mark pouted like a berated puppy when Amelia handed him a much smaller portion. He wasn't fat, he was muscular, but his broad shoulders and short height made him look slim, at best. In all fairness to Amelia, Mark's and Apollo's slices were more than fair, while Pluto's looked like a sliver next to mine.

She explained that she had many pictures of Jenny, Paul and Beth before Anna was born, and a few more of Tommy, though she wasn't sure there were any pictures of Anna. The girl was elusive.

"I just thought this might help you find her. I hear you boys are investigating the happenings at Jenny's house, right Pluto?"

She sat down and cut a bit off her pie with her fork.

"Yes," said Mark as he began flipping through the album, then he turned to me and said, "you should look through this, you're the only one who's seen her."

Babcock raised his eyebrows and Amelia set her fork down. I looked at the couple and, for the second time that day, explained what had happened the night before. As I talked, I saw Amelia's eyes fill up with tears, and when I got to the part where Anna kills Tommy, I left out the fact that she spit on him. I could tell that probably would've sent Amelia over the edge. When I was done, Apollo told them about what he and Mike Monroe had seen from outside the house.

"Murphy?" Babcock asked when Apollo mentioned Anna's companion.

"Yeah, David Murphy," I answered, "I found out through one of their classmates that he was Anna's boyfriend, and we know now he was involved in the killings."

"Kevin Murphy was the guy I told ya performed Jenny's autopsy. It's way too much of a coincidence, I wonder if they're related."

"I bet, Pluto," Amelia turned to her husband, "maybe that's what they had on him? Maybe he knew about the Peaceville murders and the police cover-up," she went on, "I mean, there was obviously a police cover-up. No suspects? No murder weapon? Not one single clue uncovered? I don't buy it, and Jenny didn't buy it either, she always thought there was something fishy going on."

"Where is the doctor now?" Apollo asked.

"Dead. Spent the last two years of his life in a coma. He was in a car accident about a week after Jenny's death. He had just enough time to write up that phony autopsy report. Now it all fits. This girl and her boyfriends are genuine serial killers."

The grimness I'd felt in the car had settled itself over our table, despite the bright sunshine and hot day. We looked down at our plates and I began to nibble on my untouched pie. It was raspberry and it was delicious. I wondered if Amelia had made it herself. I closed my eyes as the warm and buttery taste of the dough filled my palate, while the tart sweetness of the raspberries sent the glands on the side of my mouth all a-flutter. When I opened them, everyone was eating their piece with such gusto that the grimness had vanished again.

"What if she's dead?" Amelia suddenly set her fork down and looked up, "What if Anna is dead?"

"What do you mean?" I asked, looking around. Everyone else had also stopped eating and was looking at her in stunned silence.

"Well, how else could you have seen her? You said she came to you and leaned over as if to say something," she went on, "how could she have known you were there if that had been like a replay of what happened years ago?"

I was speechless. She was right, we were all supposing Anna Jenkins was still alive and at large somewhere, but there was no way of knowing; she had disappeared since she went to college.

"But," Mark spoke up, "why would they still be haunting Jack? Wouldn't her death have put them to rest?"

"Maybe not," Apollo scratched his nose as we all turned to him, "maybe what the spirits want is that she be officially recognized as the murderer. *If* she's dead, because I really don't get the feeling she is. I think that would've turned up in the Google search, some obituary or something."

I nodded. I didn't think she was dead either, but still...

"Nah," Babcock said, "I would've found something out. I've been looking for her for years. In my opinion, she changed her name. Probably even before enrolling in college. I believe Jenny's murder was planned down to the last detail, as well as her family's."

"Michigan State University" Amelia spoke, "that's where Jenny told me Anna had gone, but when we looked for her there, there was no one by that name. I just always thought she transferred out after Jenny's death."

"Or," Mark waved his finger, "she never went there. I mean, what if she told Jenny she was going to Michigan State and then just went somewhere else? That would definitely cover her tracks."

"Maybe she stayed around here. After all, her boyfriend moved here for her. She can't have come from so far away just to kill her aunt," I looked at Babcock and Amelia, "by the way, is there a computer we can borrow? I just remembered we still don't know who David Murphy is or what he looked like."

Babcock got his daughter's laptop. He set it down on the table and we huddled around, looking expectantly, as it started up. I've never understood why we all do that, staring at it is not going to speed up the process.

I logged into the website Doris the Librarian had shown me and typed the name in the search box under the Peaceville North High yearbooks. We got a couple of hits, an Alex Murphy for one, (Mark smiled and gave us two thumbs up—he loved *Robocop*), a David Beacham, but no David Murphy. I put my head in my hands and sighed.

"Try the other school," Apollo said behind me.

I ran the same search in the Peaceville South High School website. Nothing.

"What the hell?" Babcock asked, "Who is this guy and where did he come from?"

"Does this guy even exist?" Mark asked.

I nodded and said he had to, since Kathy had also been in love with him. They all had to know each other from somewhere. Apollo was quiet and pale, like he was doubting what he had seen. Mark had his finger over his mouth in a pensive gesture, trying to think of some logical explanation. Babcock and Amelia both looked completely confounded. I'm sure I had a similar expression on my face.

"Maybe," Mark spoke up waving his finger again, "maybe, he went to a different school, like a private school?"

"And what, they met somewhere else?" I asked.

It was possible. There were hundreds of different ways kids could meet. Maybe David Murphy had gone to school with them as children, and then moved to another district. Or maybe they had met at a summer camp, or a recreation center. If that was true, then we were looking for a needle in a haystack.

"Why don't you do a regular Google search for David Murphy?" Apollo looked at me.

I typed in the name and came up with what seemed like a thousand hits. Then I searched for "David Murphy Peaceville, MA" and as the page was loading, it suddenly began to rain cats and dogs. Maybe, while we were all huddled around the computer we didn't notice the storm clouds rolling in. We sprung up and began gathering everything so as to get in the house as soon as possible.

I closed the laptop and ran to get out of the driving rain. It was coming down thick and hard. Freak storms were not unusual in New England, but this was ridiculous.

Apollo and Babcock gathered the dishes, while Amelia followed me with the photo album shielded by her chubby arms and chest.

Mark, the Eternal Hungry Man, made a beeline for the remaining pie and, as I stepped out again to aid someone, I saw him run across the yard, trip, and with the pie held out in front of him, fall. He didn't let go of his precious pie, and as fate would have it, buried his face in it when he hit the ground, thus ruining the very thing he was trying to save.

Amelia cried out as she rushed to help Mark, and I ran towards the backyard table where some stuff had been left behind.

I passed Apollo sprinting with a pile of plates in his hands and a big smile on his face and the rumble of his laughter blending with the thunder above. He had seen what would later be known as The Death of Pie, and almost fell himself as his knees buckled, weak from laughing.

Babcock was behind him, running with two glasses in each hand and one under his arm. His head was inexplicably thrown back, chins to the wind, while his belly jiggled like Jell-o under the unsteady baby-like run his short, fat legs equipped him with.

I grabbed the remaining glasses and cutlery, and was dashing back to the house when suddenly, I felt a strange warmth behind me as the world lit up all around. I was lifted off the ground and the last thing I remember was Amelia's waddle and Mark's dejected stride as they rushed toward the sliding doors.

CHAPTER NINE

Out of The Frying Pan

When I woke up, everyone was looking down at me. I turned from one face to another. What the hell had happened? There was only one face I didn't recognize, but I was sure it was Babcock's daughter because she looked like a much younger version of Amelia (goose-like demeanor and all), and she was just as chubby as her parents. She was standing close to Apollo and kept glancing up at him with puppy-dog eyes. Apollo appeared not to pay attention—he's very good looking and he's gotten used to women gazing at him.

"Dude," Mark said as our eyes met, "you almost got struck by lightning."

I blinked. My head felt heavy, my muscles ached and my mouth was dry. I was in a hospital bed, wearing one of those gowns that close up in the back and leave your tush hanging out. I also had a walking cast on my right leg.

"At least I didn't kill the pie," I croaked.

Apparently, it wasn't funny.

"I'm all right," I said.

I made a motion to sit up but was held back by Amelia's gentle, yet firm touch on my shoulder.

"The doctor will be here soon to check on you. He said lightning strike victims often have injuries that are not immediately noticeable."

As she spoke, her eyes filled with tears. They cut right through me. I didn't feel too hurt, save for the pain in my ankle and the heaviness of my head, but the concern in her eyes made me uneasy, as if somehow, everything had changed forever.

"I saw the whole thing," Apollo spoke softly, "when I got to the house, I turned around to see if anyone else needed help, and the lightning struck the table. You were already halfway across the yard, but suddenly you were lifted off the ground and pushed into Amelia's rose garden. It blew your shoes right off and somehow fractured your ankle."

I looked down at my arms and legs and noticed there were scratches everywhere, as if I'd been mauled by cats.

"The shockwave from the lightning traveled through the yard and got you as you were running. It probably wouldn't have reached you if you'd been closer to the house," Mark explained, "at least you're awake now, so that's good."

"Wait," I said, "how long have I been out?"

"It's about midnight now, so it's been a while," Babcock answered, "you hit your head pretty hard against a rock and we called 9-1-1 immediately. They brought you here to the hospital in Brunswick. You gave us one hell of a scare, kid... By the way, this is my daughter, Abigail. She just came home from a college graduation trip."

He pointed to her and I smiled and nodded as our eyes met. She blushed and smiled shyly.

I touched my head and felt a huge bump just above my eyebrow. *Sheesh Johnny-Boy, one inch below and you'd have hit your temple. One inch below and you'd have been in the morgue.*

"There's more," I turned to Mark as he spoke, while Abigail glanced up at him with a 'kiss me' look on her face, "they said I should call your family, but I couldn't get a hold of your parents, so, I, um... called, um...you know..." He looked around embarrassed as I realized whom he meant.

"YOU CALLED MY SISTER?"

I felt a small pain in my lungs as my voice came out, as if I'd been running in the rain. My parents were traveling through Eastern Asia for the summer and it was difficult to get a call through as they were somewhere in the Indian jungle, but my sister...*Oh jeezus.*

"Yeah," he looked down at his feet, "she said she'd try to catch the next flight out."

"Call her back and tell her I'm all right, and there's no need to come." I looked sternly at Mark. I loved her, but she could be a handful.

"What's wrong with your sister?" Amelia turned to me, her hand was still on my shoulder and she placed her other hand on my forearm in the most maternal gesture I'd felt in a long time.

"Nothing," I said, "I love her dearly and we're pretty close, but if I had to describe her in one word, I'd say she's fiery."

Amelia smiled softly.

"She's my big sister," I went on, "so if anything happens to me, she turns fierce. When she found out I was being bullied at school, she almost got expelled for defending me. She was known as "The Nerd Avenger" after that."

I still remember Matt Russell lying on the ground grabbing his crotch after the kick she gave him. I recalled how proud and embarrassed I had been. The term 'ball-buster' had taken a whole new meaning.

Suddenly I burst out laughing as I pictured her in a match against Anna Jenkins. People looked at me weird and I was about to explain when Mark's phone rang and he went out of the room to take the call. Presently, he came back and, placing his phone in my face, took my picture, and went right back out.

"I guess it's proof of life," Apollo shrugged.

Mark returned, looking relieved.

"Sammy's staying put," he said, smiling contentedly.

The Babcocks looked confused.

"Sammy, Samantha—my sister. She's a Kindergarten teacher in Sacramento. Went out west for college and stayed there."

"Wait, your sister's name is Sam? As in *Sam Adams*?" Babcock burst out into a hearty laugh and I rolled my eyes. Apollo joined him, and soon, everyone followed suit.

"She said the only condition was that you keep her updated and call her yourself," Mark went on, still chuckling, "so here, knock yourself out."

He tossed his phone to me.

"Yours is dead, by the way," Apollo said as I took it, "the lightning killed it."

I wasn't surprised, Mother Nature had failed in her mission to end me, so her consolation price had been my phone. And the pie.

They turned to leave as I put the phone to my ear. Abigail kept glancing at me as she walked out. She gazed at me the same way she'd gazed at Apollo and Mark, and for some reason I felt better; as if this signaled that my looks could contend with theirs. Apollo told Mark he smelled like raspberries and butter and Mark punched him in the arm as they disappeared. Now that I was all right, that delicious pie was the biggest tragedy of the day.

I called Sammy and explained what had happened. I told her everything. I know my sister, and unless she has all the information right off, she'll pester me with questions; what was I doing in Maine, who's Babcock and how did I meet these people, yadda-yadda-yadda. When I described the Babcocks, she burst out laughing.

"Seriously?" I heard her between yuks on the other line (she laughed like me), "Amelia and Abigail? And they remind you of geese?"

Her laughter grew in intensity and I asked her what was so funny.

"Amelia and Abigail Gabble are the geese in *The Aristocats* ! You know, that old Disney movie? I've seen it a thousand times with the kids and they crack me up. They're my favorite characters."

She laughed a while longer, and I could feel some tension dispel, as if she laughed her worries away. I've always loved that about my sister, once she lets loose, she's worry-free. I've often wished I could handle stress like her, or Apollo. They know how to let stuff go.

We talked until the doctor came in with a nurse to check on me.

"Sam, I gotta go, doctor's here," I tried to cut our conversation short as the doctor hovered just inside the doorway.

"Put him on!" Sam's voice was so loud I was certain he heard her.

I tried to mumble excuses, but Sam just kept shouting into the phone and insisting she speak with the doctor. I sighed and motioned to him.

"My sister," I mumbled as I reached the phone out to him.

"JOHN ADAMS, PUT THE DAMN DOCTOR ON THE PHONE NOW!" Sam bellowed into the room as the doctor took the phone.

They talked for a while. I suppose she kept asking him questions about the incident, my condition and any future treatment necessary, because I heard the doctor say that I seemed to be fine and that they were keeping me overnight and maybe tomorrow as well. He said the head injury seemed to be just a bump, but that they were going to run some tests anyway to check my brain function and fully evaluate me. He told her that physically, I was mostly unhurt, save for the fractured ankle (actually, it was just the fibula) and a few scratches and bruises, that I would be sore for a few days, and that they would prescribe painkillers for the leg. I would be in a walking cast (Aircast, he called it) for about a month.

I heard her getting excited on the other line as he explained that lightning strike victims often developed neurological and psychological disorders due to the electrical charge that had coursed through their bodies, but that he thought that was unlikely with me, since I hadn't been struck directly; but still, those closest to me should watch for personality changes and whatnot.

Meanwhile, the nurse took my pulse, checked my vitals and temperature. I was relieved when the doctor told Sam that he thought my prognosis was good and that, since he had seen there were people close to me, he didn't think it'd be necessary for her to come here.

The doctor walked over and handed me the phone, signaling she was still on the line. I put it to my ear.

"Jacky, don't worry about a thing. I'll call the 'rents and I'll tell them there's nothing to worry about, but you're not getting rid of me that easily. I'm still coming to you, even if I have to cancel my trip to Lake Tahoe."

"Don't cancel!" I exclaimed.

I'd forgotten she'd told me she was going next week with some girl friends and I didn't want her to miss her trip. I knew she'd scrimped and saved all year for that, even bypassing movies and the most basic entertainment to have enough money to go; I thought she'd have to dip into her savings to cancel and come here instead. Besides, she'd sounded so excited about it the last time we spoke, that the energy and excitement of that conversation had shone some sort of cleansing light on the Funhouse and had lifted my spirits. I'd almost said I wanted to go too.

"Don't cancel your trip, Sammy, please don't! Mark and Apollo are here, I'll be all right, I promise. I'll call you every hour on the hour if I have to, really, but don't cancel."

"Okay," she sighed, "but I'm still coming to you when I get back, so you better be ready. Tell Mark and Apollo I'll skin them alive if they don't take good care of you."

I chuckled as we hung up.

"Your sister is..."

I looked at the doctor.

"Fiery? Passionate? Volatile? Crazy? Energetic? Kick-ass?" I interjected as he racked his brains for a word.

"Indescribable."

The tests results arrived and Doctor Richardson said everything had come back normal, but that he'd still like to keep me under observation for another day. So I remained at the hospital until I received a clean bill of health.

Meanwhile, the Babcocks took the guys to Jenny Jenkins's house; Mark landed in the emergency room as well when he tried to climb the rotted stairs and put his foot through a step. His prize was six stitches on the inside of his right shin and a tetanus shot. Needless to say they found nothing useful on the ground floor.

"I wonder," I turned to Apollo, "what if the real find is upstairs?"

"Could be," Apollo made a pensive face, "but then, if Jenny is the ghost, why would she try to keep it hidden?"

"Did you guys actually see anything?" I asked.

"Yeah, we got the same manifestation you described before. I get the feeling she wasn't pushed down the stairs, but thrown out of a window or something. After the light floated up to the second floor, there were noises as if furniture was being moved around and then one long scream. I imagined that there was some kind of struggle, or maybe Jenny was trying to block a door or something and then got pushed off."

"Hmm," I scratched my head. "It wouldn't have been too difficult to move the body to the bottom of the stairs. After all, Anna probably wasn't alone, that David Saunders claimed to have been with her. I think we need to find a way to get up those stairs, maybe try and follow the light up."

Apollo shook his head and said that's exactly how Mark had gotten hurt. He'd tried to run up the stairs after the light but he hadn't been fast enough before the steps rotted again. He was lucky he'd only gone up three steps, otherwise, he might've fallen right through.

I spent that Sunday night at the hospital, while the Babcocks insisted Apollo and Mark stay with them. Abigail was beside herself. She was obviously very shy and the guys were either totally oblivious to her jejune flirtations, or just plain ignoring her. When I asked them about it, they rolled their eyes and said that, although she was a nice, quiet girl, at twenty-two, she was much too young and most definitely not their type. It was true, Mark had a tendency to like hot bimbos and one-night stands; and, while Apollo's girlfriends seemed great at first, they quickly turned into 'bossy, soul-sucking hags' as Mark had once put it. My last relationship had been a toxic disaster and I'd decided to lay low on the dating scene for a while. Even so, Abigail Babcock *was* too young, and not my type either.

I talked to Sam often during my stay at the hospital, and kept her updated on everything that was going on. I was surprised she was so understanding. I never imagined she'd be the type to take tales so fantastic as this in stride. She said it came from being around kids all the time; they came up with the weirdest stories and she'd gotten used to them. She told me that sometimes, children's fantasies had some sort of hidden truth behind them; but that in her experience, the most incredible ones were just imaginative tales the kids came up with. I wondered if she believed my mind was playing tricks on me, so I asked her what she thought about my ghostly happenings.

"I know you're telling the truth," Sam said, "your tales are fanciful in the Tolkien, Narnia or Earthsea style, and you've never liked ghost stories. I mean, Scooby-Doo used to give you nightmares, remember?"

She chuckled, pushing images of childhood sleepless nights to the forefront of my mind.

"That said," she went on, "I'd really like it if you didn't go back to that house, at least not alone, and not until we figure this out. Jack, really, please consider staying with Mark or Apollo or someone else. I'm still coming to you, and we'll figure out what to do."

I rolled my eyes. It was emasculating when she behaved like that, as if she was the white knight charging in to save the damsel in distress. *She's always been like that, Johnny-Boy, she's always been Lancelot on a quest to save Guinevere.* I suppose this instinct to protect the defenseless makes her so great at her job; she's amazing with kids and she's even won Teacher of the Year Awards in her district. I used to wish I were more gung-ho like her, until my grandfather told me that we were the perfect pair: *where you are weak, Johnny-Boy, she gives you strength; but when Sammy-Girl falters, you have the fortitude to pull her through.*

Sam's fears of me staying alone in the Funhouse were unfounded, since I was simply not allowed to stay there by anyone. Very early Monday morning, Apollo and Mark drove back to Massachusetts in order to be at work on time. They'd entrusted me to the Babcocks, who had behaved like real caring and loving people. But even so, their attentions were short-lived, since, upon being wheeled out the hospital's main entrance, I found myself facing Apollo's mother, Lupe, her hands in her pockets, elbows tucked at her sides, and smiling. Apollo had inherited that stance from her.

She said I was to stay with them until my leg healed and that Tallulah was inside signing me out. I tried to tell her that was not necessary, that I would be fine and that there was no need for me to impose.

"Ay, Yack, eet ees no imposee-cheeon," she said in her heavy Mexican accent, "we love to have joo overrr."

Lupe was in reality an average height woman, although she looked tiny next to Apollo and Tallulah. She had brown skin, straight black hair and emerald green eyes. Apollo had once told me her father was German and that's how she had inherited the light eye color. Apollo took after Tallulah's family more, but he had inherited Lupe's natural tan, only his skin was a lighter shade. He had also inherited her smile, and as she smiled down at me and spoke in her joyful manner, I couldn't refuse the offer to stay with them.

I fell asleep on the backseat during the drive home. When I woke up, we were already pulling up in front of the Funhouse. Tallulah said they'd help me get some things together as I slowly got out of the car. I hobbled to the door and had just opened it when Mike Monroe came hurrying across the street.

"Aah ya okay, kid?" he called, rushing to my side and looking down at the cast, "I've been calling ya to see how ya aah, since ya didn't come home all weeken'. I got no answah so I was worried, and I lost Apollah's numbah."

"I'm fine, Mike, but my phone isn't," I smiled at him, "I just had a little accident."

"That don' look little to me," he said pointing at my injured leg.

I introduced Lupe and Tallulah and told him what had happened in Maine. Tallulah explained that I would be staying with them for the duration of my treatment and that we were just going to get some of my things. Lupe also offered him the contents of my fridge, if it was all right with me. I nodded and laughed. It takes a mom to think like that, I would've just gotten some clothes and toiletries and left the few perishables to slowly rot in the refrigerator. I hadn't been able to cook elaborate meals for a while now since the power went out so much, but I still kept the necessary foodstuffs in it.

We went inside and, while I got what I needed, Mike and Lupe raided my fridge. Lupe told me that she would put anything she could in the freezer. At least the power outages only lasted a few minutes and not a few hours, otherwise the stuff in my freezer would be no good either.

The house was still spotless and seemed quiet. The couch cushions were still stuck to the ceiling and Tallulah scolded me like she would a child when I tried hanging from them. Mike said there had been grumbling over the weekend, but the screeching was louder now, and that he had seen Tommy playing in the yard like he used to. Once, he had thought he heard someone dropping their bicycle on the driveway, but when he looked there was nothing there. "Fuh some reason, kid, there's been moah spooky sh…(he glanced at the ladies) stuff goin' on since ya moved in than evah befoah."

As I slowly limped down the stairs with a duffel over my shoulder and my laptop bag, I saw Tallulah bending over by the back door.

"What's wrong little boy?" I heard her say, and as I walked over, I saw little Tommy's ghost squatting and crying.

"I'm sorry Jack got hurt," a tiny hollow voice said, only it seemed to come, not from the little boy, but from somewhere beside me.

Then he vanished. Lupe was still in the kitchen chatting with Mike, and, as Tallulah straightened up and saw me, she put a finger to her lips, letting me know I wasn't to say anything. Perhaps Lupe didn't know about what was going on, or wasn't ready to accept it. I recalled that she hadn't seemed to pay attention to Mike when he had explained the goings-on over the weekend.

When I declared I was ready, we walked out to the car; Mike, asked us to "wait heah," and quickly rushed back to his house, carrying a boxful of food. He hurried right back out and, panting, presented me with the most beautiful and elaborate cane I had seen since my grandfather's passing. It was made of a red wood and had a golden Chinese dragon coiling itself up around the shaft. Its mouth was open as if trying to eat the big blue glass ball that served as the handle. The tip of the cane was also gold and shaped like tongues of fire. When I said I couldn't accept it, he insisted.

"'Twas one of my dad's," he said, putting it in my hands, "he had two and I hahdly use eithah of 'em. Ya need it now more'n me, kid. Ya can give it back when ya don' need it anymoah."

I thanked him and said goodbye. We drove off. I looked back at the Funhouse and thought I saw a blond woman on the stoop, as little Tommy clung to her legs. She looked familiar, but I couldn't place where I'd seen her before, and I felt this strange sensation, like when something in real life reminds you of a dream you maybe had.

"Good news, Jacky-Chan!" Sam yelled into the phone on Thursday night.

She had a habit of adding little words to my name when she was in an especially cheerful mood. I've never had the heart to tell her that part of the reason I got bullied at school, was because she would sometimes call me Jacky-O, Jacky-Bee, or Jacky-Loo or whatever spontaneous cute name she came up with. She never called me Johnny-Boy though, that name had been reserved for Grandpa only. It was an unspoken pact between us—she didn't use his nickname for me, and I didn't call her by its counterpart: Sammy-Girl.

"Rhonda's dad had a heart attack so we had to cut our trip short."

"How is that good news?" I said appalled.

"It's not. It's terrible news," she still sounded upbeat though, "but that means I can come to you sooner!"

"Still not sure that's good news."

"Oh-my-gosh you're such a jerk," she giggled, "but no matter, I'll be there tomorrow night."

"Sammy, there's really no need," I sighed, "I'm staying with Apollo's family and I don't want to impose on them further if you come. They've already done too much."

In the past couple of days I hadn't been allowed to do anything for myself. And, gosh, how they fed me. The ladies kept saying I was much too skinny and needed some meat on my bones. They had also taken my iPhone and my MacBook to the Apple store for repairs. The iPhone had been replaced immediately and the computer had been sent to the company's repair shop; but still, I felt like I kept adding on to my debt with these gestures. It felt both good and awkward to be so pampered, but when I thought about how much I owed in return, my stomach turned into the typical worrywart's knot. I already owed Apollo for the pair of jeans that had to be cut in the emergency room, not to mention Mark for the long distance phone calls on his phone, Mike Monroe for the ridiculously luxurious cane, the Babcocks for calling the paramedics and the roses I destroyed, and now Lupe and Tallulah for their attentions. If Sammy came to stay with them, it would just be one more thing on my tab.

"No problem," she said cheerfully, "I'll stay at your house! I've never been in a haunted house before."

She sounded thrilled.

"It's really not that great."

"Sure it is, it's just that you're a scaredy-cat."

I couldn't disagree with that. I remember how, as children, I used to cling to her back when we had to go into the darkened upstairs on our way to get ready for bed.

"Sam, really, please reconsider," I knew this was my last chance to convince her before she put her foot down, "I'm really well taken care of, there's no need."

"Jack," she sounded serious now, "you could've died. I don't know what I would've done if that had happened. I want to see you. You can't stop me."

"Sam, really..."

"JOHN ADAMS, I AM COMING TO SEE YOU AND THAT IS FINAL!"

I'm sure all Japan heard her.

CHAPTER TEN

Into the Fire

"Put some muscle into it, Shrimp!"

Mark was trying to pull the couch cushions down while Apollo leaned against the wall, heckling him.

"I don't see you trying, Lurch!" he grunted.

Mark had managed to pull himself up and put his feet on the ceiling. He was trying to push with his feet, as if picking up something heavy off the floor, only upside down. His face red, he was sweating profusely.

It was Friday evening and we were in the Funhouse, waiting for Sam to let me know she was at the airport. She was taking the red eye from Sacramento to Boston and would be here early tomorrow morning. We would drive directly up to Osprey Cove after picking her up. She wasn't content with seeing just one haunted house.

I watched them, amused, as I sat on one of my living room chairs and rested my injured leg on the other. I don't know why we'd decided to spend our Friday night at the Funhouse just waiting for scary shit to happen, but here we were.

"Jack," Sammy said when I answered my ringing phone, "I'm almost finished packing. My friend Diana will be here soon and we'll be taking a taxi to the airport. I'll call you before we take off."

She explained how, coincidentally, her friend Diana had booked the same flight and would be visiting some relatives in New Hampshire. They'd meet at Sam's place and would go to the airport together. I asked her if Diana had also gone to Tahoe, and she said no, and that she hadn't seen her in a long time. She chatted on and on about how great the trip had been until the heart-attack and that I should go to California as soon as my leg healed, and so on, until her doorbell rang and we hung up.

Meanwhile, the guys were still fruitlessly trying to get the cushions unstuck. I was getting bored, unable to do much. My ankle hurt and, even with the special boot, it was difficult to walk. Mike's cane helped some, but I still avoided stairs and had to sit for long periods of time. The painkillers made me drowsy, and I had spent much of the past week dozing on Lupe's couch.

My phone pinged with a notification that "Samantha Adams was tagged in a photo with Diana Sanderson" on Facebook. I figured I'd take a look at this Diana person and see if she was pretty. Sammy had lots of girl friends but none were really good-looking. I couldn't understand why. She was very pretty herself, with light brown hair, hazel eyes, an upturned nose and a pouty mouth (Mark had once said she had the most kissable lips ever); but for some reason, unfortunate-looking girls gravitated towards her. Mark, Apollo and I would sometimes spend an evening looking through her Facebook page, saying rude things about their appearances.

I yawned and spun the cane on its tip with the palm of my hand, waiting for the picture to load. There was Sam, smiling big and looking up. She had one arm around her friend who seemed uncomfortable in the picture, and I could tell the other was holding the phone up high, taking the selfie. The caption read "with Diana Sanderson on our way to the airport! Be there soon, little bro!"

Her friend was not exactly what you would call beautiful, she had a long thin face, pale and framed by long black hair so straight it seemed to stick to her skin. If anything, she was bland; but there was something about her eyes, and the look that she gave the camera made me wonder if I'd seen her before.

I looked closely and suddenly my heart skipped a beat. *This* was *Diana Sanderson?* I started breathing hard and clutched my chest, while the cane fell with a clank onto the floor. The walls seemed to close around me and the air felt thin. I felt myself spinning as my world crumbled. Apollo noticed my distress and rushed over, while Mark still clung to the cushion with his feet on the ceiling.

"Jack, what's wrong?"

"It's her! Diana! She's with Sammy!" I panted, showing him the phone, "Anna! Diana is Anna! Anna Jenkins is with my sister!"

Apollo opened his eyes wide, and I heard what sounded like a growl at the back of his throat as he looked at the picture. There was no mistaking it; the face hadn't changed much from the sallow, blond teenager we'd both seen as she killed her brother, and those cold blue eyes with their unfeeling gaze were unequivocally hers. *"There's been a lot more stuff going on since you showed up, kid,"* Mike Monroe's voice swam in my head, *"it's nevah been anythin' like this."* And in that instant, I understood that it wasn't about keeping *me* safe, it was about keeping

Sammy safe; Anna Jenkins was friends with my sister, which meant that Sammy was in trouble.

Two things happened at once: everything went quiet while the power went out, and Mark crashed to the floor as part of the ceiling collapsed, couch cushions and all. Apollo rushed to Mark as objects started flying around the room and lights flickered. I tapped my phone, hoping it hadn't died with the supernatural power outage, but the screen was black.

"NO! NO! PLEASE, LET ME CALL MY SISTER! PLEASE! LET ME KEEP HER SAFE!" I yelled at the walls, and just like that, the activity stopped and my phone restarted.

I called Sam three times on her cell phone but she didn't answer. Thankfully, when I tried her landline she picked up.

"Sam! Get away from her! Diana is Anna Jenkins!"

"You sure?" Sam said, "Oh my God." Her breath quickened.

"Yes! I saw the picture you posted. She dyed her hair black, but it's definitely her!"

I was desperate and helpless, there was nothing I could do. I was stuck in a sweaty cast and my sister was miles away, alone with a killer.

"Shit...I told her everything," Sam's voice was an octave higher, "Jack, she knows everything!"

"That's right," a strange cold voice chilled me as I heard a thump and a groan on the other line.

The call dropped and I redialed immediately, but didn't even get a ring-tone, which meant the phone was dead.

Tears welled up into my eyes as I imagined the worst. Anna could've killed Sam with one single blow. She could be dead now, bleeding horribly from her head while Anna cleaned everything up.

"Jack!" Apollo was yelling at me, "Jack! Can you hear me? Call Sam's cell again! I'm calling 9-1-1."

I looked up to see he had his phone to his ear. Mark was slowly getting up.

"Listen," Apollo spoke into his phone, "I don't know if there's anything you can do, but there's a woman in Sacramento that's being attacked in her home. I know because we were on the phone when it happened and the line was cut off," he put his hand over the speaker and asked me for Sam's address.

I was still shaken and it took me a second to remember it. Mark crawled over and took my phone from my shaking fingers. Dust and debris floated all over the room as he moved, and there was blood dripping down his forehead.

"I'm calling her cell," he spoke slowly, as if trying to stay awake, "even if she doesn't answer, the ringing might drive Anna crazy, or someone else might hear it. She lives in a duplex right? Hopefully the other family will be mad enough to ring her doorbell."

He pressed the call-ended button and tried again, and again, and again.

After what seemed like a long time, I pulled myself together and took the phone from him, and like him before, called her number over and over. It was the only thing we could do. He lay on the floor and grabbed his head, groaning.

Apollo came over and laid his phone on the coffee table, saying that somehow, the 9-1-1 lady had gotten through to the Sacramento police and they were on their way to Sam's house. He said we were still on the line with them and that the phone was on speaker. There was an ambulance on the way here too.

I looked at him, dazed, and nodded. I was still trying to connect with my sister.

"Jack," Sam whispered as the call finally got through.

"Sammy, get outta there!"

"Shhh, I'm hiding in my closet," her voice shook as she whispered, "I can't get out. She blocked the doors. She beat me bad, I can barely crawl."

Her voice broke and I heard a soft wheeze. My stomach went to my feet when I realized she was crying softly.

"I'm so scared, Jacky, I'm so scared."

"Sammy, hold on, please." My voice broke too. "The police are on their way. Apollo called them, help is coming."

There were muffled sounds in the background, as if someone was breaking all her things in the other rooms. As the noise grew louder, I heard some kind of distorted singing, or chanting. It was creepy to say the least, and my sister's breathing got quicker still. There were loud booms and my sister squealed.

"Sammy," Apollo spoke softly and calmly, "the 9-1-1 operator needs to know if she's armed."

He had taken the phone from me, put it on speaker and set it on the table alongside his.

"She's got my softball bat," she sobbed, "she hit me with it, over and over. It think my arm is broken. It hurts like hell. She also knows where the kitchen knives are. I couldn't grab anything for myself."

Boom!

It was louder now and I heard Sammy's breath hitch, followed by whimpering. I imagined Anna Jenkins hitting the wall with the damn bat.

"Sam-my, where are you?" an ugly singsong voice came through behind Sam's quick breathing.

"Sammy, hold on, please hold on," I whispered.

My sister's fear seeped into the room with us. This was new; Sammy had never been afraid. I'd always been the scaredy-cat, the one who'd had to sleep with the nightlight on, the one hiding under the covers. She'd always been the one to make fear leave. She could walk into a darkened room without turning the lights on with ease, or sleep peacefully in absolute blackness. Nothing fazed her, and she was always ready for whatever life threw at her. I'd heard my parents say once that if anyone could rule the world, it was her. Now, hearing the panic in her breath, I felt so helpless.

"Just hold on," I pleaded.

"I can't do it, Jacky, she's stronger," my sister whispered into the phone, "I'm too scared."

Boom!

Anna was taunting her and the taunts were getting closer. Sammy screeched softly and sobbed quietly. I've never known Sam to be so helpless. I never thought that she'd be the one to give up; that she'd be the one to just roll up in a big ball of fear and die. I've always thought that would be me.

Boom!

I jumped at the sound. She must be in Sammy's bedroom now where my sister was hiding, there was no escape.

Sam was quiet, and we could hear Anna Jenkins rummaging around her room, chanting, calling out to her. I heard crashing sounds as Anna seemed to break everything in the room. I worried the sound of breaking bones would be next, then tried to shake that horrible thought away. My sister was badly injured and all I could do was be scared. I remembered being shown the last moments of Tommy Jenkins's life. I was most likely listening to the last moments of my sister's life now. Tears streamed down my face. The one time I should've been defending my sister, I was too far away. The one time I should've stepped up to the plate, I was helplessly listening while some monster took my sister from me. I longed to see her, to hug her, to have her by me, instead of in that closet.

Boom!

I turned to Mark for some rational explanation, but he had sat himself up with the aid of the cane, and was leaning his forehead against the dragon. His knuckles were pale against the red wood of the shaft, and faint sobs came from him. Apollo was white as a sheet and looked fierce. I could tell he felt as powerless as me.

Boom!

"Sammy-Dooby-Doo, where are you?" I heard Anna chuckling and she sounded like the Devil might.

Why was this happening? Was this the before-and-after moment of my life? I had been so indignant when forced to watch the ghost of a little boy die, and now I was listening to my sister's last quick breaths as she kept quiet in the closet.

Boom!

Suddenly, it hit me. Suddenly, I understood why the house had shown me only Tommy's death. It was like Tallulah had said, every past instant of your life led you to your present, and everything had a reason. Suddenly I knew how to awaken the fight in her and save my sister.

"Sammy-Girl, she spit on him," I said as the guys looked up, "she killed her five-year-old brother as he lay in his bed and then she spit on his body. He thought it was his mommy coming in the room."

Boom!

Sammy's breath slowed and a door creaked open; Anna chanted in the background.

"YOU BITCH!" Sam screamed and the sound of a struggle boomed out of the phone speaker and into my living room.

I imagined my sister lunging at Anna Jenkins and fighting for her life. I put my hand to my mouth and sobbed. The Nerd Avenger was back! The Geek Protector inside my sister flew out of that closet and charged. Amidst the screams and the growls, it seemed to me that my sister was the real Caped Crusader, the real Superman and every superhero ever imagined lived inside her and had exploded out in that moment. Nothing could anger Sammy more than the thought of harm being done to a child, and now, my sister was fighting to save herself, and to avenge Tommy, and Beth, and Paul, and Jenny.

Suddenly, there was silence on the other line. We held our breaths and waited. I dared not imagine what might have happened. Had Anna won and killed Sammy? The thought of spending the rest of my life knowing Sammy had died because of me cut my soul into little pieces.

The sound of sirens in the background was music to my ears, and we heard big heavy footsteps in the room.

"Sam?" I called out, "Sammy? Are you okay? Sam?"

We heard men's voices and a lot of movement.

"SAM!" I yelled.

"Who's this?" One of the men answered. I assumed it was the paramedics. *Oh please let it be the paramedics!*

"I'm John Adams, my sister is Samantha Adams and she was attacked in her home. I need to know if she's okay," I took a deep breath and closed my eyes. *Please don't let it be the coroner!*

"There's a woman here but I don't know if it's your sister. Can you describe her?"

I gave a quick but full description, down to the kidney-shaped birthmark on her neck.

"That's her," the man answered, "she's alive. She's unconscious and we need to get her into the ambulance immediately. I assume this is her phone? Is this the best number to reach you at?"

"Yes!" I almost laughed out of relief, as the sirens drowned out the paramedic's voice saying, "Samantha Adams, thirty-three years old, multiple trauma..." before we were cut off.

I sat looking at the phones still on the table. They'd both blinked 'call ended' moments before and I felt as if I was in a bad dream I couldn't wake out of. Was Sammy okay? Was she going to die? I wished I could teleport myself into that ambulance and go with her to the hospital. I put my face in my hands and sobbed, while our own sirens approached.

"D'you guys think that's rust... or blood?"

Mark was woozily pointing where the ceiling had fallen. There, amongst the cushions and the debris, lay what looked like two camping axes, the blades gleaming red in the electric light. My skin crawled as Apollo walked over and knelt down beside them.

"I think it's rusty blood. They must have fallen when the ceiling caved in..." he said as the sirens drowned out his voice and we heard footsteps coming to my door.

He looked at us wide-eyed before quickly shoving the weapons under the couch with his foot. He put his finger to his mouth and we understood. There was no way to explain two bloody axes amidst the debris without the police getting involved, and something told me that it was best to keep this quiet for now. The thought that had been nagging me before we left for Maine tugged at the back of mind. I still couldn't shape it into anything coherent, but I had the feeling that if we told the police we had the Jenkins murder weapons, things would go from bad to worse quickly.

CHAPTER ELEVEN

Only the Beginning

We were in Lupe's living room. Apollo had gone in the ambulance with Mark, while Mike Monroe, who had rushed out as soon as he saw it pull up, had given me a ride to Lupe's. It had been more than four hours since I'd last heard my sister's voice and I still had no news of her. I'd tried calling a few times but I think the phone had been turned off. So it wouldn't distract the doctors, I hoped.

I'd set my phone down on the coffee table and stared at it, wishing it would ring. Apollo had wrested the cane out of Mark's hands and handed it to me as the ambulance door had closed before us, and now, I was the one holding on to it for dear life. I kept twisting it in my hands, in sync with the turning and wringing of my stomach.

Lupe and Tallulah were on either side of me on the love-seat and rubbing my back. They'd made me tea, and brought cookies and had done everything to try and calm me down, but I was still a ball of nerves. Mike had left to lock up the house, but had made me promise to let him know as soon as I'd heard from Mark or my sister. I didn't mention the axes to him.

We looked up as the front door opened and Mark, with a bandage around his head and leaning on Apollo, walked in. They told us the injury had been minor, although dramatic since the head tended to bleed a lot. He'd been allowed to leave as long as he was watched all night for signs of a concussion. Other than that, he had a huge bruise on his back from falling off the ceiling and some on his arms and chest from the ceiling falling on him. Apollo helped him lay down on the big couch, then sat in Lupe's rocker.

No one spoke. We all looked at the goddamned silent phone. Why didn't someone call? Was my sister dead? Was she alive? In a coma? Paraplegic? What?

Images of every sickening scenario of what might be happening were parading through my head, my stomach hurt from all the worry and I felt like tearing my hair out.

Suddenly, the little device came to life, showing me bright and happy the picture of Sammy making a goofy face that I'd set up for her contact. Her ringtone, *The Muppets'* "Manamana", sounded out loud and clear throughout the house.

I clicked the answer button and put the phone to my ear, too scared to speak.

"Johnny-Boy," my sister's voice flowed through me like manna from heaven, "I'm all right."

"Thank God," I breathed, "thank God, Sammy. It's all over."

I looked up at everyone and beamed. Lupe threw her hands up in the air and crossed herself, while Mark pumped his fist, and Apollo laughed quietly (I didn't know he could, he usually roared). Tallulah hugged me and kissed my cheek.

I put the phone on speaker, set it back down on the table and was about to let her know everyone could hear her, when she said, "It's not. She got away. I think she might've even made the flight to Boston, although I really don't see anyone letting her on the plane the way I left her," she giggled a little and I felt like Christmas had come early, "she owes me a pair of Manolo Blahniks."

Man-oh whats? I looked at the guys and they looked as confused as I did.

"You hit her with your shoes?" Tallulah asked and enlightenment dawned on our faces.

"Yeah," she answered, "Tallulah? Is that Tallulah?"

I quickly told her who else was in the room and she went on to tell us how she had jumped out of the closet with her shoe in her hand and tackled Anna Jenkins onto the floor. Then, Sammy had found herself on top of her and began beating her with the shoe. Anna was still strong enough and somehow wrestled herself free and hit Sam on the head with something hard, but she didn't know what.

"I think the heel stuck her in the eye and she deserved it, but she clobbered me and I passed out. She must've heard the sirens and that sent her running. The police told me there was no one else in the house."

"Joo are lacky she did nat take jor phone,"

"It wasn't on me when she attacked, I grabbed it from my nightstand as I crawled into the closet, and she must not have seen it as she ran off."

"But you're okay?" I was worried there might still be some serious damage.

"Yeah, my left arm is broken, but besides that, I'm okay," she sighed, "I'm still coming to you, the doctor said I could leave the hospital in a couple of days, and the police already took my statement. They sent out a search for Anna, but still, I'm not letting that bitch anywhere near my little bro."

I started to protest, but Tallulah put a hand on my arm as if saying 'let her finish',

"Besides, I really gotta see that haunted house of yours."

She was relentless, there was no getting the idea of coming to Boston out of her head. I begged and pleaded her to stay home, I threatened, I teased, but like always, Sammy won.   *She's as hard-headed as a mule, Johnny-Boy, give it up,*   Grandpa's voice sounded in my head, and I sighed as we hung up.

I looked at my watch and saw that it was too late to call Babcock, so I texted to let him know Anna might be on her way. The battery was drained and I hoped the message got delivered before it shut down.

I laid my head back on the sofa, yawned and closed my eyes. I was exhausted. I sat like that while Lupe and Tallulah fawned over Mark. It felt good not to be the center of so much care. It felt good to be ignored again. I loved Lupe and Tallulah; but two affectionate ladies worrying over an invalid was a bit suffocating. I would never tell them that, of course; but I'd gotten used to taking care of myself since my family had moved away, and I missed the sense of independence it gave me.

The room gradually became quiet as I drifted away. In my mind I saw images of Anna Jenkins entering her brother's room and raising the axe, only this time, the little blond head wasn't Tommy's, but Sam's. I tried to scream but couldn't. The axe came down, the blood splattered, she spit and left the room.

I followed her.

I was the guy; I was David Murphy and as the thought struck me, I realized I was asleep. I was aware this was all a dream, but no matter how hard I tried, I couldn't wake up. Instead, I followed her to her parents' bedroom, and as she attacked her sleeping mother, I lifted my arm and my own axe came down on her father, who had barely woken up. We kept at it, hacking away at the bodies until we were both soaked in their blood. It was a hell of a party. We laughed and laughed as our axes struck over and over again. Then, when the blood had stopped flowing, we kissed.

She led me to her bedroom and inside, she knelt down in the corner and lifted the carpet. She pried apart two wooden boards, and taking the insulating material out, put the two axes inside. She put everything back in its place and began undressing. I grabbed her by the waist and kissed her.

She pulled my T-shirt over my head, and as I pushed her down on her bed, she undid my fly. I climbed on top and slid my hands onto her breasts...

I had to wake up.

This was all a dream, but it was too vivid, too real, and somehow I knew this was them showing me what had happened. I was screaming inside, and as I tried to wake, Anna grabbed my neck and whispered in my ear "no Jack; stay and watch."

I struggled against Anna's hold and when I heard Tallulah's voice calling me, I tried to reach it, but I was too far away. Anna was on top of me now, and as I pushed her away with weak arms that seemed to make a herculean effort, I heard a loud booming thump that hooked itself onto my sternum and pulled me out of the dream. I opened my eyes. I was back in the living room and the women were both looking at me. The cane had rolled off my lap and the thud of the dragon's head on the floor had jerked me awake.

"Yack, are joo all rrright?" Lupe said and I was about to answer when Mark groaned. He was lying down on the couch, eyes closed and moving his head side to side, deep in a dream.

"Anna," he moaned, "we have to leave. Give me your clothes."

"Okay," Apollo answered in an unusually high-pitched voice. He was still on the rocker with his head thrown back, and his eyelids were trembling rapidly. Lupe moved towards her son, but Tallulah held her back and said to listen.

"I'll see you at my place, baby," Mark said and Apollo giggled.

Then, his giggles turned to small girlish sobs and wails.

"How's that, sugar?" he still spoke in that creepy, high-pitched voice.

"Perfect," Mark answered and blew a kiss.

As we watched this exchange, I felt my head fall back and my eyelids getting heavy again. I saw Tallulah holding on to Lupe, who was crying, as my eyes drooped and darkness closed in around me.

I was back in the dream. I was kneeling behind a hedge, with the bundle of bloody clothes under my arm, and there were police cars everywhere. I saw a much younger Mike Monroe talking to an officer.

Anna was talking to a man in civilian clothes, who was jotting things down on a small notepad. She was perfect; the tears were real, and she was even shaking.

I got up and began walking. I walked down several streets until I came to a square house with green siding. It had two stories and a gabled roof. The mailbox read 'Murphy' as I walked past it. I opened the door, went upstairs and laid down on what I knew was my bed. I closed my eyes.

In my brain I was still Jack and still in the dream; but in body, I knew I was David Murphy, and I was letting everything happen. Jack was scared shitless, and yet David couldn't feel anything inside, he had no emotion. David Murphy was calm, cool and collected; something Jack Adams never was.

Suddenly there was a knock at my door, and the man I had seen talking to Anna came in. I knew him as my uncle. I smiled as Anna (Apollo?) followed. They walked in the room, Anna smiling behind his back but looking contrite and grief-stricken when he turned around.

"Did you have something to do with this?" he asked gravely.

He was infuriated ('shittin' kittens' as Mark would say) but was keeping his voice level and composed, just as he had been trained to do. No one answered. He looked me in the eye and, behind the anger, I saw an immense fear in his face. Fear of me. Fear of Anna.

"Right," he knew the truth, "I'll handle this."

I smirked; Mr. High and Mighty Detective William Sanders of the Peaceville Police Department was going to take care of everything. He walked out the door, while Anna and I burst out laughing.

I opened my eyes and found myself back in my body, back in Lupe's living room. I had laughed myself awake and as the laughter rolled out of my throat, I realized I wasn't the only one laughing. Apollo and Mark were laughing too. Lupe was crying over Apollo as she shook him awake, and Tallulah was tending to Mark.

"Um..." was all I could say as Tallulah turned and rushed over to me.

The guys were both awake now and the only sounds were Lupe's stifled sobs.

It took Tallulah a few minutes to convince Lupe that everyone was all right. She sat Lupe down next to me and I put my arm around her as she sobbed quietly into my shoulder. Mark and Apollo had started to complain about the fuss Lupe was making, when Tallulah gave them a look that undeniably said 'shut the fuck up', before going in to the kitchen. The guys had remained quiet and motionless since, like two berated children at the principal's office.

Mark lifted his eyes and silently asked me what was going on as he moved his eyebrows up and down.

"We all had the same dream." I said.

The guys blanched, and I realized they had no idea what the extent of that nightmare had been. I was the only one who had woken up in the middle of it and then been pulled back in, while Lupe and Tallulah had witnessed the whole thing from the outside. It had been disturbing watching those two play out the roles of Anna and David, so I can only imagine what it must have been like for the women to watch all three of us.

Tallulah came back and handed Lupe a steaming cup. She said it was Sleepytime tea so it would help calm her. We sat quietly as Lupe's sobs died down and she sipped her tea.

"I think we need to look for this detective," I said softly, hoping I wouldn't get Tallulah's stony look too.

"I think there is a lot we need to talk about," Tallulah said calmly, "but it can wait."

"No," Lupe's voice was surprisingly firm, "I want to knoh what's go-eeng on."

Everyone looked at me and I gave her a very summarized account of what had been happening in my house. I decided to spare her the details and she seemed thankful for it.

"So," Apollo spoke sheepishly, "what happened just now?"

It was not like him to be shy. I think he still felt the chill of Tallulah's erstwhile condemnation.

"Jack fell asleep while we were looking after Mark," Tallulah looked straight at him, "and, while Lupe got him a cup of tea, Jack started making strange noises in his sleep."

She explained how, while they were trying to wake me up, no one realized that Apollo and Mark had fallen asleep too. We told them what we'd seen while I was awake, and the women finished by explaining what had happened afterwards.

I had acted out the part of David Murphy, Apollo that of Anna, while Mark had been, first David in my wakefulness, then the detective that had covered the murders up. Between the five of us we managed to piece together the events of that night. The thought that had been nagging me since the week before, finally (and belatedly) took shape; the article relating the murders had never mentioned the detectives' or police officers' names.

Now, in the aftermath of that dream, it was obvious. The detective investigating the case was David Murphy's uncle, and he had known about everything, but had covered it up. Mark described the paralyzing fear he had felt as Detective Sanders in David Murphy's room. He explained how angry he felt at the man's fear, and how unacceptable it was that a grown man did not have the balls to oppose a teenager and do what's right. He was shaking and punched one of the pillows on the couch.

Apollo talked about how he'd felt elated as Anna, and I stated how calm and collected David Murphy had been in his bedroom, as if he'd known all along that Sanders would keep it quiet. I avoided their eyes when I explained how much fun the killing had been for David, though I had been horribly guilt-ridden myself. Apollo lowered his head, red-faced.

"Yes," he whispered, "like Jack said, Anna was having fun, but I was ashamed."

Then, he put his head in his hands. When he looked up, I saw him wipe something from his eyes.

"Why would you both feel ashamed?" Tallulah asked, " *You* didn't kill."

"But I could feel the girl's mirth as she killed her parents, and that's just wrong. To feel such pleasure over those despicable actions and know that, while it wasn't me, there was nothing to be done about it."

"Yeah," I said looking down at my hands, "it was like watching yourself stripped of your own humanity, and knowing it's the worst thing you could ever do, but loving it at the same time."

"David Murphy felt no remorse," Mark interjected, "I was him too for a bit, and he felt no remorse. Worse, he felt proud."

"Yes," Apollo looked at Tallulah directly, "Anna felt the same thing."

"Well," Lupe spoke up, "I am glad joo all feel this—eh—chagrin. As a mother, it means that we all did something rright, it means that we, the parents, rrraised human beings that act and feel like human beings. I am proud of joo boys."

Lupe's warm smile brightened the room a little.

"Lupe is right," Tallulah said, "and on that encouraging note, I think we should put this all behind us for now and get some much needed rest. There is a lot to do tomorrow. For starters, we need to warn Detective

Babcock about Anna, and find this detective Sanders. I hope Mark, that when we do, you can refrain from punching him like you did that pillow. Although I'm tempted to do so myself."

I told them I'd already texted Babcock and we agreed we would call him first thing in the morning. I had been staying in the guest bedroom on the ground floor on account of my cast and, for only an instant, I felt like an outsider as I watched Mark and Apollo walk up the stairs. The feeling dissolved almost immediately when they called goodnight.

I woke up in a panic when it occurred to me we'd never followed up with Mike Monroe, and more importantly, hadn't warned him about Anna possibly being on her way to Boston. If she managed to get here tonight, she'd probably head straight to my house and Mike might be in danger.

I turned on my phone, which I'd left charging. It read three a.m.

"Hullo?" Mike sounded tired and I was embarrassed to have called him so late.

"Mike, I'm so sorry to wake you, it's me, Jack,"

"Ya didn' wake me kid, is everythin' okay with ya sistah?"

"Yes, she's fine, in the hospital, but fine. Mark is okay too, but I have to warn you, Anna Jenkins got away and she might be on her way here. I know it might be too late, but is there somewhere you could go?"

"No worries, kid, I'm at my brothah's; we jus' got back from the hospital. The ol' faht thought he was havin' a haht-attack, but it was only indigestion." He laughed loudly and my worry subsided. "But it's good to know, I'll impose on 'im until she's found and all is ovah, it's the least he can do aftah the scare he jus' gave me."

Relieved, I lay back down and drifted off to sleep.

CHAPTER TWELVE

Where in the World is Anna Jenkins?

"Jack, your descriptions are very sparse."

My sister was sitting on the bed in Lupe's guest bedroom, with my newly repaired MacBook in her lap and reading this, my private journal, which recounted the occurrences at my house. I had decided to let her read it instead of having to explain everything again. Besides, when we were growing up, my stuff had always found its way into her hands.

"What do you mean?" I asked, taken aback. I'm pretty sure my descriptions of the hauntings were accurate and abundant.

"Well, your description of Jenny Jenkins's house and Osprey Cove are quite thin," Sammy went on, "I mean, you're a writer, you're supposed to be able to describe everything down to the last detail, not "the ceiling was very high and had some beautiful cornices" (she spoke in a lower register, in an attempt to mimic me). You could do better than that, you know, be more elaborate."

"What? Like Mom?"

"Oh God no, she's much too elaborate," we laughed and Sam continued, "you know she once spent a whole hour on the phone describing some funky dream she'd had. Seriously, I think she could've given Dickens a run for his money."

"Has she ever given you directions?"

She shook her head no, her hair flying about like a headbanger. Her hairstyle was similar to the ones Bon Jovi had sported in the early nineties. It barely touched her shoulders and the slight waves made it look permanently tousled. She looked fresh, breezy and like a young girl.

"She once gave me directions to the new house down south, and went on and on about which highway exit *not* to take. She kept saying things like, you'll come to a gas station just before an exit, that's not the exit you wanna take. After that there's a rest area with a sign pointing to another exit, that's also *not* it, and so on. By the seventh time I cut her off and was like "woman, which exit is it?""

Sammy pealed with laughter and brushed her hair away from her forehead.

"What did she say?"

"Dad grabbed the phone and said, "Son, take exit X when you're on highway Y," and then we hung up. Easy as pie."

"I suppose you're more like Dad," she said.

"Yeah, detailed descriptions are not my style. Professors were always giving me crap about that."

She smiled.

I was lying next to her. It had been a week since Sam's assault, and Anna Jenkins was in the wind. Mark and I had picked Sammy up at the airport early this morning and I was exhausted. The cast and the painkillers made me feel like I'd been run over by a truck. I couldn't understand how she could be so upbeat with her broken arm and bruised body. She must be on painkillers too, but somehow, they didn't seem to make her drowsy.

I'd gotten the shock of a lifetime at the airport when I'd seen her coming towards us with her arm in a cast and tied tightly to her chest. She had an enormous, ugly bruise across her left cheekbone and around her eye, a gash that ran in a slant across her lips, and a giant scrape down the right side of her jawbone and across her long neck. Up close, I'd noticed other cuts and bruises on her bare arms, especially her forearms and elbows. Her knuckles and wrists were grazed too. She was limping slightly. There was also an ugly scrape that ran down her nose, and I was glad that it wasn't broken. As I'd hugged her, I'd heard her softly whimper in pain. That tiny sound had torn at my heart and made me loosen my embrace. I'd pictured my sister in the fetal position, her arms wrapped tightly around her head and her knees protecting her belly as she took blow after blow from her own softball bat in Anna's grip. She'd told me over the phone that she'd managed to trip and kick Anna and buy time enough to drag herself and crawl into her closet, but that she'd been too hurt to get to the door.

Mark's hair had shadowed his eyes but I could see his mouth pressed in a tight line as she'd approached. He'd hugged Sam softly and carefully, (I don't know if he'd heard the whimper too) and lovingly kissed her cheek. Sam had smiled and talked cheerfully as we'd gotten in the car. She'd winced a little as she'd sat down, but other than that, acted as if nothing was wrong. I'd caught Mark's eye and saw a mixture of anger, despair and hatred. I'd wondered if this is what 'thirst for revenge' looked like.

Sam had managed to convince the police in Sacramento that she was okay to travel and would be coming to Boston. On the way home, she'd told us about how she'd persuaded them by claiming that I could be in danger, that no one here knew what Anna Jenkins looked like (which was a downright lie), that she was the only one who knew anything about her, etc. She'd recounted it as if she'd rationally and calmly explained the situation to the authorities; but instead, I pictured her stomping her foot, plugging her ears and holding her breath till she turned blue, then shouting at the top of her lungs that she was coming to Boston and that's that. I'd looked over at Mark and, by his smirk, I was pretty sure he'd been imagining the same thing.

We'd talked to Babcock the day after the assault and he'd assured us he'd be keeping an eye on Saunders. He was still certain the man was implicated in Jenny's murder and that he'd kept in touch with Anna all along.

"It ain't gonna be easy, kid," he'd said on the phone, "since I've retired, I no longer have access to anything at the PD, but believe me, there's plenty of people in town that can keep a lookout on Saunders and let me know what he's up to."

We planned on driving up to Osprey Cove in the morning. It was clear to me that both houses were trying to show us what had happened, albeit in different ways, but I felt there was more to Jenny's murder. The couch cushions at the Funhouse had pinpointed the hiding place of the murder weapons, and I had a hunch that Jenny's house was hiding something too.

In the past week, I'd gone back to my house a couple of times, flanked by Apollo and Mark and backed by Mike Monroe and his trusty shotgun, but nothing had been amiss. There was no sign of break-ins and the axes were still hidden; we had no idea what to do with them.

The search for Detective William Sanders (David Murphy's uncle) had led to a dead end, literally, since a simple Google search had revealed that he, his wife, sister and brother-in-law (last name Murphy) had been killed in a car accident about eight years after the Jenkins murders. The obituary read that there were no surviving relatives, which had brought up the question: who in the hell was David Murphy? And where was he?

Tallulah figured it was all a set up, that somehow David Murphy had faked his own death, or falsified town records. As for me, I was pretty sure there was a connection between Murphy and Saunders. I hadn't seen what Murphy looked like in that eerie collective dream we'd had, and the guys hadn't seen Saunders on our trip to Maine, but if Saunders and Murphy weren't related somehow, then I was Donald Duck.

"All right, Jacky-Doo," Sammy said closing the computer, "grab that swanky cane of yours and let's go to the Funhouse!"

The house loomed over us, dark and dreary as always. I glanced at Sammy and wondered whether she felt the same dread, or sadness or whatever it was that emanated from the house, but she seemed comfortable and excited.

The thing about Sammy is that she is more in touch with her inner child than many adults I know—including myself—so I wasn't really surprised when I saw her almost leaning out the car window as we pulled up to the house. She gave a little squeal of delight as Tallulah parked the car. You'd have thought we had arrived at Disneyland.

Mike Monroe crossed the street as soon as he saw us. He was still staying with his brother, but we'd agreed to meet today so Sammy could see the house. I introduced them, while Tallulah made her way to the door.

"Jack," she said, "the door is unlocked."

"What? No way, I'm certain we locked it the last time we were here."

Mike Monroe made his way to the front, and shotgun at the ready, gently pushed the door open with his foot. He walked in all stealth-like and pointing the gun in every direction, just like in the movies. I had to fight back a sudden fit of laughter, and Tallulah softly pinched my arm. She was struggling to keep a straight face too, while Sammy, shoulders shaking, had opened her mouth wide as if laughing, though no sound came out. Mike had told us to wait outside, and disappeared as he went into the dining room. When he sneaked past the open door he gave us a nod, and signaled to stay where we were.

He climbed the stairs and moments later, walked back down, the shotgun by his side and his stride relaxed. I guess there was nothing new with the house. Maybe I had forgotten to lock up, but I didn't think so. Maybe Anna had been here, but from what I could see, everything was in its place.

The first time we'd returned to the house after the ceiling had fallen, Apollo and I had been stunned to find that everything had been cleared up. The hole in the ceiling had been fixed and the debris had been cleaned down to the last speck of dust. There wasn't even a crack in the ceiling paint where the couch cushions had been. My heart had raced when we'd realized the axes might be gone, but sure enough, they were still under the couch where Apollo had pushed them. We'd tried to move them to a safer hiding place but found they were stuck to the floor, just as unmovable as the couch cushions had been on the ceiling. Good, the Funhouse wasn't going to let anyone have them, and they were safely hidden from view. Babcock had said that was perfect, since we hadn't actually removed any evidence, and if anyone asked, we could easily say they'd probably been shuffled under the couch while we were helping Mark.

Sammy browsed as if in a toy store. She looked in the parlor, around the bookcases, perused the kitchen, opened drawers and cabinets, ran her fingers over the dining room table and walked out onto the deck—my favorite part of the house. I awkwardly bent over the living room couch using Mike's dragon cane as support and checked that the axes were still there.

As I stood up, I saw an old man lying on the whole length of the couch. He was dressed in a brown suit and his hands were crossed over his chest. The eyes were closed and I could almost see little cartoon X's over the eyelids. Tallulah put her hand on my shoulder as I breathed heavily and my heart raced.

"Don't worry," she was calm and her voice was soft, "he won't hurt you."

"Why are there X's over his eyelids?" I asked. My whole body was shaking badly now, and I wanted to run away.

"That's probably just your mind letting you understand he's dead. I don't see any X's, but his lips are blue to me," she softly stroked my back and went on, "Jack, my darling, it seems you have a very symbolic mind."

I looked at her blankly and wished she'd explain. I wanted to take my mind off the dead old man on my couch, and thought that maybe if I didn't look at him, and completely ignored the fact he was there, he'd just go away.

"What do you mean?"

"Well, it appears that your mind lets you understand things that are beyond the scope of our five senses through visual symbols, like the X's on this gentleman's eyes. In cartoons, I believe that means death, right? Or like how you always say that you can almost see other people's thoughts. If you paid more attention to your instincts, I'm sure you'd notice there's a relation between an image in your mind, what's happening around you, and what you feel compelled to do."

"Is that good or bad?" I asked, "Does that mean I'm psychic?"

"It's neither good nor bad, it's just the way you are," she shrugged, "and no, I don't think you're psychic, but you are definitely more receptive than most. I suppose that's why you're so imaginative, and that's very helpful in your chosen profession. It's one reason your stories are so good."

I looked down at the dead man, and felt compelled to say something, but had no idea what. Should I keep the current conversation going, or redirect towards the elephant in the room?

"It may also be why they show you what happened here so easily," she waved her hand around, "they probably kept throwing your things until they figured out how to show you pictures. After all, they had to get in your dreams to get through to Mark, for example. His mind is hermetically sealed."

She chuckled softly, then suddenly broke out into her almighty roar of a laugh and declared he should now be known as Tupperware Mark. As if to prove her point, the image of Mark kneeling in front of Tallulah in queenly garb while she tapped his shoulders with a sword (*I now crown thee Sir Mark of the Tupperware*), suddenly popped into my head, and I chuckled. The one 'ha' came out constricted and nervous.

"What about Apollo?" I asked. *You can keep dancing around, Johnny-Boy, but at some point, you're going to have to address the issue of the dead man on your couch!*

"Apollo's mind is wide open, but he mostly senses emotions, as opposed to seeing symbols. For example, if he were here, he might sense the lack of this gentleman's heartbeat, instead of seeing X's on his eyelids."

"Tallulah," I leaned closer and whispered, "how long do you think he's been here?"

"Oh, many years Jack," she whispered back, "he's been dead for a long time. This is just them showing us the past again."

"But why?" I asked.

"Perhaps because this is something we need to know," she shrugged, "don't let it get to you. All will come to light, you'll see."

We heard the back door close as Sammy walked in. She began to say something, but stopped mid-sentence as she entered the living room. I saw the color fall from her face. She stared at the couch, then at us and shakily pointed her finger.

"Is there a man on the couch or, am I seeing things?" Her voice trembled, slightly.

"No, he's there," I said, nonchalant. Having the upper hand on my sister for the first time ever felt so good that even the fear and uneasiness gave way a little.

"Who is he?"

I shrugged.

"We shall find out soon enough." Tallulah answered, as she invited Sammy to come closer.

Sam hastily came up beside us and we looked at the man, waiting for something to happen.

"Jeezus Christ!" Mike Monroe exclaimed behind us, "That's Jeff Jenkins!"

He had walked in the living room, unnoticed, and we turned around, aghast.

"That's Anna Jenkins's grandfathah! He died just before little Tommy was boahn. Remembah I told ya kid, that Anna said his death had been the befoah-and-aftah moment of her life?"

Mike said that Jeff Jenkins had been a nice, easygoing man. He'd been widowed soon after Paul and Beth had moved in; Anna must have been around three or four. He said he remembered meeting the grandmother just before she died, and that Mike's own wife, Rosie, had wished she'd gotten to know her better. There was nothing odd about Jeff Jenkins and the Monroes often had him over for dinner.

"Someone always stayed home with Anna," he went on, "that was one of the things that nevah fit quite right. The whole family was invited ovah, but it's as if they nevah wanted to bring her to othah people's houses. And if they did bring her ovah, they watched her like a hawk."

Anna Jenkins had been riding her bicycle around the block the day the grandfather died. It had been an unforgettable day, he said, since it was also the day Tommy was born. Mike remembered seeing her smiling and happy and free as she'd whooshed past his house over and over. He said that after he realized she'd had something to do with the murders, that image of her kept popping into his mind, and, it seemed like she'd looked expectant and excited, as if she was looking forward to something wonderful.

When Anna had walked in the door, the grandfather had been agonizing. Mike said that Paul himself had mentioned the whole family had been with him when he died, and that fit with Anna's story about walking in and finding her grandfather dying on the couch, surrounded by his family. But that day, there'd been nothing suspicious, he said; the hearse had come quickly and the body taken away, while Beth Jenkins was rushed to the hospital to bring little Tommy into the world.

"D'you think she had something to do with his death?" Sam asked, just a tad too upbeat.

"I didn't think so, but now, who knows?" Mike shrugged, "I've often wondahd what life in that house was like."

"Maybe he was her first victim?" I asked.

I don't know why, but a sudden vision of a circle of elephants came to mind. I racked my brains for the meaning, but couldn't put anything to words, as if I couldn't reach the thought.

The room suddenly got cold and the cicadas outside became very quiet. I took Sammy's good arm and whispered to her that the Horror Show was about to begin. Tallulah rubbed her arms to warm herself and Mike stuck his hands in his pockets. Sam squeezed my hand, took a deep breath, and exhaled white mist. I felt her body tense, not from fear but from bravery. I glanced at her and thought I saw her dressed in armor, her broken arm against her chest, holding a shield.

Her jaw clenched and she scowled as the room began to spin. It gradually spun faster and faster, while I felt I was turning in the opposite direction, like on the teacups ride at Disney World. Suddenly, it stopped and we were still in my house, but the furniture was different and there was a strange warm glow about the rooms, as if the real sun were coming in through the windows, not the fake cold sunlight that seeps into the Funhouse.

There were noises behind us. We turned around and Sam planted herself in front of us, her good arm on her hip, like the Man of Steel, ready to take on General Zod. I turned last. There were chills running down my spine, and all I wanted was to jump in bed and pull the covers over me.

I was ashamed of my fear, but there was nothing I could do about it. No matter how hard I try, I've never been able to steady myself. It's as if Sammy had gotten the nerves-of-steel gene and I had gotten the nerves-of-mush gene instead. It was unfair, and I thought that at the very least, I had to pull myself together in front of Mike and Tallulah. No way I was going to let two old people be braver than me.

A blond woman walked out of the kitchen. She was very pregnant and slowly waddling towards the deck with glasses in her hands. I recognized her as Beth Jenkins.

"Wait, honey, let me get that," a man's voice wafted in from the deck followed by the very much alive Jeff Jenkins in his brown suit. He took the glasses from her and let her pass. He looked straight at us and beckoned us to follow.

Sammy didn't hesitate one instant, and with her head held high, stepped forward with her good hand in a fist, as if walking out to a duel. I was dying of fear, but not to be outdone by the old folks, I hesitantly inched forward. Tallulah wrapped her arm around my elbow and let me lead her, as Mike moved up beside us. The gesture gave me courage and Tallulah's fingers digging into my arm made me feel much better. I understood now, I wasn't the only one scared half out of his wits, Tallulah was too, and Mike's ashen face told me he was frightened as well. Only Sammy was unshakeable. Maybe that night with Anna had been her before-and-after moment, and now she felt that there could be nothing to be afraid of.

The family was outside, milling around a big, white table with a plexiglass top. Jeff Jenkins was setting the glasses on it, while a much younger man, tall, thin and brown-haired was talking and laughing to a woman only slightly older than him. I supposed this was Paul Jenkins and as I looked closer at the woman, I saw an unmistakeable resemblance between her, Paul, and even Jeff. It wasn't that they looked exactly the same, but there was something about them, their expressions, their movements that clearly said, 'family'.

With a pang in my heart, I realized who this was. I was looking at Jenny Jenkins herself, alive and well and about seven years younger than she would've been that Christmas Eve she died. Amelia Babcock was right, Jenny Jenkins was beautiful in a very modest sort of way. She was tall and thin, like her father and brother, but graceful too, with a long neck and a naturally straight nose most women pay thousands of dollars to have. She was dressed like a librarian, in gray slacks and a blue blouse buttoned up to the top. Her brown hair was in a pony tail, but I bet that on weekdays at the library she wore it up in a bun.

"I wonder if she was ever a ballerina of sorts," Tallulah whispered beside me, and I told her I'd ask Babcock about that.

Beth had settled into a white plastic chair and was fanning herself wildly with a magazine. Anna was nowhere to be seen, presumably riding her bike around the block. A clock somewhere struck noon and I looked at Mike Monroe. I think he was looking around for Anna and when our eyes met, he shrugged.

"You think she's on her bike?" I whispered to him. I don't know why we whispered, the Jenkinses didn't seem to know we were even there.

"I dunno," he whispered back, "I remembah she was ridin' around in the aftahnoon, not durin' lunchtime, but then again, my wife an' I were havin' lunch ourselves."

We heard a voice coming from the kitchen. It was the same unemotional voice I'd heard during my sister's attack and I looked over at Sammy. She had tears in her eyes and was shaking badly, but she still held her head high. I put my arm around my sister, leaning us both on Mike's cane. Sammy reached up and squeezed my hand with bone-white fingers.

A pre-teen Anna Jenkins walked past us. She was blond and pallid and very skinny. She was carrying two plates laden with food.

"Mom, Dad," she said coldly, "I didn't know if you wanted to serve the food in the kitchen or bring it out, so I brought these."

She set one of the plates in front of Beth and the other in the adjacent place-setting, before sitting down herself.

Paul and Jenny rushed into the kitchen like lightning, while Beth warmly thanked her daughter and smiled at her, telling her the food smelled delicious. When they came back out, he was carrying the remaining plates and she the big pot of food. Jeff was eyeing his granddaughter suspiciously, and, once again, the image of elephants in a circle with their backs to each other, came to mind. I thought that maybe it was Jeff trying to tell me something, but what?

They all sat down at the table and, for a moment, it broke my heart to think that such a nice family would soon come to a horrible end. Beth raised a forkful of food to her mouth, and Anna smirked. I opened my eyes wide; I knew she was up to something. I looked around the table, but no one in the family seemed to notice. There was a glint in her eyes and I now understood what Mike Monroe had meant. That was 'The Look'. Sam squeezed my hand tighter while the dragon head dug deep into my other palm. I realized I was holding onto that cane as if it was the only thing that could save us from harm.

Jeff Jenkins looked up and, as our eyes met, I saw the circle of elephants again, only in that instant, one elephant was running out of it. And I understood. I understood that Jeff Jenkins was that sacrificial elephant that had chosen to die in order to save the rest.

"Look!" he exclaimed, "There's a hawk flying above us." Beth put the fork down without eating a bite.

And while everyone, including Anna, looked up, he quickly and quietly switched plates with Beth, and without a second's thought, took that first bite on Beth's fork. He made a pained face, then began stuffing forkfuls in his mouth.

"NO!" Sam and I screamed, while Tallulah put her hand over her mouth and Mike raised his hands to his head. With every bite, Sam bent forward as if she had stomach pain and cried that it was poison.

The room spun again, and then we were back in my house, as if we'd never moved. Sam fell to her knees and retched, once, then twice. The retching continued for a while, but nothing came out, although I thought I saw a green haze surround Sammy and evaporate. I tried to bend down despite my broken ankle and hold Sam, but Tallulah got to her first and led her to the couch. I sat next to her and stroked her hair as she laid her head on my shoulder and sobbed. It occurred to me that, just the week before, I'd sat on this very couch and wished desperately to be with her.

Mike sat down in the armchair that hid the axes and sighed, his head hung low.

"And heah I'd always thought the cansah had gotten him," he shook his head, "I dunno if the family knew, but Rosie and I did. We'd bumped into him at the clinic a couple o' times when she got sick."

Sam was quiet the whole drive back, as if her naturally bouncy self had been placated by the incident at the Funhouse. She seemed a little green, and I noticed that every once in a while she would pass her good hand across her eyes, as if wiping away tears invisible to me from the front passenger seat.

No one spoke beyond polite conversation and the making of plans for the evening, when we would be meeting up with Apollo and Mark after their workday was over. They were to sleep over at Lupe's, and tomorrow early, we would be driving up to Osprey Cove and meeting the Babcocks at their house. Lupe would stay home with Jude.

I didn't want to talk about what happened, so as soon as we got home, I excused myself and sat down at my computer in Lupe's guest bedroom. I didn't want to talk, but I knew that I had to get what happened off my chest quickly and the best way to do it was to write about it.

Sammy entered the room a few minutes later and laid down on the bed. I couldn't see her face, but I heard soft sobs and sniffs, and though my heart ached for her, I knew it was best to leave her alone. I listened to her as I wrote and noticed her breathing gradually calmed and soon she was fast asleep.

When I was done, I grabbed the cane and ambled to the other side of the bed and laid down on my back, next to her. She was on her side with her back towards me. My eyelids soon drooped and I fell asleep, still holding on to the cane.

I don't know how long we slept, but when I roused, the light in the room had shifted. I turned towards Sam, who was now facing me, her good hand under her cheek and her eyes big and wide. Her shoulder-length hair fell onto the pillow and framed her face like feathers.

"I knew she was weird, I didn't know she was dangerous," she whispered, "if I'd known, I'd never have befriended her."

"How did you meet?" I whispered. I'd let go of the cane while I slept and figured it must have fallen onto the carpeted floor.

"In college. We took a class together and had to buddy up for a project. It never occurred to me that she would one day try to kill me. I should've listened to all my friends when they said she was too strange."

"Yeah," I sighed.

"Thank you, by the way. Thank you for giving me the strength to fight her."

"I didn't do anything," I answered, "you've always had that strength within you, I just reminded you of it."

"Johnny-Boy," her eyes welled up with tears. This was the second time she'd used Grandpa's nickname, and I guessed that for her, it came out naturally in difficult circumstances, as it did for me. There was comfort in that name. "I'm really scared that one of us isn't going to come out of this alive. She doesn't seem to have a problem with murder, and I think she killed once in Oregon too."

I raised my eyebrows and beckoned her to go on.

"Do you remember my friend Stan?" she asked, "I used to talk a lot about him and I'm sure you met him once when you came to visit me."

I began to shake my head no, when an image of a thin, geeky-looking guy with glasses popped into my head.

"Yeah-yeah-yeah-yeah!" I exclaimed, "He was a nice guy. I remember, everything was Stan this and Stan that. Whatever happened...Wait, didn't he die?"

Sam adjusted herself, her eyes welling up with tears, which she blinked back. She had met Diana and Stan when they'd been assigned to work on the same project together. They'd become fast friends and soon, Sammy had developed a deeper interest in Stan.

Sammy never spoke about boyfriends and I always assumed it was because she didn't have many, or none that were really important, but now, she confessed to me, guys never really liked her back. I couldn't believe it, my sister was good-looking, intelligent and, if you knew her well enough, and learned how to be around her, she could be really fun. She was enthusiastic about almost everything, and it had taken me years to realize that if I let go of my natural worries and apprehensions, her enthusiasm was contagious, and it would lead to some of the most interesting, if not fun, times in my life. I told her that.

She waved the comment away, and said that it didn't matter, that nothing had happened with Stan. He told her he'd never seen her as anything other than a friend and that he was interested in someone else.

Soon after that, Stan and Diana (Anna, actually) had become a couple. They'd dated through college and when Stan had asked her to marry him, she'd agreed. Sam and Stan had remained close, despite her unrequited love, and in time, she said, she got over him and saw him only as a friend. After they graduated, Sam had distanced herself from the couple, but still kept in touch.

"I wish I'd known. I wish I could've kept him away," she told me as she wiped tears from her eyes.

"I'm sorry Sammy, I didn't know you were going through all this. Why didn't you tell me?"

"Don't worry about me, I got over Stan, and really, when I think of him, I don't feel any kind of love-love for him at all, just nostalgia for a lost friend. I didn't tell you anything because I didn't want to worry you. I know you, I know you'd have taken my sadness and disappointment upon yourself and made yourself sick. After all, there was nothing at all you could've done. You're a natural worrywart and sometimes, the least you know about my troubles, the healthier it is for you. I can handle myself in matters of the heart, and besides, back then, you were getting started with your career, looking for agents and stuff, and I didn't want to add to that stress."

I sighed. It was just like Sam, taking on the world by herself.

"What happened to him?"

"Not long after they married, the brakes on Stan's car failed on the highway. It was a route he took every day, but somehow, as he was driving on a curve that overlooked a cliff, he lost control and flew off. Killed himself instantly."

Sammy broke down in tears and I let her cry for a while. When she calmed herself, she went on about how a guy she'd been dating at the time wasn't surprised that the brakes had failed.

"You see, Jacky, this guy, who was a prick and shall therefore remain unnamed, was into cars and knew a lot about mechanics. He'd driven that car with Stan about two days before the accident and claimed that he'd thought there was something wrong with the brakes. He said he'd told Stan, and Stan said he'd get it taken care of. The strange thing was that the car was practically brand new, there shouldn't have been anything wrong with those brakes. When I mentioned this to the prick, he said that sometimes even brand new cars had their defects and that only an expert investigation could determine fault. The experts came up with nothing suspicious, but even so, after what's happened here and what she did, I think she might've had something to do with Stan's death."

"What makes you say that?"

She rolled herself onto her back. Diana claimed to be grief-stricken and wanted to distance herself for some time. One day, barely a month after Stan's death, Sammy was at a grocery store and thought she heard Diana's voice in the next aisle ("I still can't stop calling her Diana, Jack, even though I know now that's not her real name"). She sounded like she was talking to someone on the phone. So Sam went around the aisle to see if it was her and say hello.

"It was her, Jacky. As I walked into that aisle I only saw a glimpse of her face as she turned, but I heard her saying, "It's all done baby, I'm free again. Did you take care of yours yet?" That statement left me cold, and I just stood there as she walked away. I told the nameless prick about that and he said I was probably mistaken."

"Did you ever ask her about it?"

"Yeah," Sam rubbed her nose with the back of her hand, like she used to do as a kid when she was done crying, "she totally denied having been there and having said anything at all. So we just left it at that. I broke up with the prick soon after, and Diana and I gradually lost touch when I moved to Sacramento. We sometimes emailed and saw each other only sporadically, but we've been quite distant these past years; until about the time you bought your house, come to think of it. It's like Mike Monroe said (it's really quite impossible to just call him Mike right? The Monroe just rolls off your tongue), pieces just fell into place. I only wish they'd fallen into place sooner."

"Yeah..." was all I could say, as an uncomfortable thought formed at the back of my mind, and my stomach twisted with guilt that I was to blame for their re-acquaintance, "I'm just glad they didn't fall when it was too late."

"Amen to that, Jacky-Lee."

"Hey Baloo, guess what? We saw ghosts today!" Sammy squealed, delighted, as Mark walked in the door.

She'd gotten into the habit of calling him Baloo since I'd mentioned to her he reminded me of a bear; and by Mark's scrunched up face, I could tell he hated it.

Sam had gotten back to her energetic, bouncy self soon after Lupe had knocked on the door to offer us a snack. We'd gladly accepted, and with each bite, Sammy's color and smile had come back, bright as the summer afternoon outside. Now, she was all excited about what she'd seen. I didn't think she'd forgotten our talk, just like she'd never forgotten about Stan, but rather, she'd managed to put it all behind her. It was remarkable how easily she could do that.

"Why? What happened?" Apollo said, smiling as he gave her a big, tender hug, while Jude stood up on his hind legs, eager to meet the new person his master was greeting.

"Let's have dinner first, then talk about it," Tallulah said, walking out of the kitchen, "I'm famished, so I just ordered us some pizzas. No mushrooms for Apollo, no anchovies for Jack, extra cheese for Sam, and inexplicably, no pineapple for Mark."

"There's something just wrong about pineapple on pizza," Mark rolled his eyes at Tallulah, "and *normal* people agree."

It was one of the happiest dinners I'd had in a long time. Apollo told us about this crazy old woman that lived just a few blocks from his apartment ("you guys should see her, she looks as if Hell had spit her out"); Mark told a funny story about something that had happened at work, and Sammy talked about each and every one of the quirks the kids in her classroom had. I had nothing cheery to say, so I just sat back and enjoyed the conversation. Meanwhile, Jude kept us all on our toes every time he tried to sneak away with a slice. The little beagle absolutely loved pizza; it was his very own forbidden fruit.

After dinner, we sat in the living room, while the women brought out warm drinks and dessert. I think we all expected Lupe to excuse herself once it was time to bring up the topic of Anna the Axe and her Great House of Screams, but instead, she sat down quietly on the rocker with a cup of tea in her hand. Everyone looked around uncomfortably, not knowing whether to bring up the subject or not, until she looked up, and, noticing our awkward gazes, said, "Ah no, chuss beecos I don' wan' to go tomorrroh, dahsen't mean I don' wan' to knoh what joo cheel-dren are getteeng into."

"Well, then, in that case, let's begin," Tallulah said as she raised an eyebrow.

We talked about what we'd seen at the Funhouse and about Jeff Jenkins's sacrifice, while Sam gave a much summarized version of her acquaintance with Anna. She told them about Stan, but left out her own feelings towards him and, for some reason, the nameless prick. I thought it weird and looked at her closely trying to figure out why. I had the feeling there was something about that relationship that Sammy wasn't saying, and it wasn't good.

"I wonder why Anna would've told Mike her grandfather's death had been such an important moment of her life," Apollo said taking a little cube of some Mexican fruit-candy Lupe had brought out ("eet's called 'ah-teh' Yack, joo should try eet.")

"I think it's because he was her first victim, although she didn't expect him to be," I said, taking a piece with my fingertips and sniffing it, "I think she meant to kill her very pregnant mother."

I popped the dark red cube into my mouth and hoped I wouldn't throw up. It was absolutely delicious! It's sweet and tangy taste filled my mouth and I smiled big at Lupe, who said that the one I tried was made of quince.

"Once again, it's all about Tommy," Tallulah said as she sipped her tea, "for some reason, she hated him from the very start, even before he was born."

"She was probably envious about him getting more attention than her," Sam said, "I've talked about it with my kids whose mothers are expecting again. They're so used to being their parents' focus of love and attention that they fear the baby is going to take it away. Maybe that's what Diana—I mean, Anna—felt. She's always been the jealous type. I never understood it until now, but she used to scare away guys that paid attention to me and not her. Now that I think of it, it was as if she felt she was the only one worthy of anyone's attention. Plus, I don't think she has a problem with killing. She was laughing wildly as she was beating me, and it wasn't that crazy fake laugh like in the movies, it was a real laugh of pure pleasure."

I winced at the thought of anyone hurting my sister, and the shame of what I'd experienced in that strange dream welled up again. I looked at the guys. Apollo's hair was hiding his eyes, but his shoulders were slightly hunched forward as if he were a berated child, while Mark looked at Sammy like he was ready to strike anyone down that so much as thought of doing her harm.

"That crazy bitch is going to pay for everything she's done," he said turning to Sam, his fist in a ball.

They were sitting next to each other on the big couch and Mark put his arm around her protectively. Sammy didn't wince or go stiff, instead, she seemed to grow more at ease. Tallulah and Lupe exchanged knowing glances and I decided to ignore them. The last thing I wanted was to think about my best friend shtuppin' my sister. I shuddered. *Ewwsh.*

"But there's gotta be more to this than just showing us her hate for Tommy," Apollo, who was sitting next to Mark, spoke up, "I mean, we already figured that out, so why show us the grandfather's death?"

"Maybe to take a body count?" I said, "I mean, I bet he was her first, but since then, it's been...(I counted on my fingers) five more people, the four remaining Jenkinses, and Stan. That we know of."

"Does that make her a serial keeler?" Lupe asked, "Like in that cho, *Creemeenal Minds*?"

Everyone shrugged, though we all agreed that *Criminal Minds* was a good show.

"What about the Murphys? They're dead too," Mark said, his arm still around Sam, "I really don't think it's a coincidence that all of David Murphy's family died suddenly in a car accident. It's as if they're both leaving a very spotless trail of bodies in their wake."

"And what about Anna?" Tallulah said, "We still don't know where she is, and I find it very strange that the door to the house was unlocked, yet everything was in its place."

I suddenly saw an image of Anna forcing the door open, yet unable to come inside. I closed my eyes and let the image flow. I tried to follow Tallulah's advice about listening to my instincts, and somehow, I got the feeling that the Jenkinses were planting this image in my mind. I don't know why they connected with me so easily.

"What if she couldn't get in?" I asked, "What if, somehow, she's forbidden to go into that house?"

Everyone looked at me, and I felt as if I'd said something totally embarrassing or wildly inappropriate, but I couldn't figure out what.

"You think there might've been some kind of brouhaha when she tried to go in?" Sam asked, "But what did she want? I would've thought she'd be smart enough to think you wouldn't be there."

"She probably went to get the axes," Apollo said, "it's a very big piece of evidence against her; hell, our only piece of evidence. Everything else is pretty much conjecture."

"Then the Funhouse wasn't about to let her take them away; after all, even *we* can't move them," I said, "I bet that's what happened. I bet the ghosts all banded together to kick her out, or to keep her out."

"Makes sense," Tallulah spoke up, "so far they've done everything to help you help them, I'm sure they aren't about to let their murderer destroy the evidence. I still feel we're missing something, though."

Suddenly, it was all too much. I felt a great weight bearing down on me, as if I was being crushed by stones and I couldn't understand why this was happening to me. Haunted houses and ghosts were my worst nightmare. As a child, I had to sleep with a nightlight for more years than I care to admit because of my fear of ghosts. I couldn't walk into darkness without almost peeing myself. Halloween was the worst holiday ever (I used to run away screaming whenever my sister happily watched *Disney's The Legend of Sleepy Hollow*) and, jeez-louise, even Scooby-Doo scared the shit out of me. Hell, if I'd been one of Bluebeard's wives, I'd have never opened the goddamn door out of pure and simple fear of what might lay behind it.

"Why me?" I said burying my head in my hands, "Why is this happening to me?"

"Because of Sam," Tallulah rubbed my back as we sat together on the love-seat, "because sooner or later, Sam was going to get in Anna's way. And Anna gets rid of everyone that does. I think that when they realized the connection between you, they worked extra hard to find a way to get through to you. I think that's what those messages on the wall and the computer meant, "Keep you safe". Not just you, Jack, but both of you; eventually your path was going to cross Anna's too, and if you hadn't bought that house, we might've been attending both your funerals one day."

"But why did it have to be ghosts?" I looked at her through misty eyes.

"It's what's remained of them. And perhaps, it's also because it's time for you to work on managing that particular fear. Remember, you won't experience anything you can't handle. Your spirit guides, or whoever you believe in, will always make sure of that."

"Perhaps it's the lesser of two evils," Apollo joined in, "I think dealing with your fear of the supernatural is better than dealing with the murder of a sister."

"But there's always been spooky stuff going on, even before I bought the house," I whined. "Why is it worse with me?"

Sam looked at me with eyes so big they practically looked like dinner plates.

"Because they cannot rest, and it became much more important to connect with you than with anyone. I have a feeling that the one that caused all the previous trouble was Tommy, you know, the screaming and the throwing of things around? I have a feeling he's the one that's more restless, since he's the one that probably never understood. It's almost as if he were throwing a tantrum.The parents knew they might end up dead by their daughter's hand someday, so their main mission was to protect Tommy, who had no idea he was in danger." Tallulah said.

Tommy's "mommy?" whisper rang out through my brain again, and I felt like crying. I wonder if I'm ever going to stop hearing that little voice.

"Poor baby," Sammy spoke, "he must feel like a caged lion, unable to go and unable to stay, never knowing why. Not understanding why his life was cut so short." She balled her hand into a fist and angry fire shown in her eyes. Mark pulled her just a tad closer.

"And I think there may be something about you two, that makes them more powerful, if you will." Tallulah went on, "Somehow their supernatural powers (she made air quotes with her fingers) grow when they're around you both. Look at what happened today; until now, they hadn't been able to affect anyone physically until Sammy came along."

"Why?"

"Energy, perhaps? I don't know. Maybe you both have some sort of spiritual energy they can tap into more easily than with anyone else. Not to mention that they must absolutely keep you safe because of Sam's connection with Anna."

We sat quiet for quite some time. Mark kept his arm around Sam, who kept opening and closing her fist, probably trying hard to fight back the helpless anger that Tommy's ghostly existence incited in her. I'm sure she was going to do everything in her power to make Anna pay for what she'd done to the little boy. Lupe sipped her tea, while Tallulah stroked my hair as she would a child's. Apollo played with Jude.

"Why would Jeff Jenkins kill himself instead of calling Anna out?" I asked, "I don't get this family, why all this protection of someone so evil? Why did he sacrifice himself? It doesn't make sense to me, but then again, I don't have a child who murders. "

"It's systems psychology, Jacky, the theory that any system, say a family, will do anything it can to keep functioning. In this case, I think only Jeff and Jenny, who were somewhat outside the immediate family unit, realized there was something wrong with her. Maybe after Jeff's death, Anna's parents began to believe it too, and so closed themselves off to shield others from her, and sent Tommy away as much as possible to keep him safe. The grandparents are often the first ones to notice when something is wrong, and perhaps Jeff ate the poison to plant some doubt in Beth's and Paul's mind, or maybe it was just his first instinct, after all, Mike Monroe said he had cancer."

Now it was my turn to look at Sammy like she had something on her face.

"What?" she said when everyone remained silent and staring, "I took some psychology classes in college, they are handy if you want to work with kids."

"Hmm," I said, "it's in like the book that Babcock gave me, *Innocent, Evil…*" I broke off as I suddenly remembered the dream I had when I'd first started reading. I realized now that dream had not been a dream, but an image the Jenkinses had shown me. It had been the moment Paul and Beth realized Anna Jenkins was capable of murder.

People looked at me, waiting for me to go on, but Apollo spoke, picking up on my train of thought,

"Yeah, in the book, when the grandmother realizes…"

Sammy cut him off by throwing a pillow at him.

"I haven't read it, jerk! I'm gonna start tonight!"

The clock on the wall struck midnight, and Lupe declared it was time for bed. She said we all needed to get some sleep, since tomorrow was going to be a big day and that we had a long drive ahead of us. I didn't counter by telling her that two hours isn't really that long, because I was certain it was going to feel like forever.

"I theenk joo will all find some answers in Maine tomorrroh."

CHAPTER THIRTEEN

Heigh-ho, Heigh-ho, to Jenny's House We Go

"OH MY GOD YOU COULD BE TWINS!" Amelia Babcock exclaimed when she saw Sam and I standing side by side as I finished the introductions.

She wasn't wrong, we look very much alike, we both have light brownish-blond hair, but my eyes are stink-water green instead of hazel.

"Yes, but Jack, with his square jaw, looks like a boy, and Sam looks like a girl," Tallulah smiled, "I once knew a pair of siblings; *she* looked exactly like the father, and *he* was the spitting image of the mother. Neither was very popular in school, I'm afraid."

Sammy playfully batted her eyelashes and giggled, pretending to be demure and coy, but then turned serious and, in that knightly pose of hers (back straight as an arrow, arms at her side and lightly turned-up chin), looked right at the Babcocks and said,

"I want to thank you all so much for everything you've done for Jack. I'm so sorry if his accident destroyed your garden. Please let us know if there's any way we can repay you for your kindness."

Her voice sounded full, as if it came straight from her heart, and a lump went to my throat when I noticed Sam's torn lips quiver.

Amelia went all misty-eyed and hugged Sam (who winced discreetly), then, holding Sammy's face in both her hands, said in a broken voice,

"Oh honey, don't you worry about some flowers and there's nothing to be sorry for. You and your brother are alive and that's repayment enough. If you can help us get justice for Jenny and end this matter, *we'll* be in your debt. I know it doesn't seem like it, since it was such a long time ago, but we loved Jenny Jenkins very much and her death took a bad toll on us, and now it's time to move forward. We can only do that if Anna is behind bars."

She hugged Sammy again, while Pluto affectionately slapped my back.

Abigail appeared from the kitchen and, glancing awkwardly at Apollo and Mark, greeted them in a somewhat cold and matter-of-fact voice. She was warmer when Babcock introduced Tallulah. When she saw me, a huge smile spread across her face. She was about to hug me when she caught sight of Sam and her effusive greeting died. Abigail looked taken aback by the presence of another young woman and seemed to be almost jealous.

"Abby, this is my sister, Sam," I said, trying to smooth out any roughness arising from Sam's presence, "she's come to help us, all the way from Sacramento. She knows Anna Jenkins better than any of us."

Sam smiled through broken lips and held out her hand. Abigail took it, diligently looking Sammy up and down, like she was scanning her and registering Sam's tall, thin figure, simply dressed in jeans, sport sandals and a Van Halen T-shirt. I looked at the guys and they both shrugged; we'd already known that meeting Abigail Babcock today was going to be awkward.

Back in Massachusetts, they had both told me about the night they'd spent in the Babcock's family room. Apparently, they'd both gently turned down Abigail's pretty obvious advances. Now, I guess I was the only option left, and to make matters worse, had turned up with another woman at my side, however much we looked alike. I wondered if Sammy had been this boy-crazy in college. With a pang, I realized that was when she'd fallen in love with Stan.

"You okay?" Abigail asked, "They told me you'd been attacked."

"Yeah," Sam replied brightly, "Anna's no match for Manolo Blahnik." Abigail chuckled.

"Wanna check out the mall later?" She smiled up at Sam.

"Sure, but I'd rather check out Osprey Cove's one and only haunted house first," Sammy smiled back, "I'm a sucker for that shit."

"Oh yah, Jenny's house is both creepy and awesome at the same time. You should see the place, it hasn't changed since she died. I was really little so I don't remember her much, but in high school, I used to go there when, y'know, life got to be too much."

"Yeah," Sammy assented brightly, "in high school life was always too much. Jack here used to hide out in the library, and me, well, let's just say I knew where to ride my bike so I wouldn't be bothered. We all need a place to go sometimes. Do you still hang out there?"

"Sometimes; the house doesn't change, but something's different now."

Apollo raised his eyebrows and asked her to explain. Abigail turned to him with a stony look that melted after only an instant. I thought I saw both regret and disappointment pass before her gaze turned warm. She looked at Mark and the same thing happened. In that instant, Abigail

Babcock cut her losses and accepted the fact that neither Apollo nor Mark was for her.

"Since I came back from Europe, the house seems different. Nothing can be moved still, but instead of that light that goes up the stairs, I thought I saw human figures. And once, when I walked around the house towards the cliffs, I heard a woman singing. I asked Mom if Jenny could sing, and she said she could, but she hardly ever sang in public."

"That reminds me, Pluto," I said turning to Babcock, "was Jenny some sort of dancer? Like a ballerina?"

"Yes," Babcock replied, as my eyes met Tallulah's, "she was going to be a professional ballerina, but she was in an accident in high school and her knees never healed quite right. I know she used to dance at her house, but her chances of dancing professionally were shot. How did you know?"

"Cuz we saw her," I said, "actually, we saw all of them."
The Babcocks looked surprised, and Tallulah suggested that we all sit down instead of standing around the parlor. Amelia then proposed we all have a late breakfast and talk about what's going on.

The women went into the kitchen while Babcock led us out to the backyard. This was the first time I'd been back since the accident and it felt strange to see the white iron table still there. I'd almost expected it to be split in half like some sort of symbolic Narnian Stone Table. But it looked perfectly fine. The rose garden looked like a giant had stomped all over it. Apollo put his arm around my neck in a brotherly fashion, while Mark lightly punched my arm.

As we set the table, I caught Abigail alone and apologized for cutting her off the way I had. I said that we had a lot to tell and that somehow, I was pretty sure it would all make sense with what she'd been experiencing at Jenny's house.

Amelia went all out with a breakfast of sunny-side-up eggs, bacon and sausage. In between bites, we told the Babcocks about Jeff Jenkins's deadly sacrifice and Tallulah's theory of how Sam and I made the Jenkins ghosts more powerful.

"Hmm," Amelia said, "that might just fit with what Abby said. She was still in Europe when Jack went to the house, so maybe it was his presence that changed everything."

"Actually, I think it's Anna's acquaintance with Sam that's making them work harder to help them," Tallulah explained. "Sam is the connection. For the first time since the murders, there's the possibility of putting Anna behind bars. Before that, there was nothing to tie the Jenkinses to Anna's life."

"So, where is Anna now?" I asked.

"I think she and Saunders have some sort of hideout no one knows about," Babcock answered, "I've been keeping an eye on him, and friends in town have too. No one's reported anything odd about his behavior, but then again, Anna is very elusive."

"It makes sense," Sammy spoke up, "they'd need somewhere private to plan Jenny's murder, and to keep in touch with each other. What's this Saunders like? Does he have a family? A wife? Kids?"

Babcock shook his head, and said that, as far as he knew, Saunders was unmarried and childless. He didn't have any known family in Osprey Cove and he hardly ever took vacation. He was always at work on time and did his job well enough. He wasn't the most intuitive of policemen, but since Babcock's retirement, he'd taken over the job of detective because there was no one else. The staff had changed over the years, and Babcock had been the last holdout from the days of Jenny Jenkins; some had died, others, like the former Chief, were hospitalized or in need of constant care, but most had retired to warmer climates.

"He lives in an old house on the edge of town," Babcock went on, "and it's always struck me as odd that a single guy like that would choose that kind of place to live in. It's a Victorian, like Jenny's, but not nearly as big, yet too big for one person. There seems to be nothing wrong with the guy, but he's always rubbed me the wrong way, and talking to my friends, I'm not the only one who thinks that. He's polite, you know, and well-mannered, but something about him is off."

"Yes," Amelia joined in, "and he doesn't have many girlfriends. I've seen him around town with different women a couple of times, but sporadically, and always someone from outside of town. My friends say that he doesn't date Osprey Cove women, though some of their daughters wouldn't mind if he did."

"My friend Jane lives down the street from him and says he's really weird, like loner weird, you know; and also that lately he's been more reserved than usual," Abigail piped up, "she says that he hardly leaves his house and that the neighbors had to talk to him about mowing his lawn. It looks like he hasn't done it in a few of weeks. "

"Maybe he's hiding Anna," Mark suggested, shrugging his shoulders, "I mean, she needs a place to stay, right?"

We pondered and talked a while longer, until Sammy tapped the table and gleefully said we should go see Jenny's house.

"Do you think you can walk there? Or would you prefer to take the car?" Amelia asked when we were done clearing the breakfast dishes.

I looked down at my cast and then out the kitchen window. It was a beautiful day, and I told Amelia that walking would do me some good, and that with Mike's cane as support, I could probably make it to the house and back.

"It's not too far, right?" I asked when I saw her doubtful expression.

"No, just a couple of blocks, I would say about a fifteen minute walk," she looked pensive for a moment, "let's do this, why don't we take the car too, because I'd like to stop and get some groceries some time today. That way, if you feel too tired, you can get in the car anytime."

"That sounds like a good idea," Babcock jumped in, "Abby can show you guys the way and we'll meet up at Jenny's. It's too hot for me, I'd rather go where there's AC."

It was decided that Abby would walk with us to Jenny's house while Tallulah, who claimed to be a bit tired, would go in the car with the Babcocks.

We were strolling past the Moose Crossing Diner when Sammy, who had been walking beside me, suddenly stepped behind me. Apollo took the opportunity to step into Sammy's empty spot. Abigail was walking in front with Mark, when she suddenly stopped and said hello to someone. As Mark stepped aside, I saw that she was coldly greeting David Saunders. He paused and looked us up and down.

Sam clutched the tail of my T-shirt and pressed her forehead against my back. I felt her breath quicken and she started to tremble. It made my spine crawl, and I almost pulled away when she whispered, "Please don't let him see me, Johnny-Boy, please don't let him know I'm here."

Her voice was oozing fear and something else I couldn't quite place. Anger? Surprise? She transmitted these sensations into me like osmosis and I began to tremble with her. Alert and wary, I imagined Sam and I were like two cats with curved backs because of the presence of dogs nearby. I clutched my cane with both hands, ready to pick it up and use it as a weapon if need be.

Apollo didn't seem to notice Sammy's distress, but as Saunders walked by, Apollo stepped aside to let him pass, at the same time shielding Sam, while I pivoted slowly to face him. I knew it would be difficult for Saunders to see her, since Sammy, who stood tall for a woman at five foot nine, was still shorter than the both of us. But even so, I reached and pulled my sister in front of me as we left Saunders behind us. Apollo resumed his place next to me, and I thought I felt Saunders's intensive stare at my back, as if he was trying to see through me and seek out Sammy.

When Apollo put his hand on my shoulder, his warmth passed through me, relaxing me. Sam was walking in front of us, her hips swaying and her head held high, as if nothing had happened, but her knuckles were white under the tight ball of her fist.

"So," Mark spoke up, "that's the famous David Saunders."

"Yep," Abigail replied, "he's such a creep."

I was about to ask Sammy what was going on, but the look she gave me stopped me cold. Instead, I asked Apollo if that was David Murphy. He thought for a moment and said he couldn't be sure. The David Murphy he'd seen in the dream and the David Saunders he'd just met, were similar. They had the same body type and physiognomy, but there was something about Saunders that differed from Murphy. He couldn't place what, but for some reason, he couldn't say with any kind of certainty that they were one and the same.

Sam walked quietly the rest of the way. She seemed to have lost the spring in her step, and grew morose. I worried that there was more to her acquaintance with Anna than she was saying, but I also knew that if I asked her now, she would shut me down. No one else had noticed her distress.

At the house, Abigail opened the door while Sam went around the side as the guys filed in after Abby. I couldn't run after Sam, so I did my best to hurry and catch up with her. In the yard I saw her sitting on the edge of the cliffs Babcock had mentioned. She was hunched over, her good hand covering her mouth and her hair falling in front, shielding her eyes. Her knees were pulled up tight to her chest. As I neared, I noticed her shoulders were shaking up and down and I heard quick sobs.

"Sammy-Girl," I sat down beside her with the help of my cane, "what's going on?"

She looked at me through the tears, and in her eyes I saw such an immeasurable pain that I almost burst into tears myself. Instead, I put my arm around her as she sobbed on my shoulder. I had never heard her cry like that and it wrung my heart. Her tears wet the front of my shirt and soaked right through to my skin. Gradually, her breathing slowed and her sobs quieted. I don't know how long she cried, but everyone was still in Jenny's house and everything seemed quiet.

"That Saunders was the Nameless Prick, but back then I knew him as David Murdoch," she wiped her cheeks with her hand, "I met him at a house party soon after Diana (Anna) and Stan got engaged. They were there too."

"Sammy, did he hurt you?"

"Oh Jack," her lips quivered, "I never wanted you to know."

"Sam, what happened?"

My heart beat faster. She straightened up, but kept her knees close to her chest. She breathed deep and began in a voice so broken and cold that I hope never to hear again.

"I broke up with him because he hit me. It happened soon after I bumped into Diana at the grocery store following Stan's death. It was just once, we were on a date and it was outside a restaurant. But that once was one too many. About a week after I told him I didn't want to see him anymore, I was leaving for school. When I opened the door he was standing there. I didn't have time to react as he pushed himself inside and locked the door. I tried to run away, but he caught me by the hair and pulled me back. He hit my head against the wall and that was it. I was done for. He was already inside me when I came to, and he beat and raped me for the rest of that day. Jack, he was insatiable and I had no chance. I couldn't run away, I tried hitting him, but I wasn't strong enough. He just laughed at my attempts to defend myself. He laughed the whole time. He *liked* it and the more I screamed, the more he enjoyed it. It was as if sex couldn't be pleasurable without causing pain and humiliation. He said horrible things to me, things no man should ever say to a woman. And when he was done, he just left. Disappeared. He left me on the floor, bleeding. I don't know how I managed to get to the phone. The police looked for him everywhere, but he'd completely vanished. There was no record of him, no paper trail, nothing. His apartment was empty and clean. The case went cold, and soon after that I moved to Sacramento. I started over and came out on top." Sam's voice was ever so distant, as if she was just a robot, spitting out facts.

"Why didn't you tell me about this? I thought we were close. I thought we were very good friends, not just siblings."

"We are close, Jacky, and it's because of that, I chose not to tell you. I didn't want you to think less of me. I didn't want you to think I was weak, and stupid, and easy, and that I couldn't see a bad guy coming from miles away. I didn't want you to think that I had provoked this, that I had *let* this happen."

Tears were rolling down Sam's face again and her cut lips were quivering so badly she could barely speak.

"Sammy," I grabbed her good hand in both of mine, "look at me. I would never think that of you. Never, ever. You're the strongest person I know!"

"But *I* thought that of myself, Jack. *I* thought those horrible things about my own person. For the first time in my life, I felt weak and stupid and I didn't want anyone to know that, least of all you. You take everything onto yourself, what was I supposed to do? Dump this on you? Make you sick with worry, and anger and despair? Don't look at me like that, Jacky, it's what would've happened and you know it. Even if we'd known where he'd gone, what could you have done? Beat him up? Did you think I was going to allow that? I know you, brother, we *are* close, and I know you so well, that I know you would've come to fight, like the knights you love to read about, and defend my honor, and you would've lost. Against that guy, you would've lost. I'm pretty strong, and I'm pretty resourceful, and I didn't stand a chance. There was no way I was going to let my little brother get seriously injured or killed by some bastard that's capable of assaulting someone he's supposed to be in love with. Can you imagine what he would've done to you?" She took a deep, shaky breath, "Besides, how do you even *begin* to tell your brother you've been raped? I couldn't say it, the words just dried up in my mouth."

She was right, there was nothing I could've done against a guy like that. I'm not weak, but I'm not very strong either, and physical activity has never been my forté. That was my sister's realm, mine was words. In a way, I was like Bastian Balthasar Bux in the *Never-ending Story*, a weak-bodied child who only wished he was strong; and she was Atreyu. And yet... She should've come to me.

It pained me. My sister had been abused. She was a victim. Beaten and sexually attacked (*raped, Johnny-Boy, the word is raped. Be a man and call it what it is*) by a man she thought was good, and I was none the wiser.

"I'm not a victim, Jack. I can see in your eyes that you've labeled me as such, but I'm not. I was raped, and I was victimized, but I am *not* a victim. And I will *never* be one."

Her bottom lip quivered as she stood up and assumed that knightly pose of hers, which, in that instant, went from impressive to downright amazing.

"I'm okay, Jack. It's in the past, I've put it behind me. I've put him behind me. He hurt my body, Jacky, but he never hurt *me*. My *self* remains untouched, so don't let him hurt *you*. Don't let him hurt us."

"Okay," I said, awkwardly getting up, "I promise. I just wish you could've let me help."

"You did help. You pulled me through. Believe it or not, in your blissful ignorance, you did more than the cops and the group therapy and the psychologist ever did. Without you, I'd be a different person."

"How?"

"Remember when I used to call you everyday and we'd spend hours on the phone, talking about absolutely nothing? And how we'd video chat using those funky effects that made our faces look so funny that we'd spend an entire night laughing? That was how. And your stories, your amazing stories. I couldn't wait for the next one. I felt like they pulled me out of my body and my life and took me to all these different worlds where Good abounded and there was no violence, and no pain and no despair. Just the sound of your voice reminded me of what it was like to be happy and that gave me the strength to move forward... And I did. Believe me Jack, in spite of what happened, what he did, I *am* happy, and you're a big part of that." She put her hand on my shoulder, "Now it's time to move forward again. The sooner we finish this, the sooner we can put Anna and David behind us."

I hugged her and we stood like that for a moment.

"Is that why you started with the martial arts?"

"Yeah, that's why I got into Aikido and Tae-kwon-do. I swore I would never let anything like that happen again."

"Apollo does Tae-kwon-do," I blurted out.

"I know, we've always talked about sparring some time. Have never gotten around to it, though."

"Do Mom and Dad know?"

She shook her head.

"I've never told them, but I think Mom suspects. It's not something you bring up in conversation."

She looked up at me.

"Really Jack, this was years ago. I'm over it. I was just surprised when I saw him. Suddenly everything just fit. He was at that party because of

Anna, he dated me because of Anna. Now, I think it was him she was talking to on the phone that time in the grocery store. I think he was going to beat and rape me whether I broke up with him or not. She got Stan out of the way, and it was his turn to get me out of the way. I don't know why he let me live though."

"To break you," I said, with a certainty that surprised me, as if something deep inside had whispered the truth, "he let you live because he wanted to break you. He probably wouldn't have felt any satisfaction if you were dead. It was more fun for him to hurt you like that and let you live with it. He probably thought you were never going to figure out the connection between the two of them."

She pondered that a moment and nodded, "And if I ever realized who they were and what they were capable of, he probably would've attacked me again to keep weak, stupid, broken Sammy in her place."

She raised her chin and rubbed her nose with the back of her hand, "Sucks for him; he never even came close to breaking me."

I kissed her forehead and told her she could tell me anything, anytime. She stood up on her tiptoes and kissed my cheek. We've never been a touchy-feely family, but none of us had ever been in any kind of danger before. Now, in the past week, I'd almost died and she'd almost been murdered. Somehow, the physical contact was comforting, as if we were both making sure the other was all right.

We put our arms around each other and walked back to the house. I felt like my life had changed, but I couldn't say whether for better or worse. Sammy was right, sexual assault was not something you told your brother so easily. Saunders, or Murdoch as she'd called him, had changed her life and he had indirectly changed mine too. Even though I knew it had happened years ago, I felt an overwhelming helplessness. Once again, my sister had been in grave danger and I couldn't do a damn thing about it.

"Have you had any boyfriends since?" I whispered as we came to the front walk.

"A few," she shrugged, "but nothing to write home about, y'know. My relationships have always been short and sparse."

"Why?"

"I dunno... You know how people always say that all men are the same? Well, I've never believed that. I've just always thought that I haven't met the one who's different," she sighed, "I'm in no hurry, Jack, and I've always known that I don't *need* to be with a man, so it's cool.

I'm fine by myself and I *like* being by myself, and until that changes, why waste my time on guys I don't really love, and who don't really love me?"

She had a point. After my relationship with Megan had ended, I realized that sometimes it was best to be alone. That sometimes dating someone just to date could lead to a very unpleasant experience, or more than one.

"What about girls?" I asked smirking.

"*So* not my thing," she playfully bumped me sideways with her hip, "I'm straight as an arrow, Johnny-Boy, and that's irrevocable."

"Yep, me too."

"I know. I found your porn a few times, remember?"

I threw my head back and laughed.

CHAPTER FOURTEEN

Osprey Cove's One and Only Haunted House

We walked to the front door, and Babcock's car pulled up. We waited until they got out and went in together. Mark, Apollo and Abby were standing around the parlor.

"Has anything happened yet?" I asked.

"Course not, dude," Mark rolled his eyes, "we only just walked in."

I opened my eyes wide and met Sammy's gaze. She had gone pale, and looked both confused and scared. She mouthed a silent "how?" but I had no answer. I'm sure we'd been out back much longer; much, much longer. I'd even tried to think up a story about what had taken us so long.

"Just now?" I asked, hoping no one would think the question was weird. Sammy shook her head and put her finger to her lips.

"Well, duh. Dude, you're such a space cadet. Abby was opening the door when the car with the old people pulled up. Really where's your head, man?"

I shrugged and Mark shook his head with a sheesh.

"Who're you calling old?" Tallulah pinched Mark's ear, "There are no old people here."

"Well, you're no spring chicken, I can tell ya that," Mark retorted, while Babcock playfully grabbed the back of his neck and told him not to sass his elders.

Sammy laughed and Apollo's roar rang out through the house. I was still disconcerted about that weird time-lapse but figured Sam was right, I should let it go, otherwise we'd have to explain everything and I didn't think Sam would want everyone to know she'd been abused. *Time stands still in this house, Johnny-Boy, and today it paused so you could both talk.*

We went further into the house, and Babcock told us we could look around but to stay away from the stairs. Not one of us, he said pointing at each of us, was light enough to stand on the rotted steps. Sammy was looking at the stairs like she was willing to try anyway. I whispered to her that she should ask Mark to show her his stitched-up leg. She looked longingly at the stairs again, sighed, and walked away.

Apollo had gone further into the back of the house when he called to us. Mark and Sammy rushed over, while Abigail slipped her arm around my elbow and looked up at me smiling. I sighed.

"Abby, I..." I had no idea how to tell her she had no chance with me, but she cut me off saying,

"It's okay, Jack, I know. I'm too young, not your type, blah-blah-blah. I got the speech from the other two, and it's true, you guys are right. But I'd still like us all to be friends, just friends, if you agree."

I nodded, and smiling, told her I'd like that too.

We'd come to the room that Jenny had moved into. Mark, Sam and Apollo were looking at a shelf full of CDs, while I noticed that the one next to it held an impressive collection of vinyls.

"Dude, you gotta check this out," Apollo said, "I'm really liking this Jenny."

He pointed to the CDs, and I glanced over their spines. Jenny Jenkins had a lot of classical music, especially ballets, but I couldn't figure out what was so amazing about that.

"So? She used to do ballet, remember?" I said, looking at Mark and Sammy who were both smiling with mirth.

"Look closer, dude."

I sighed and looked again. Right next to Prokofiev's *Romeo and Juliet* was...Bang Tango! I chuckled and kept reading. Next to it was Aerosmith, Rush, Journey, Boston, Deep Purple, Tesla, Bon Jovi, Led Zeppelin, Kansas and even Great White!

"Sammy, this is right up your alley!" I exclaimed.

She smiled and held up her hand in the Metal Horns sign the great Dio had taught us metal-heads and hard-rockers worldwide. Sam was a huge fan of hard rock, prog rock and heavy metal music, although I also knew her shelves and iPod were replete with Disney and other kid's music as well.

"So?" Abby shrugged.

We all looked at her, nonplussed. Mark seemed to ruffle himself and blinked wildly.

"So! What do you mean "so?" This woman had an amazing taste in music!" He turned to us, while I shrugged and smiled at Abby, "D'you think if she'd lived she would have moved on to heavier stuff? This is still pretty easy-listenin' if you ask me."

"Well, does Symphony X answer your question?" Apollo said kneeling in front of the shelf.

"You're kidding?" I said, while Apollo shook his head smiling, and pointed at one of the cases. Sure enough, it was their debut album.

"Wow, she must've bought that shortly before she died," Sammy said, "d'you guys remember we went to their concert together that Christmas when I came to visit? It was so awesome."

"Yeah-yeah-yeah," Mark said, "they played "The Odyssey" as the encore and we'd already been standing up for like four hours straight and the song is like a half hour long. My knees and my back were killing me, but I didn't care. They totally brought the house down."

"Yep, I remember you'd just moved to Sacramento, but insisted on spending a white Christmas here, instead of all of us hanging out in sunny California," Apollo said smiling.

My heart skipped a beat when I suddenly realized why Sammy had been so adamant in coming to the Boston winter that time, and Apollo's unknowing smile dug a knife into my heart. She'd been trying to get away from rape.

I turned away and noticed that Abigail looked as if she felt left out; even Sam's comment about a concert we'd all attended together seem to pinch her somewhere inside. I asked her if she went to concerts with her friends, and she said not really. Her friends weren't very musical and she didn't have many friends to go with in the first place. Apollo asked her what kind of music she listened to and she said she'd always liked Kelly Clarkson. We nodded and said something noncommittal, before dropping the subject.

Apollo, still kneeling in front of the CDs, tried to take one out, but claimed it was stuck. I wasn't surprised, Babcock had said that nothing in the house could be moved, I suppose this included the CDs.

"Why's everyone milling around here?" Babcock said behind us.

The Babcocks and Tallulah walked in, and we were about to mention Jenny's choice of music when suddenly, the hi-fi on the desk turned on and its turntable whizzed and cracked to life. We all looked at each other as The Rolling Stones' "Brown Sugar" boomed out. The walls groaned and I got that feeling they pulsated, when Amelia said, "Jenny, honey, is that you? What is it you want to tell us? We already know that you liked rock music, but what do you need? How can we help you?"

The music grew louder and louder while the women covered their ears and screamed to turn it down; Babcock, who was next to the system, was unable to turn the dial or shut the system off. I covered my ears when the music got too loud for me. The women ran out of the room, followed by

Apollo, Mark and myself, and only Babcock remained. He must be losing his hearing.

"Okay, Jenny, we get it, the song is important, but please, it so loud it hurts!" Abby yelled over the noise.

Gradually, the volume lowered and we filed back in.

"I wonder what that was about," Mark said.

Sammy opened and closed the little prominence over and in front of left ear, the one she hadn't been able to cover because of her broken arm. The song ended and began again, although now it was set to a pleasant volume.

"I know she's trying to tell us something with that song, but what?" I said, worried that Sam might lose hearing in that ear. It certainly did seem to make her uncomfortable.

It struck me that Sammy was the most important person in the room to me, and that I should've realized sooner her hearing might be damaged and covered her ears myself. Once again, I'd failed to protect my sister. Once again, she'd taken all the blows. I hadn't been there when she was assaulted by Saunders, or when she was almost beaten to death by Anna, but now, I should've gotten her out of that room sooner. My failure to protect her, and the dark lump of her confession, weighed deep in my heart and I felt like crying. Saunders hadn't just forced *her* to live with rape, he had forced *me* to live with it too; and added to that the failure of my one job as a brother: to look out for her. She caught my eyes, and seemingly reading my gaze, sighed and smiled a sweet smile of resignation. I think she knew in that instant that Saunders *had* gotten to me, regardless of my promise earlier. *Let it go, Johnny-Boy*, my grandfather's voice sounded in my head, *she's her own person and allowed to live her own life. You can't always watch over her, just like she won't always be able to stand up for you. Let go, you'll only make yourself sick over circumstances you can't control.* I sighed and was brought back to the moment by Apollo's voice.

"What album was that song originally on? I only recall it on compilations," he was looking at the CDs, "I figure it must be important to Jenny."

"*Sticky Fingers*," Tallulah said without hesitation.

Everyone looked at her amazed.

"What? Why're you so surprised, Pollo? Did you really think I didn't listen to Rock in my youth?"

Apollo shook his head, mumbling that he'd always thought she only listened to weird New Age and World Music; Mark and I looked at her open-mouthed and Sammy beamed.

Just then, a vinyl flew out of the shelf and hit Apollo on the side of the forehead. He groaned "ay" instead of "ow" and rubbed the spot with the palm of his hand. It landed on the floor, the words *Sticky Fingers* blaring at us. As Apollo bent down, a small piece of paper slipped out of the sleeve and flew up, covering his eyes. He reached up and grabbed it.

It was an old photograph of what looked like a nineteenth century family. The father, in suit and sideburns that extended down the face, sat front and center; while the wife, and their two daughters stood behind him. The girls' long, puffy dresses and elaborate lace, as well as the man's suit, denoted wealth and status.

I looked over Apollo's shoulder as he turned the picture over. 'Hiram Jenkins and Family, 1854' was written on the backside, and next to it was a drawing of a square, with inner rectangles that ran in an angular spiral, and ended in a black square in the middle.

We passed the picture around, and when Sammy turned it over, she said, "I know what this is! It's a quilt block!"

Everyone looked at her surprised.

"Do you quilt, honey?" Amelia sounded utterly confused. Sammy didn't look like someone who could sew two stitches together, and I knew for a fact she couldn't.

"No, but my friend Gabby does, and she's always showing me her patterns and going on and on about quilts. She said that it was once believed that quilt blocks were used as codes for the Underground Railroad, y'know, to guide the escaped slaves to safety, and she showed me a few patterns and told me their supposed meanings. I think that myth has been debunked now. Anyway, I wasn't really paying attention, but I'm pretty sure this was one of them."

I tried to remember what this Gabby looked like; I was almost certain I'd seen her on Sam's Facebook pictures, but couldn't place her among the circle of Sam's unattractive girl friends. Mark and Apollo were racking their brains too. Apollo met my gaze, opened his arms wide indicating a big girl and shrugged. Mark nodded and gestured that maybe she was short. I suddenly saw an image of a particularly unfortunate-looking girl, with simian features and crooked teeth; fat, short, with big geeky glasses, complete with unibrow and 'stache; and smiled at them, rounding my fingers over my eyes as if wearing thick rims. Mark put his finger across his philtrum like a mustache and Apollo nodded fervently that that was the one.

"You jerks been laughing at my friends on Facebook again?" Sammy asked, crossing her good arm over the cast. She'd been watching our exchange.

"Us?" Mark was mockingly indignant, "Nevah!"

"What's wrong with your friend?" Abby asked.

"Absolutely nothing, she's a wonderful person, very caring and kind, and if *some people* focused on that, they'd forget she's not exactly pretty."

"Frickin' ugly, I'd say," Mark said, as Sammy punched him on the shoulder, then, deciding that wasn't enough, grabbed his nipple between her thumb and forefinger and twisted it. Mark winced in pain; Apollo and I automatically covered our chests with our arms and chuckled. Sammy was a Purple Nurple maestro.

"Okay, children, time to focus now," Tallulah's voice rang out over Mick Jagger's (the song kept repeating itself), "Sam, do you remember what this sign or block meant?"

Sam raised her eyes to the ceiling, as if trying to look into the back of her mind, then shook her head.

"I think it had something to do with logs, but I can't remember."

Tallulah took the picture from Sammy and turned it over and over in her hand.

"I wonder," she said after a few moments, "the picture, the song and the block; is it possible this area was part of the Underground Railroad? Did it ever get to Maine?"

"Yeah, it did," Abby answered, "there are known sites in Topsham, Brunswick and Brewer. Portland claims some too. I studied at Bowdoin College, where Harriet Beecher Stowe's husband taught when she wrote *Uncle Tom's Cabin*, and my friend Jane worked at their house, which is now a museum."

"Oh my God," gasped Amelia, covering her mouth with her hand, "do you think this was a station? Do you think Jenny's ancestors were abolitionists?"

"Jenny was a librarian, right? She might've found something out," Apollo spoke up, "but what does that have to do with her murder? How would this being a safe house for escaped slaves before the Civil War affect Anna?"

"Maybe Jenny found some concrete proof that slaves were hidden here," I scratched my head, "but maybe it's only indirectly linked to her murder."

"Yet Jenny wants us to know this," Babcock said, as the volume turned itself up again, showcasing Jagger's yeahs and woos.

Suddenly, the picture flew from Tallulah's hands and out the bedroom door. Mark and Apollo ran after it, followed by Tallulah, Babcock, Sam and Abby, while I brought up the rear as my cast forced me to. It had made me useless and slow.

Amelia wrapped her arm around my elbow and ambled with me after them. Mike's kitschy cane went clack, clack, clack on the wooden floor and I kind of felt like a Gilded Age dandy with different women on my arm for any occasion. All I was missing was a top hat and tails.

Everyone was milling around the stairs; the picture was on the rotted steps. Mark was looking around the area and feeling up different parts of the walls, floors and railing. We all knew it was impossible to get up to where the picture was resting, so I think Mark the Engineer was looking to get around that. He stopped in front of the stairs and let his gaze climb up them.

"What if," he said shaking his finger like a scolding parent, "what if...Jack, gimme your cane."

I reluctantly handed it over, while Babcock came up beside me, as if letting me lean on him if I needed.

Mark tapped the steps with the tip as if feeling for a certain spot, then suddenly spun it around and swung the cane over his head, letting the dragon come down hard on one of the middle steps. The women exclaimed that he would break it, but all it took was that one blow for the bottom of the staircase to come tumbling down. The cane looked unscathed.

"Shit," he said looking down where the stairs had been, "I'll be damned."

I came closer and saw that, instead of a floor, there was giant hole in the ground. It was less than a story deep and I figured most people could climb or shimmy themselves down it without much assistance. Apollo was probably thinking the same thing and without hesitation, jumped into it easily, his shoulders and head remaining above ground as he stood up. The hole was barely wide enough for two people at a time, and it seemed that the only way to move was farther under the stairs. It occurred to me that the hole, rectangular and narrow, was just like a shallow grave; but I quickly brushed the thought away.

Apollo bent down and started carefully lifting some of the fallen steps out and laying them on the floor beside the stairs, their jagged and splintered edges making me tense. I'd taken shop in high school, only to realize that I hated working with wood and getting all splintered up.

He cleared most of the debris, then took out his phone from his pocket and turned on the flashlight feature. He shined it in front of him and crouched down under the splintered steps.

"I think there's a door here or something," Apollo's voice came out from under the wood, and we heard a hollow clanking, as if he was knocking on a brass knocker, or trying to open a bolted door.

"Dwarf, gimme the cane," he said peeking back out. There was dust and debris on his hair and shoulders.

"What for?"

"I think I can pry or knock it open."

"Then get outta there Frankenstein, and let the pro handle it before you hurt yourself," Mark shook his head, "one wrong move and the whole staircase could come down on your head. Sheesh, (he rolled his eyes) oxygen must not reach your brain at such an altitude."

Apollo reluctantly climbed back out. He brushed against Mark and punched his ribs in passing.

"Why's everyone beating me up today?" Mark complained, rubbing his chest.

I suggested he should try holding his tongue more often. Mark looked daggers at me, slid down less easily and stood up, only the top of his hair protruding out.

"Mark, honey, are you feeling all right? You seem a bit out of sorts," Amelia asked him, then immediately turned to me and whispered, "he's kind of grumpy, don't you think?"

"He's probably just hungry. He gets crabby when he needs to eat. And he always needs to eat," I said, as Mark simultaneously grumbled something.

"What's that, sweetie? I didn't quite get that," Amelia turned her attention back to him. Apollo and Sam were both snickering and Tallulah's arms were crossed on her chest, her index finger covering her mouth. I could see a faint smile across it.

"I'm hungry!" Mark growled louder.

Amelia fished in her purse, saying that she thought she might have some kind of snack since she always carried something for Pluto, who also got cranky when hungry. She dug out a mushed Snickers Bar, opened the wrapper and reached it out to Mark, whose eyes were shining as he licked his lips. Babcock intercepted it, claimed it was his, and ate half of it in one bite.

Mark's face went from hopeful, to dejected. Sam, Apollo and Tallulah could no longer hold back their laughter. Abby and I joined them. Meanwhile, Mark tried to climb out and grab the chocolate before Babcock ate the rest. He had one knee on the edge of the floor and the other still in the hole as he extended his arm in a final attempt to snatch the candy, when Babcock popped the last bit in his mouth, made 'yummy' sounds while chewing, then declared it was delicious and that it hit the spot as he licked his lips and rubbed his jiggly belly. Amelia was covering her mouth with her hand and looking at Babcock in disbelief. Mark lowered his head and slid back down the hole.

He grumpily took Apollo's phone and the cane and walked under the stairs. He was completely hidden from view but we heard shuffling, clanking and tapping; then, one loud boom and crack that echoed throughout the house. Dust flew out and we covered our mouths and coughed. Mark was still inside the hole, but the remnants of the staircase above stayed in place.

"Holy crap!" he yelled.

Apollo jumped down and peeked under the stairs. Sammy bent her knees on the edge as if ready to jump down, but Tallulah put her arm on her shoulder and told her to wait. The guys filed back out into the open and said there was some sort of passageway, but we needed some big flashlights since our phones wouldn't be enough. Mark added that hard hats would come in handy too. He was about to climb out when the walls pulsated again and Apollo's phone went dark.

I felt a strange coldness behind me, like a hollow, like something was missing, or rather, like a door had been opened. Sammy had gone pale, and Tallulah's lips were sealed in such a tight line that they'd practically disappeared. Abigail was wide-eyed; Mark and Apollo stood quiet, stiff as boards. I broke out in a sweat and my heart pounded so loud I thought it would come out my ears. Amelia turned and dug her fingers into my elbow. Babcock was panting.

I turned around, slowly, shaking like one of those vibration machines that Fugly Gabby used for exercising (she had once posted a photo online and commented that "New Year's Resolution Number One was bought and paid for, on to New Year's Resolution Number Two: diet and exercise!") and nearly screamed like a little girl. I managed to clamp my mouth shut before I made a fool of myself and took quick shallow breaths. *You should be proud of yourself, Johnny-Boy, at least you're not diving under the covers anymore, or running away.* As if I could run with this goddamn cast.

Jenny Jenkins hovered right in front of me. She didn't look like she had in the Funhouse when we saw the death of Anna's grandfather. Then, she had seemed as if she'd been alive, real; like, if you reached out and touched her you'd feel flesh and bones. Now, she looked filmy, somewhat faded and translucent. She was wearing a gray skirt that reached beyond her knees, tall black boots and a green turtleneck sweater with small embroidered snowflakes across the top of her chest. She was smiling, and I felt Amelia shake as she held on to my arm, sobbing softly. Babcock was still panting, and I thought for a moment that he might be having a heart-attack, but I couldn't take my eyes off Jenny to look at him. She was beautiful with her salt-and-pepper hair in a braid, and I was surprised that she was so young. When Babcock had told me she'd had difficulty climbing stairs, I'd imagined a much older woman, hunched over and completely white-haired.

I looked into her flickering eyes and saw something familiar, as if there was something hidden about her features that reminded me of a face I've known all my life, but I couldn't place either the characteristic that gave me that sense, or the face it resembled.

She reached out and touched my cheek, and I felt soft, cold dew on my skin. The feel of her almost-touch didn't transmit anger, or hatred or regret, but rather love and kindness and safety, and I felt a lump build in my throat. I hadn't experienced any sort of physical contact with the Jenkinses since the hauntings had started and I had never imagined it would be like this. I'd always thought they were stuck here out of the hatred and revenge they must have felt at Anna, but now, it seemed like there was something more.

She turned and touched Babcock's shoulder in a friendly gesture. Tears were running down his cheek and I realized his heavy breathing was actually an effort to constrict his sobs. Then, she moved to Amelia and gave her a light hug. Amelia went stiff and gasped, exhaling with a long moan.

Jenny sidled over to Sam and Abby. Her walk was slow and stiff, as if she couldn't bend her knees, and for the first time I noticed the cane in her left hand. It seemed to be made out of some sort of black wood, and it had a golden dragon coiling head down around the tip. I couldn't see the handle covered by her fingers, but it struck me how strange it was that her cane was so much like mine, only opposite. *It's just a coincidence, Johnny-Boy, both canes were probably made by the same craftsman around the same time.*

When Jenny came to Sam, she reached up and kissed her forehead, then turned towards the hole, stroked Abby's hair in passing, and pointed under the stairs. Mark and Apollo looked at her open-mouthed. Jenny compressed herself into a ball of light and flowed between them into the passageway under the stairs.

"We need to go down there," Babcock's voice was full and broken, "I think Jenny means to show us something."

I looked over at Tallulah, who was completely pale, covering her mouth and shaking her head softly, in a no-it-can't-be gesture. She kept looking at me, then at Sam, and I was about to ask her what was wrong, when suddenly a big loud groan echoed throughout the house and broke the spell Jenny's presence had cast on it. The groan had come from Mark's direction, and as we looked at him, his grumbling stomach betrayed him.

"What?" he said, rubbing his tummy, "I really *am* hungry!"

"Okay, then, let's take a lunch break," Amelia sounded shaky, yet composed.

"No!" Tallulah was firm, "We need to go down there now, Jenny is waiting."

Amelia looked at her amazed, Tallulah didn't look like a bossy person, and she wasn't. Sammy inched forward, and Apollo reached up to help her. When Mark realized Sammy wanted to jump in, he quickly shoved Apollo against the hole's wall, and slipped and tripped toward Sam. When he'd found his footing, he reached up and took Sam by the waist, slowly lowering her into the hole. I pursed my lips and felt my cheeks burning. Now there were three people in a hole that was wide enough for two, and Mark and Sam were squeezed together too close, while Apollo tried to make himself thin as paper and shuffle away.

To say I was uncomfortable with this scene was an understatement; I wasn't quite sure how I felt, but I did not like this closeness my best friend was trying to have with my sister. *Relax, Johnny-Boy,* grandpa's voice spoke softly, *she's already had the boyfriend from hell. Mark can't be that bad.*

"Sam," I said, my voice lower and hoarser than usual, "let Mark the Builder go ahead and pave the way under the stairs, we can't all fit in that hole."

Mark looked up at me surprised, and his eyes darkened as he met my gaze. He was trying to read me and my irrational behavior. I knew there was nothing inappropriate about my best friend dating my sister, not in theory anyway, but I'll be damned if I let Mark's womanizing ways hurt her. I didn't know if he wanted a relationship or a one-night-stand, but the thought of them bumpin' uglies before going their separate ways was gross and wrong. If Mark was just looking for a good fuck, he'd have to look somewhere else. I don't know if he understood my thoughts, but he quietly turned and went under the stairs.

We heard some grunting and shuffling and steps, followed by what sounded like another door creaking open.

"Jeezus Christ! You guys have to see this!" Mark's voice was muffled and he sneezed.

Apollo shrugged, and let Sammy shuffle past under the stairs. I wanted to kill him too. He should be going first, he shouldn't let them be alone in the dark together; but when I saw him help Abby down, my anger subsided. After all, he was caught in a moral crossroads: be a gentleman and make sure the path ahead is safe for a lady with a broken arm, or be a gentleman and help everyone down. He chose to let the lady go ahead, and help those who would have more trouble climbing down, myself included.

"Mom, Dad," Abby's voice floated up from the bottom of the hole (she was *that* short), "I think you and Tallulah should stay here. It might not be safe for you all."

The older women exclaimed that they weren't staying, and Babcock let out a sonorous "hell, no!"

Abby mumbled "okay, then", and went under the stairs.

Tallulah held herself back and I ambled to her as Amelia huffed and panted down. I meant to ask her what had troubled her about Jenny's presence, but she just squeezed my arm and signaled to Babcock to go on, then whispered,

"What do you know about your ancestors, Jack?"

I was taken aback by the question, I didn't think there was any reason to ask me about that now.

"Nothin' much," I shrugged, "my grandfather once said we'd been here since the first settlers came from England. He said his grandfather had told him one of our ancestors had sailed with John Smith, but even he didn't believe we went that far back. Why?"

"I don't know," she whispered as Babcock tried ten different ways to shimmy his short, blubbery body down, while Apollo stood arms outstretched, "but I wouldn't be surprised if it all came full circle today. What did you feel when you saw her? Did you notice anything about her features?"

"Honestly, I thought that something about her reminded me of someone, but I couldn't say what or who."

"Makes sense," she said taking Apollo's hand now that Babcock was wiping his forehead with a handkerchief, his hand resting on the truncated steps, catching his breath. Amelia had already gone on ahead, and I could hear the murmur of their voices coming from the dark.

"Makes sense that one would have a hard time noticing the resemblance between oneself and another, however slight and diluted it is," Tallulah went on as Apollo lowered her down.

"What?!"

But she was already gone under the stairs.

It was my turn now, and as I inched forward, I tried to find the best position to lower myself without further breaking my injured ankle. I shifted and turned in circles, almost like a dog looking for a place to sleep, before I opted for awkwardly sitting and sliding down on my bum. Apollo was patiently waiting for me and smiling.

He caught me as my good leg found the floor and helped me steady myself with my cast.

"What was that thing with Mark?" he whispered as I reached up for my cane which I'd left on the floor above.

"I don't know, but I think he wants to bonk my sister and I'm not sure I like that."

"Hmm, not surprised," he said as I shuffled past him, "he's always had a crush on her, and we haven't seen her in a long time. She looks good, y'know, in spite of the bruises; you should feel proud. She could look like Fugly Gabby."

"True, but you know he plays the field, and I don't want Sammy to get hurt."

"Nah, don't worry 'bout that, she's strong and independent; she can take care of herself and handle him no problem. Just take it easy, Jack." He said as he ducked under the stairs after me.

Apollo had no idea just how strong Sammy really was.

I bent and walked down a narrow, dank tunnel with wood beams on the very low ceiling, but walls completely made of rounded or jagged stone. I was sure this had been used by the Underground Railroad, but had no idea when it had been built. For all I knew, it had come with the house. As if answering my thoughts, I heard Tallulah saying that as an Anthropologist she couldn't determine the age of the tunnel, but that if we really needed to know, she could ask Lupe, who was an Archaeologist, to come take a look once this whole ordeal was over.

I saw a faint rectangular light ahead and realized they'd all gone through a small door. I walked through it and into a small room. Everyone had managed to pack themselves in and, as I shuffled inside, I felt as if they were somehow squeezing themselves farther in to the walls to let me pass.

I tried straightening up but the ceiling was too low, which left me no choice but to stick my neck out like a turtle as my shoulder blades brushed the ceiling. When my eyes adjusted, I saw writing on a perfectly white, smooth wall. It contrasted deeply with the tunnel and the rest of the room, as if the modern feel of that one wall had broken through the aged ruggedness of the tunnel. I looked closer at the writing and realized it was a family tree. In front of it was an old desk with dusty papers strewn about, and a big kerosene camping lantern which someone had lit. The lantern illuminated the whole room, making it somehow cozy, despite the damp feel of the tunnel. In the corner there was a big combination safe. I heard a far, muffled, thunder-like rumbling through the walls and I wondered if it was going to rain.

"I knew she'd dabbled in genealogy, but I never imagined this" Babcock whispered beside me, "she started soon after Tommy was born, come to think of it."

"Oh, she was hardcore, honey," Amelia looked at Babcock, "she spent most of her free time going through papers and working late in the library. I thought it was just a hobby, something to keep her occupied. After the accident, she couldn't dance well anymore and in the five years of Tommy's life, the condition of her knees kept getting worse." She wiped tears from her eyes and looking around at everyone, continued, "I used to help her sometimes, and we'd spend hours just talking and researching and, oh my God, how I miss her." Amelia broke down as Babcock put his arms around her, burying her face in his shirt.

I examined the wall closer, Sammy was mysteriously quiet through all this and I looked down to make sure she wasn't holding Mark's hand. The wall had names, dates and lines connecting all the people and, as the family tree grew, photographs and daguerrotypes had been added. The very last was a Polaroid picture of a little blond boy, and next to it, that of a cold sallow teenage girl.

"Jacky, look," Sammy said pointing to a name, "that's Hiram and his family, from the picture."

Sure enough, there he was Hiram Jenkins, born 1811 and died 1864. He had married Mary Jackson. They'd had four children: Mary Anne Jenkins, born 1837, died 1899, then Hiram Jackson Jenkins, who'd died a baby; Samantha Maria Jenkins was five years younger than her sister and had died in 1915. Finally there was John Hiram Jenkins, born 1855 and died 1931. I followed the path from his name down to Thomas Jeffrey Jenkins, born 1991 and died 1996. I touched Tommy's name, his death had started all of this and somehow I felt a sense of conclusion as I stood in front of that wall.

Suddenly, Sammy gasped and shakily pointed at a name.

"Arabella Samantha Mason," Sammy read aloud, "born 1881 and died 1983. Jacky, that was our great-grandma's name! And Dad always said she'd lived past a hundred."

"Are you sure?" I said stunned, "There could be more people with the same name."

"I know, but look, she married Hannibal Adams and they had a son, Oliver Adams. That's grandpa! Look at the birthdate; it's 1905! Grandpa was born that year. It's definitely him!"

Sammy was looking around with a big smile on her face, and I felt the ground pulsing beneath my feet as I realized she was bouncing on her heels.

I still couldn't believe it, so I traced the line back from Oliver Adams to Samantha Maria Jenkins. She had married John Mason and had a son who'd married a woman named Miller. Together they'd begotten Arabella Samantha Mason.

Next to Arabella's name was a black and white picture of a woman with a baby, and as I looked closer, I almost saw Sam's gaze peeking out at me from under the strange woman's brow. There was also a faded daguerrotype of Samantha Maria Jenkins, and I thought I saw my grandfather's scowl as she looked serious into the camera. I then traced the line; the tree ended with Samantha Adams, born 1982 and John Adams, born 1983.

"Is this possible?" I said turning to Tallulah.

"I saw the resemblance between you two and Jenny when she showed up today," Tallulah nodded and smiled, "it's only noticeable when you're close together, but there's something about your cheekbones and forehead maybe; it made me wonder whether you were related."

"Wow," I was about to go on when Sammy spoke up,

"Oh my God, Jacky, it all makes sense now. Grandpa once told me it was Grandma Bella who insisted that the next girl born to the family be named Samantha and the next boy John. Since Dad has no siblings, it fell onto us. She also insisted no one ever be named or called anything even close to Ann."

"There's no way your grandma could've known about Anna Jenkins," Pluto sounded strange, as if he'd just been brought out of a deep sleep, "Jenny never mentioned any cousins. She always said it was just her and Paul."

"Dad has always talked about Grandma Bella being strange and saying weird things that made people cringe. Things that nobody could ever know about, or hadn't happened," I said, "he said she was always blurting things out; like, one time, when they were going on a trip across the Appalachian trail, just before they found out Mom was pregnant with Sammy. Grandma Bella stopped them, claiming that Mom had to be careful with her little girl. She died about a month after I was born. I wonder if they ever knew we were related to the Jenkinses; shit, we grew up in Bedford, that's pretty close to Peaceville."

"I don't think they knew anything," Amelia spoke up. "I just remembered that when I was helping Jenny research, we found some letters from the turn of the century, correspondence between John Hiram Jenkins and a Boston law firm. Apparently, John Hiram had gone out west during the Klondike Gold Rush and completely lost touch with his older sisters. When he returned home to Osprey Cove, some time before World War I, I think, he found the estate totally abandoned. I've forgotten what else the letters said, but apparently he was trying to reclaim the Jenkins property, something to do with a false death. I remember Jenny and I joked about writing a novel based on the man's life."

Apollo, Mark and Abby just stood in stunned silence. I don't know how I was keeping calm myself. I'd just found out that I was related to Anna Jenkins, and, for some weird reason, I didn't care. It was as if Anna wasn't a part of this, although she was the reason we were all here. Somehow, it just didn't fit that Sammy and I could be related to such a cold-blooded murderer. I felt detached from her and her crimes, they were beyond me, and I suddenly understood what Sam meant when she'd said Saunders had only hurt her body, not the real person in it. I think she had detached herself from him, whether during the attack or after, and just as he couldn't hurt her anymore, I myself felt nothing for Anna.

"Oh my God, I'm such an idiot!" I slapped my forehead, " *That's* how it all started! *That's* how they knew!"

People looked at me confused.

"Just before the 'keep you safe' message appeared for the first time, the ghosts had messed up my closet and had thrown a box of Grandpa's stuff on my bed. In it was a notebook he'd kept with the Adams family history. That's probably when they realized I was related to them. That's when everything changed."

"Didn't you read it?" Apollo asked.

"I tried, but only got as far as 1756. Grandpa's penmanship was for shit, most of it is illegible, but now it all makes sense. Suddenly, I wasn't just some schmuck who'd bought the house. Suddenly, I was a member of the family, and in Anna's way."

"Anna's way to what? How did she even know about you? And besides, what did she care?" Mark asked.

I was dumbfounded.

Suddenly, the combination on the safe in the corner began to turn. It rotated forwards and backwards between clicks and flung open. Inside I saw a bunch of papers and some boxes. One of the papers flew out like a shot and hit me clear in the face. I didn't have time to block it with my arms, but it bounced off and landed on my raised hands. The title read "Last Will and Testament." It was folded in thirds, and it hovered above my hands as it slowly straightened itself out.

"I, Jennifer Jenkins," a woman's voice boomed from the walls and enclosed the room, "being of sound mind leave my estate and all my worldly belongings to my only living relatives and last descendants of my line, Samantha and John Adams, children of Oliver and Meredith Adams..."

I felt chills as the voice sounded out our birthdates and went on to list all that we were supposed to inherit. This house and everything in it had been left to both of us, to do as we pleased with it. Sammy was given the red box in the safe, while I was bequeathed the other box, a blue one. Sam grabbed my arm and buried her face on my shoulder. She'd become agitated as the voice had read on, and now she was almost hysterical. As the voice died out her sobs mixed with giggles rang out through the room. Mark moved to touch her, but Apollo held him back.

I had suspected Sammy was not financially comfortable; education didn't pay well, and I had supposed she'd spent the last of Grandpa's inheritance coming here so suddenly. I knew she worked hard and enjoyed her independence and, like me, preferred not to ask my parents for money. They were both retired now and it was only fair that they spend their pensions on themselves, not their kids with low-paying jobs.

"Hey Sammy-Girl," I whispered, "don't get too excited, this might be just like Geraldo and Al Capone's safe. There might be nothing."

"Don't be so quick to judge that, Jack," Apollo spoke softly (if I looked like a turtle under the low ceiling, Apollo looked like *Count Duckula's* Igor), "if it's true that Jenny's ancestor came back from the Gold Rush and, not only reclaimed this house, but rebuilt and maintained it, there might be more than you imagine. And Mark, that's your answer. This is what Anna really wants. Although how she knew about this is beyond me."

"Go on, man," Mark said, "go see what's in that safe so we can get some chow."

His stomach grumbled noisily, chorused by Babcock's and Abby's.

I let go of Sam and shuffled toward the safe. I doubted I could take anything out, since nothing could be moved, but to my surprise, the contents of it were surprisingly light. First, was a dusty Trapper Keeper with dolphins on the cover. It was almost bursting with papers. I passed it to Apollo. Next, I took out what looked like an old diary with flowers printed on the cover, which Mark took from me. Then, as I slid it out a red box I was surprised how incredibly heavy it was. It was a big deep lockbox, its key safely on the lock. This was Sammy's but I asked Babcock to take it, since it felt too heavy for Sam and her one sling-less arm. He took it and immediately plunked it down, panting that it weighed a ton. Mark offered to exchange the diary for it and awkwardly slid and shuffled the box over, leaving it at his feet; I presumed he would pick it up before leaving. Finally out came the blue box, my box, and it was also a lockbox, but only this one was shallow and nowhere near as heavy.

When the safe was empty, I stood up, blue lockbox under my arm. People were looking at me as if I were Moses or something, just waiting for me to part the Red Sea and lead them out of Egypt. I squeezed myself between them. Being the center of attention has always made me uncomfortable and today was no different. I wasn't a leader, Sammy was the leader and now, even she took a backseat. She'd calmed down since her almost hysterical outburst, though I could still see her imagination running away with her.

I crouched and passed through the small door, with Sammy and the others following me. I walked back up the tunnel and stopped so suddenly Sammy bumped into my back. The door was shut.

Sammy whispered, "What the fu...?"

"What's the hold up?" Mark's voice boomed from behind, drowning out Sammy's f-bomb.

"The door is shut," I said, trying to open it, "it's completely and totally sealed."

I leaned my weight against it and pushed, but it didn't budge one bit.

"What now?" Abby said in the low light of the cellphone flashlights.

"I imagine we have to go back and try to find another way out," Tallulah sounded calm.

I suppose that, like ghosts, close space didn't faze her either. I certainly didn't like it. Faced with the prospect that I might be stuck here forever, I realized that I hated it. I felt the walls close in on me like never before and got anxious. I just wanted to get out of here, and as my heart raced, my breath quickened. I had never felt claustrophobic before; but then again, I'd never been stuck with a gazillion people in a tiny tunnel under the ground.

As people shuffled and grumbled back towards the room, I felt like pushing myself through them, in a dangerous and stupid effort to get out. But there was no getting out. There was only one teeny-tiny room, lit by one teeny-tiny lantern. I was sweating, and as people moved like Sunday drivers at a stoplight, I began to panic.

I followed them back down the tunnel, and as they all squeezed back into the room, I stopped, I didn't want to go in. Instead, I leaned against the far end of the tunnel wall, and sat down to cry. That's when I realized that the wall wasn't stone, and as I slid my back down it, my elbow bumped against something metal.

"Ow!" I exclaimed as a tingly sensation crawled up my arm. I let go of my box and rubbed my elbow, but whatever I'd bumped into, had gotten me right in the funny bone. Sammy who'd remained in the threshold, pointed her cellphone light at me.

"Jack, I think that's a door."

I looked and realized what had bumped me was a handle, and yep, I was leaning against a door. I stood up and turned the handle.

The door creaked open and there were some more stone steps, but— oh, thank God—further down I saw natural light, and, without thinking twice, grabbed my box and stepped through it.

Suddenly the box flew out of my hand and stuck itself to the tunnel ceiling like a pancake. Sammy gasped as she looked up, then snickered. These ghosts had a thing about sticking stuff to ceilings. I tried to pull it down and, just as I thought, it didn't budge.

"Dude, is there a way out or not?" Mark sounded desperate.

"Just leave it, Jacky," Sammy said, "I don't think Jenny wants us to take it out."

I nodded, stepped through the door and slowly climbed down the stairs. I felt like I was in one of those nightmares where you try to run but your legs won't move. I wanted to run, but with my cast and the cane, it was impossible.

After what seemed like forever, I came to the light. It was an opening, and as I stepped through it, the ocean breeze hit me full in the face. When my eyes adjusted, I realized I'd walked out of a cave onto the pebble beach under the cliffs. The waves were breaking thunderously to my left, and the only way was to go right around a big rock.

I heard Sam stepping out behind me; I offered her my hand, and she took it. As we walked around the rock, the beach opened up onto the ocean. The cliffs were on our right, and the formation of the rock behind us kept the cave from sight.

Abigail popped out onto the sand and it looked like she'd just appeared out of nowhere. From the beach there was no way to tell there was a cave among the rocks; it looked as if the beach ended with the waves that broke into an indentation of perfectly smooth and tall monoliths that formed the cliff walls.

It was a perfect hideout, and Sammy's voice rang through my head, *everyone has a private place to go when life gets to be too much* . This was Jenny's place.

People popped out one by one, each looking confused and disoriented. The guys and Babcock came out empty-handed.

"Sorry, dude," Mark said when he saw me looking at his hands, "Sam's box flew out of my arms and stuck to the ceiling. I guess we have to be in there to open it."

Babcock and Apollo nodded and said their stuff was stuck to the ceiling too. Sam giggled beside me, as I shrugged my shoulders and told them it was no problem.

We followed the Babcocks down the beach and came up to stone steps that led up to the house. They also seemed to be hidden, like camouflaged among the rocks and, only if you knew they were there, would you have noticed. The steps led to a wrought iron gate flanked by two tall trees.

There was no way to get into the lawn around them, since the trees and the gate were right on the edge of the cliffs. In other words, the only way to get in from the beach was through the gate, and as far as I knew, if you didn't know about the passageway, the only way out onto the beach was also through here. You could, of course, simply hurl yourself off the tall, jagged cliffs and hope for the best.

The staircase was narrow, and we stood in single file, like on an escalator, waiting for our turn to get off. I lifted my gaze and saw that something had been worked into the wrought iron above the gate. It was an image of a tiny bird, with a long straight beak and what looked like a thief mask over its eyes.

Babcock was first in line, and I heard him jiggle some keys. Then, there was the sound of rusty metal creaking open. He went through the door and everyone followed. I asked Amelia if she knew what that bird was.

"It's supposed to be a halcyon," she said, "nowadays they're called kingfishers, but in mythology, it was a bird that nested at sea and calmed the waves and wind. The original name of this house is Halcyon Manor, although nobody calls it that anymore."

Halcyon also means a period of time in the past that was idyllic, happy and peaceful, Johnny-Boy, hopefully it's a sign of things to come.

"Am I the only one that's dying to know what's in those boxes?" Sammy spoke up as we walked back to the house. Mark spun around, his face puckered, like he'd swallowed a lemon.

"No, dear," Tallulah said, "we're all very curious, but I fear if we don't get something to eat, Mark will have a conniption."

Apollo sniggered; but when Sammy looked disappointed, he declared he was hungry too.

CHAPTER FIFTEEN

David and Goliath

Sam and I were sitting in the Babcocks' basement-turned-family room. My leg had begun to hurt as we'd sat down in Nancy's diner, and what had started as a dull throb, had become almost unbearable pain as we'd walked in the house.

I was sitting with my leg up and my computer in my lap. I had been working, but hadn't gotten too far, due to the pain, which was only now beginning to settle as the painkillers kicked in.

Sammy was lying down on one side of the love-seat recliner, she had her eyes closed and her feet up, but she wasn't asleep. She'd reached for her own painkillers as soon as we'd walked in the house.

Tallulah, Mark and Apollo had gone to check in at the Eagle's Nest Motel. Tallulah had looked completely wiped out as they'd gotten in the car, so I was pretty sure she wouldn't be coming back for a while. I had thought about suggesting we go back to the house in the afternoon, but her expression of ultimate exhaustion stopped me, and I knew that she would want to be there when we opened those boxes. After my experience with the couch cushions at the Funhouse, I knew nothing would happen to them, even if Anna and Saunders found them, getting the boxes off the ceiling would be impossible.

Abigail had received a text from her friend Jane and had gone over to her house, while Amelia and Babcock had taken the car to do some shopping. It warmed my heart to think there was enough trust between us to leave us alone in their home. Amelia had been especially attentive before leaving the house, showing us where everything was, how to reach them, how to work the appliances and on and on, almost as if we were her children being left home alone for the first time. We assured her we could handle ourselves for a few hours and that she shouldn't worry.

"Thank you, Jack," Sammy spoke, "thanks for not asking me to tell you the gory details about what happened with Saunders."

I turned to in disbelief. She was looking away from me, stroking her cast in an effort to ease the pain.

"Why would I ask you that, Sammy? It's not something I'd like to know."

"You'd be surprised how many people want to know everything when they find out you've been raped. It's pretty morbid. You and Gabby are the only people that didn't ask for more details."

"How many people know?" I couldn't imagine her shouting it from the rooftops and then keeping quiet about it from her own family.

"Not many, only my closest friends and people from Oregon that needed to know, like my superiors at work; but you know, word gets around."

"Yeah," I looked at her, and she turned to face me. I saw so much sadness in her face that my chest hurt and a lump went to my throat.

"But if you feel like you need to tell me, y'know, to get it all off your chest, you can count on me; I can take it."

She smiled and it lit up her eyes.

"No," she shook her head, "I've talked about it with the cops and the therapists till the cows come home. I'm done telling it all. I left it behind in Oregon."

I smiled and turned back to my computer. I was reading my last sentence when it occurred to me that she should call the cops that had handled her case and tell them she knew where Saunders was.

"I did. At the diner, when I went to the bathroom. I phoned them, but it doesn't matter now."

"Why not? You can get justice for what he did to you."

She shook her head.

"Statute of limitations ran out last month," her lips quivered and her eyes filled with tears.

She sniffed and wiped the tears with her fingers. I sat down beside her and put my arm around her, while she sobbed quietly into my chest.

I looked around at the Babcocks' family room as I waited for her to calm down. It was warm and cozy. The TV was down here, and apart from the love-seat recliner they also had a sofa-bed which divided the room in two. This room doubled as a guest bedroom if need be, and this was where Apollo and Mark had spent the night.

On the other side of the room, there was a bookcase leaning against the wall, and a big writing desk with what looked like a comfortable chair. I would've been sitting at it if I hadn't needed to put my leg up. Instead I'd chosen to sit lengthwise on the sofa-bed. The bookcase was lined with shelves of books (mostly young-adult fiction), and board games. There was Scrabble, Battleship, Clue, Operation, you name it, they had it. I thought about how I should probably build something similar at the Funhouse, but instead of turning the basement into a family room, it would be a man-cave, complete with fridge and bar. I would've done that when I first renovated the house, but even with Mark's discounted prices, the money had run out, so the basement had been left exactly as it had been for the last twenty or so years.

Sam's quiet sobs died down and her breathing steadied.

"Sammy," I whispered, "you're really hard up, aren't you?"

She looked up at me.

"You've got money troubles right? Did you use up the last of Grandpa's money to come here?"

"No, Jacky, believe it or not, I get paid really well at my school, even if it's still peanuts. Grandpa's inheritance was greatly depleted when I moved to Sacramento, yes, but I'm not on the street yet. I was going to look for a second job before coming here, something I could do evenings, but, plans changed."

"Yeah, because your little brother got in trouble."

Sammy had gone to school in Oregon, and immediately gotten a job in Portland after graduation, so we all thought she'd either stay there or come back home. The news of her move to Sacramento had been completely unexpected, and now I knew why.

"No, because, before I came here to rescue my little brother, I got a call from the principal. Apparently, the school wants me to head the Kindergarten program next year."

"Sammy, that's great news! Why didn't you say anything?"

"Well, because it's not set in stone, and the news just sort of fell through the cracks after Diana—I mean Anna—beat her way back into my life."

"So, you're all right? You don't need help?"

"I'll be fine, Jacky, although winning the lottery wouldn't hurt," she smiled and readjusted herself, "besides, there are other candidates and the school board has the final say, but the principal told me I had her endorsement. What do you think will happen with this thing from Jenny?"

I didn't dare say inheritance either, not yet anyway, it felt too good to be true.

"I don't know. Even though she supposedly left us her house, I don't know if that will is valid. Besides, I don't think there's enough she could have left us that would set us up for life anyway. I think we might have to contact a lawyer, but let's just focus on not getting killed first."

"For a fiction writer with a runaway imagination, you can really be the voice of reason sometimes."

We sat quiet until Sammy broke the silence by asking me not to tell our parents about the rape ever, or her promotion, for the moment. I told her I would take the assault to the grave if she wanted me to; it was her story to tell, not mine.

"Besides," I went on, "it's not like the 'rents have been easy to reach lately. They must be living it up. They called me when I was in the hospital, you know. Mom was crying (probably already imagining my funeral), and Dad was pragmatic as always. I tried to reach them after you were attacked, but couldn't get through."

"No worries, I got through and told them what happened. I didn't tell them I was attacked by a friend, just said someone broke in while I was home. Are you going to tell them about Anna and the Funhouse?"

I shrugged my shoulders and told her we probably would have to come clean about all that's been happening. If Jenny's will is for real, they should know about it. I also wanted to ask them if they knew anything about being related to the Jenkinses.

"Sammy," I said after a moment of silence, "I'm really sorry about all this, I think it's my fault that Anna Jenkins contacted you again."

"Why do you think that, Jack?"

"Well, you said she reopened her acquaintance with you after I bought the house. What if, somehow, she found out that *I* bought her old house? I know I sent you a picture of it, and I might've posted it on Facebook. Maybe when she saw the photo, she realized she might get caught? That maybe I'd find the axes?"

Sam looked pensive a moment and nodded, "Probably, but she would've only seen it if you'd tagged me in the picture. I didn't send it to anyone and definitely not to her. I hadn't heard from her, in, oh, three years? But it's totally possible. Or maybe Saunders gave her the heads up? Maybe he'd been keeping track of both houses? I don't think she knows we're related to her, though. I think it was just coincidence that *you* bought the house, and I also think that eventually she'd have tried to get rid of me for whatever other reason."

"Tallulah would say that it wasn't coincidence, that everything happened exactly the way it was meant to."

"I wouldn't worry about it much, Jacky-Roo," Sam shrugged, "all we have to do now is stay alive and deal with the situation as best we can. Doesn't matter how she found out, or whose fault it is, there's no turning back, we might as well face what's coming."

I nodded, but that uneasy feeling of being the reason Anna came back into my sister's life remained, albeit abated. It *was* possible that Saunders was keeping track of both houses, and being a detective and all, knew how to get information on whoever bought the house. Once they'd known my name, it was very easy to make the connection to Sam.

Sammy got up and went in the bathroom, closing the door behind her. I had just connected my computer to the power outlet on the desk when I heard the basement door open and footsteps start down. I didn't think much of it, just that the Babcocks were probably back, so I froze when I realized I was face to face with David Saunders.

He didn't hesitate for an instant; he punched me, and the blow knocked me to the ground. As I struggled to get my bearings and get back up, he looked down at me and, with a smile, stomped on my cast.

I screamed, then tried to crawl away and ended up facing the bookcase. Saunders quietly walked over and, with one hearty push, brought it down on me. I lifted my arms to shield my head and was pinned underneath, one arm free above my head, while the other lay across my chest, between my torso and a shelf. Everything had fallen out before landing on me, so the impact wasn't as nasty as I had expected, yet, I was still immobilized. My chest constricted and it was hard to breathe. I didn't think my arm was broken but I couldn't move it from the weight of the shelf.

There were books and games strewn about and it struck me that Saunders was making this look like an accident. My cane leaned against the desk way out of reach. I was aware that it was our only chance of salvation, the only thing we might use as a weapon, so I tried to wriggle myself towards it from under the bookcase, but it was too heavy and all I managed was to make it more painful. Trying to lift the bookcase off me with my free arm was useless.

This happened faster than it seems now that it's written it down. When a writer describes a situation he puts into words the circumstances, feelings and thoughts of his character, which to the reader, may seem like events happen in slow motion; but that's only because we don't write or read or tell as fast as we move and act, so what may seem like minutes going by when telling an event, are actually seconds, fractions of a second even.

I doubt Sammy had a chance to realize what was happening before Saunders kicked the bathroom door open and dragged her out by the hair. He slammed her against the wall and backhanded her. She managed to keep her bearings, push him and pivot away from the wall, only to find herself between him and back of the sofa bed. Saunders was big and remarkably strong, so running for the door was risky, if not impossible. Stepping further back meant tripping over the couch, and it occurred to me that her only chance of survival was to stay on her feet. Like me, she was pinned.

"Well, Sammy, did you miss me?" Saunders planted himself in front of my sister.

She managed to pivot once more so that now she was at least on the same side as the door. They were both in profile from where I lay and he was too close, creepy close.

Sammy bowed her head and tried to hunch herself over. She whimpered as Saunders began touching her; first her hair, then her face, her neck. Sam tried to cover herself with her broken arm as he pinched her breast. She tried to pull back, but he wrapped his other arm around her waist and pulled her close, his hand cupping her butt.

"Remember that wonderful day we had? How I made you scream, how you were too weak to get away? Oh, those screams of yours, I still think of them at night and how good it felt to force you open, make you mine the way no one else ever had."

"Let us go," Sammy bleated trying to cover herself as Saunders let go of her fondled breast and put his hand between her legs, "I'll do anything, just please, let my brother go, he's hurt."

"Anything, huh?" he smirked, "Then let's begin."

He grabbed her by the nape of her neck and pushed her down forcefully. She landed on her knees with a painful whack. He pulled her head back by the hair and looked down at her as he unzipped his fly and took out his penis.

"Look at me," he said coldly, but Sam's eyes were elsewhere, "look at me, you damn whore!"

She still wouldn't look him in the eye, but instead pleaded with him, told him she would do anything. He smirked.

"Damn right you'll do anything, Sammy. I am going to have the time of my life and believe me, you will not enjoy it, you will hurt and you will bleed, and your precious little brother will watch it all. But don't worry, I won't kill you, either of you, you'll both live with these wonderful memories for the rest of your lives."

He laughed like Boris Karloff.

I tried to call out but only managed an angry grunt. I flailed my free arm around but found nothing useful within my reach.

Saunders stroked Sam's face with his penis and moaned. She sobbed and tried to turn her face away. As she did so, our eyes met and I saw something in hers that froze me deep inside. It was a cold, murderous rage, and I realized that my sister was faking it; she wasn't scared, she wasn't weak, she was just waiting for the right time to act. That's why she wouldn't look him in the eye. *He doesn't stand a chance against those eyes, Johnny-Boy, and he doesn't know it.*

Saunders forced his penis in her mouth, but instead of Sam whimpering and gagging, she bit down hard. So hard even *I* felt it. Saunders screamed in pain, while blood squirted out from between them. He stepped back which gave her the space she needed to punch him in the stomach and he fell in a heap on the floor. Sam jumped up, her mouth stained with blood.

"You will never hurt another woman again, you asshole!" she screamed as she kicked and kicked and kicked. She had good technique and David Saunders had no chance to protect himself; so with one hand on his crotch and coughing from the blow to the belly, he tried to drag himself away.

"Oh no, you don't," Sam exclaimed as she quickly, but calmly, got the cane still leaning against the desk.

She grabbed it by the shaft and with her one strong arm brought it down on Saunders's head. I heard a dull thud as his body went limp. Sam wiped the blood from her mouth with the back of her hand. I looked up at her and thought I saw her wearing that imaginary armor again. My sister was a knight, she was a real knight, shining armor and all.

Sam dropped the cane and rushed over to me. She tried pushing the bookcase off me with her good arm but it wouldn't budge. She looked at me, tears streaming down her face.

"Jacky, I can't," she sobbed, looking as if this encounter had defeated her from the inside out. Her shining armor was gone and all I saw in her eyes was fear and despair. It was as if she'd used up all her courage and energy in the fight and now she was ready to lay down and die.

"Call 9-1-1," I grunted, and that seemed to bring her back, make her realize it wasn't all lost, that help could come.

She passed her arm over her eyes and rubbed her nose. She picked up the extension phone on the desk and cursed because there was no dial tone. Saunders had probably cut the line. She looked around, lunged for her own cellphone on the recliner, and dialed. My breathing had gotten even more labored and I think I finally understood people with asthma. I felt dizzy and I knew that there wasn't enough air coming in. *If you don't get out of this, Johnny-Boy, it's curtains for you.*

"There's no signal down here, hold on," she ran upstairs.

I looked up at the ceiling and wondered if I was dying, as blackness closed in.

The sound of sirens woke me up and I found myself looking into Sammy's bruised face.

"Jacky!" she wailed, "Please don't die, please don't die!"

I remember thinking I wasn't ready to die yet, when the blackness closed in again. I drifted in and out of darkness throughout the ambulance ride and always saw my sister's face first and heard her voice last.

Once, I felt myself floating and realized I was being wheeled. I opened my eyes and saw Sammy moving beside me. I looked away from her and saw another gurney being wheeled past me. There was a fat man on it, and I remember thinking before conking out again, that he looked like Pluto Babcock.

When I woke I was in what looked like a hospital room, only there were curtains instead of walls surrounding me. I heard people bustling about beyond the curtains, but the sounds soon became muffled and insignificant as my ears picked up a louder, stronger, heart-wrenching sound: sobs. Sobs so full of sorrow and despair that they soaked into my bones through the dull pain in my fingers.

As the sobs grew louder and the pain in my hand increased, the events that had brought me here came back to me in a flood, like my childhood recurring dream of a tidal wave wiping us all out. It occurred to me how strange it was that I should feel so much pain in the hand that had been free of the bookshelf.

I looked down at it and saw my sister's blondish mane draped across my arm. It fell over her face and her shoulders were shaking badly; those hopeless, broken sobs were coming from her. She was holding my hand so tight that her knuckles were whiter than my own white fingers. I tried to call her name, but oh my God, how my chest hurt as I took the first deep breath. Instead I coughed and tried to wriggle my fingers from her grip. She looked up and, loosening her grasp, lifted my hand to her lips and kissed it.

"Oh Jacky," she wept, "I thought you were dead! When I came down after calling the ambulance I saw you lying there, your eyes were closed and your lips were blue. I thought that was it, I thought you were gone forever."

I smiled and weakly shook my head. I didn't even want to try and speak, my chest hurt so much when I breathed, so instead I raised her hand to my heart. She smiled through her sobs and let go. She brushed my hair back, and I examined her face. There was a new cut under her right eye which had been stitched up and covered with one of those thin adhesive strips you see in action films; and the tear in her lips had been reopened. I was certain now that it would leave a scar and I prayed that it would not deform her mouth. Her eyes shone with the blue tint the bruises gave her hazel irises and, to my relief, I saw renewed joy and hope in them, and not the despair I'd seen when she'd tried to lift the bookcase off me.

I touched her nose and cheeks and felt strong healthy bone and smiled; my sister would still be beautiful once the bruising faded.

She understood the gesture and said, "Yeah, the doctors say I've been lucky, that there probably won't be any lasting damage to my face, save for a minor scar across my lips which might fade over time. They don't think it'll deform my mouth; after all, I can still talk. It's just a split lip. Seems I'm pretty hard-headed. I'm gonna go tell the nurse you're awake."

When she left, I took the opportunity to survey the damage. Obviously, there was something wrong with my chest, but I was breathing on my own, although I had one of those oxygen tube things under my nose. My left arm, which had been trapped under the shelf, was in a sling, but a splint, not a cast, which was both good and bad. Good because it was obviously not broken, but bad because I was now even more useless. My leg had been put up in one of those straps that hung from the ceiling and the cast was new. *Shit.* I hoped that asshole hadn't broken it in any more places.

"Mister Adams," Doctor Richardson said as he pulled the curtain aside, "welcome back."

"It's Jack," Sammy said behind him, "he likes Jack; not John, or Johnny, and not Mister Adams, either."

Doctor Richardson smiled at her and turned back to me.

"Jack, you are one lucky duck. You have a mild pulmonary contusion, but we still need some tests to make absolutely certain there is no further damage. That means that you have bruising on your lung caused by the trauma of the bookcase falling on you. There is a small fissure in your sternum, for which there is nothing we can do but pump you full of painkillers and let it heal on its own. Your arm is in a splint, don't worry, the bones are not fractured, but the shelf cut through the skin and we had to staple the wound together. There may be a permanent scar. Your ankle is healing well and there are no new fractures, but the cast was damaged so we had to replace it. You were extremely lucky, and I would suggest that you let your friends know they need to make sure their furniture is properly nailed to the wall."

"Didn't fall," I croaked, "brought down on me."

Doctor Richardson raised an eyebrow, then looked from me to my sister,

"That's why you were talking to the police earlier? Do they have the suspect in custody? Are you safe?"

"Yes, no, and probably not. I knocked him out with Jack's cane, and went upstairs to call 9-1-1. When I came back, he was gone. Vanished. He's good at that. The police said they would send someone to guard us, but I haven't seen anyone. Trouble is, he's a cop; in Osprey Cove."

"You know this person?"

"Yeah, I, uh, lost contact with him years ago. Now he knows I'm here. He broke into our friends' house and attacked us. I was in the bathroom, and Jack was already under the bookcase when he dragged me out."

Doctor Richardson looked at her quizzically.

"Do you have a picture, or a name? I need to let security know to be on the lookout for this individual. Is there someone you can call?"

"His name is David Saunders, he's tall, strong, with black hair and cleft chin. I've been trying to reach our friends—it's their house—but they aren't picking up. I'll try again."

"Apollo and Mark?" I grunted.

She shook her head and said she hadn't gotten hold of them either.

Doctor Richardson excused himself and walked out. Sammy put her phone to her ear. I laid my head back and closed my eyes. I thought I heard buzzing nearby. I listened as Sammy left Babcock a message. Then she tried Amelia. Again the buzzing and, after a few moments I heard Sammy leaving a voicemail. I opened my eyes,

"Sammy," my chest hurt so much, "call them again and listen."

She dialed, and I heard the buzzing coming from behind the curtain to my left. She heard it too and inched toward the curtain. She slowly opened it and gasped, dropping the phone.

Pluto Babcock was in the bed next to mine. He was heavily injured and his eyes were closed. There was a tube in his mouth. The curtain to his left was also open, and Sammy went around Pluto's bed, her hand on her chest.

"Oh my God, Jacky, it's Amelia," she exclaimed.

Just then, the curtain at Babcock's feet opened and Abigail walked in.

"Oh Sam!" she cried and broke into tears.

Sam put her arm around her.

"Abby, what happened?"

"They (sob) said (sob) there was (sob) a car accident," Abigail bawled into Sam's shoulder, "the doctors said they're stable and probably gonna be okay, but I'm so scared!"

Sam said that this was too much of a coincidence. Abigail lifted her head and was about ask, when she caught sight of me.

"What happened? What's going on?" she said turning from me to Sam, and I could see that she was one ounce shy of going into full blown hysterics.

I think Sam noticed it too, since she bowed her head and mumbled something that sounded like "David Saunders attacked us."

"WHAT!" Abby lost it, "Ohmygod, ohmygod, ohmygod!" She started breathing fast and fanning herself with her hands. Her lips were trembling. When Sam tried to put her arm around her, Abby smacked it away.

"This is your fault," she turned to me, "if you'd never showed up we wouldn't be in this mess! My parents would be fine and none of us would be here."

I bowed my head. She was right, I had put them in danger.

"I'm sorry," I croaked, "I didn't think anything like this could ever happen to me, you know. I'm not a hero and I should never have looked your dad up in the first place."

"Jacky, that's not true," Sam turned to me, "you did the right thing, you sought help."

Just then, Sam and Abby looked towards Amelia's bed as if they'd heard her calling. Abby rushed to her side and I couldn't see what was going on from behind Babcock's unconscious body. Sam stood there for a moment, picked up her phone and walked back to my side of the curtain, closing it behind her. She resumed her place beside the bed and looked at the phone. I could see the screen was cracked, but I guess it was still working fairly well, since Sammy clicked and swiped a couple of times and suddenly a picture of Apollo laughing popped up on the screen. Sam put the phone to her ear and waited. She left another voicemail. Then she tried Mark but didn't get an answer.

"I'm worried," I said. My lungs were on fire, but what else could I do? I had to talk, "The guys should be picking up by now. Something's wrong."

"I don't have Tallulah's new number."

I nodded and looked around for my personal belongings. She seemed to read my mind and said that my phone hadn't been among them. I thought for a minute and remembered I'd left it in the kitchen.

We sat in silence for quite a while when Abby popped her head in. She looked contrite and embarrassed.

"Um," she looked down at the floor, "I'm sorry I blew up at you. My mom woke up and the doctor said she'll be fine. Um, Sammy, could you talk to the cops with me? She said that Anna Jenkins blindsided them."

"Shit," Sam jumped up, "yeah, I'll come with you, but it's really your mom who should tell them what happened. How's your dad?"

"He's unconscious but stable. The outlook is good."

Sam whispered that she'd be back, as they both walked out. I laid my head back and closed my eyes.

I must have dozed off, because when I woke up, Mark was sitting in Sammy's place. His left upper arm was strapped to his chest and his shoulder was bandaged.

"Dude, you all right?" he said, "Sam told us what happened. Man, this has been some crazy night."

"What happened to you? Where are Apollo and Tallulah?"

"It's fucked up, right. As you know, we went to check in at the motel. Apollo and I hung out in the room for a while, watched TV and took a nap. When we were ready to leave, Tallulah said she was still tired and wanted to stay behind and keep resting. So Apollo and I were on our way back to meet you, when suddenly he realized he'd left his phone behind and was adamant that we go back and get it. I was driving, and I tried to persuade him to leave it, but he just started going mental, saying we had to go back, that he needed his phone, and it was freaking me out. I've never seen him like that, so we turned around and drove back. He bolted from the car and ran towards our room, which was next to Tallulah's. He said in the ambulance he'd seen the door ajar, because next thing I know, he's screaming and rushing into Tallulah's room. When I came up behind, I saw him wrestling with some guy in a hoodie, and Tallulah was lying on the bed breathing real hard and fast, you know, clutching her chest. As I stepped in, Apollo managed to shove him off. I grabbed the guy and was about to hit him when he turned around and stabbed me on the shoulder with a knife I hadn't even seen. As he pulled it out, I managed to punch him in the gut and Apollo grabbed him from behind and slammed him against the wall. He dropped the knife but before we could do more, he ran out. We followed but he was fast, like real fast, and all we saw was him running into the woods behind the motel."

"Are Tallulah and Apollo all right?"

"Yeah, they brought her in with chest pains and breathing hard, but the doctors think it's just a scare. She says she woke up startled when Apollo screamed, and saw some guy with a knife beside the bed. Apollo says he saw the guy standing over Tallulah, and now, Pollo has a giant gash across his chest, but the doctors said he'll be all right, nothin' staples and stitches won't cure. We're all supposed to stay overnight though."

"Did you talk to the cops? Do you know who the guy is?"

Mark nodded and said the cops had filed a report and were on the lookout.

"My first impression was that the guy was David Saunders, you know, same build and everything, but Apollo's not so certain and it all happened too fast. I didn't really get a good look at his face either, because the hood was pulled over his head. Man, Jack, this is really fucked up. First Saunders attacks you and Sammy, while Anna almost kills the Babcocks. From what we've been able to put together, Saunders and Anna attacked at the same time, but the attack on Tallulah came later, so who was it? Is it possible Saunders could've left you and gone to the motel to take care of us? But then, how did he know we were staying there?"

I shook my head and told him Sammy had left Saunders in pretty bad shape, at the very least he'd have some kind of genital injury ("I mean, she bit him, dude; right in the junk") and a head injury too. That whack with the cane had sounded pretty definitive and I'd been surprised when Sammy told me he'd vanished while she called for help.

"It's fucked up, dude, really fucked up," Mark sighed and shook his head.

We spent the night in the Emergency Room. Sammy sat with me, while Mark sat with Apollo and Tallulah who were in adjacent beds, the curtains opened between them. Babcock woke up but was still heavily sedated. He and Amelia were moved out of the ER and into a room of their own. Abby stayed with them.

If Doctor Richardson had thought Sammy was difficult, I can't imagine what he must have endured with the Osborns. Tallulah wailed, pled and complained that she was all right, that she wanted go to the motel, spend the night in a decent bed, take a decent shower, have a decent dinner, and yeah, the motel room smelled musty, but it was better than the ungodly chemicals and illness that stunk up this place. Apollo tried to calm her down and make her see reason; he kept telling her that he was spending the night here too and that he would be there beside her and everything would be all right, but that she had to listen to the doctors and because of her age they needed to observe her and make sure she was okay.

"Observe me!" We heard her yell whenMark opened my curtain, "I'm not a museum piece!"

Sammy giggled and Mark leaned against her chair.

"Everyone okay here?" he said, looking down at Sammy.

I meant to say something about staying away from my sister, but I'd been nodding off throughout the Tallulah Osborn versus Doctor Richardson match, and was now unable to keep my eyes open. I heard Sam mumble something before I fell into a deep, dreamless sleep.

CHAPTER SIXTEEN

Imposed West and Wewaxation

"Jack, how you feeling, man?"

I opened my eyes; Apollo was smiling. Light was coming in through a window and I realized I'd been moved to a new room.

"You were having trouble breathing last night, so they want you here a bit longer."

I nodded and asked him how he was.

"I'm okay, not my first battle scar but definitely my biggest," he pointed to his chest and lifted up his shirt. His chest was bandaged horizontally and also around his shoulder. He explained how the wound went down his right pectoral and across, ending just below his left ribs. I told him that he was really lucky that it hadn't been deep enough to cut anything important. He agreed and said he'd needed staples, too.

"Mark calls us the 'Stapleton Twins' now," he rolled his eyes and I tried to laugh but only coughed in pain.

"He must feel holy now with that stab on his shoulder," I managed to wheeze when the coughing stopped, "Mister Holier-Than-Thou Swiss Cheese."

Apollo burst out in his thunderous laugh, but had to cut it short from the pain in his chest.

"Ay, it's like my chest is on fire," he said patting the bandage, "at least Mikey-P is intact."

Apollo has a tattoo of the Perseus constellation and a sun symbol, both bound together by the symbol for infinity on his chest, just where his heart is. It's meant as a homage to his dead identical twin brother, Michael Perseus.

"How's Tallulah?"

"Better. All that fussing last night was for nothing. She started feeling chest pains again and the doctors say it's angina, so she has to stay here and rest. She and the Babcocks will be here the longest. They'll be okay. As you know, Pluto woke up, and he's breathing on his own now. He has multiple injuries and will be bedridden for a while. Amelia is better, she has a fractured sternum and ribs and an injured shoulder from the seatbelt, so she's not going anywhere either."

"It's good that you went back," I said, "for Tallulah's sake. What made you do it? Mark said you went mental over not having your phone."

"You won't believe me, I can hardly believe it myself, but you remember I told you guys about that crazy old lady that lives down the street?"

I nodded.

"Well, the other day, I was walking Jude, and she was sitting outside on her porch, like always, and for some reason, as I walked by she called out to me in that witchy voice of hers. She said, "Hey Boy-o, don't forget your phone, might just save yer life!" and cackled. I thought she was crazy and dismissed it, but when I did forget my phone, her words came back to me . Really, dude, I just kept hearing her voice booming over and over, only in my mind she kept saying, "might just save   *her* life". It's fucking crazy, I know, but I just couldn't think or hear anything else."

"Wow, maybe she really is a witch."

Apollo looked pensive for a moment.

"You know, I went face to face with her once, just after I'd broken up with Annabelle. She called out to me and Jude, and said something nasty, so I confronted her, and I looked into her eyes and, I don't know, man, there was something there, something I can't quite place, but I think she knows things."

"Like a psychic?"

"Yeah, something like that, only really powerful."

"Yikes," I thought for a moment, "how did you know that Tallulah was in danger, though?"

"I didn't. They gave us adjacent rooms and on the way to mine, I saw her door was ajar and thought that funny, so I peeked in and saw the guy standing over her. I rushed in, and when he turned around he slashed me, we struggled and then Mark showed up. You know what really bothers me though? How did he get in? Tallulah always locks hotel doors with the chain or bar lock and everything. "

I shrugged. We threw some theories around but all sounded unlikely. Maybe he knows how to open bar locks from the outside, maybe he used a ruse to get her to open the door, maybe he had a key. Apollo sat pensive for a moment, then looked up and said,

"What is it that Sherlock Holmes always said? Something about when you rule out all the possibilities all that's left is the impossible?"

"Yeah, something like that. What're you getting at?"

"Well, what if he was already inside? What if he knew it was her room and somehow came in and hid?"

"Scary, but unlikely, I mean, the first thing I do when I get a hotel room is check it out; you know, see the bathroom, whether there's a tub or a shower, open the closet and stuff. It would've been difficult to hide."

"Yeah, but she wasn't always in her room, she knocked on our door and asked if we wanted anything from the vending machines."

"Then that would mean that whoever he was, saw her leave and probably snuck in while she was getting a snack."

"Nah, I don't think he was inside, why leave the door ajar? Maybe, for the first time in her life Tallulah forgot to put the chain on the door," Apollo said.

I got the feeling that even he didn't believe it, and was proved right when he took out his phone, saying, "Let's cut the crap, I wonder if it's easy to open a bar or chain lock from the outside."

He googled "open a chain lock from the outside" and the first thing that came up were several videos on YouTube. We watched some of them, and yeah, it looks easy. They showed how to open chain locks with a rubber band, tape, stir stick, string and even earphone cable. Bar locks seemed even easier, all the guy had to do was stick a thick piece of paper, or—as seen on one video—the Do Not Disturb sign, between the door and the lock, close the door and push the bar out. Fuckin' easy and fuckin' scary.

"Anna is a master murderess, and an amazing escape artist," I said, "that means that this was all planned. They knew where we were going to be. Saunders probably knew Sammy and I were alone at the Babcocks', Anna knew the Babcocks would be in their car, and whoever the guy was, knew Tallulah was alone at the motel. I really don't think Saunders could've gone to the motel to try and kill Tallulah, not the way Sammy beat him. He's gotta have some sort of injury, I mean look at us, we're beat up worse than Die Hard gets in the movies; no way he's that invincible."

"Agreed, you're totally fubar ('fucked up beyond all recognition'; Apollo loved *Tango and Cash*). Maybe he doesn't feel any pain? I think there's a medical condition like that."

"No way, he screamed when Sam bit him, and held his crotch as he tried to crawl away. He definitely felt pain."

He nodded and I asked him whether he was sure it wasn't David Saunders like Mark thought, and he replied that he wasn't one hundred percent sure. He said the guy had a hood on, but he definitely had the same build as Saunders.

"You wanna know what's really scary?" I asked as he sat back and rubbed his eyes, "It's two of them versus eight of us and we're losing. Look at us, they put seven of us in the hospital in one go. These guys are aces, they're amazing at getting away with crimes. I'm sure Saunders meant to kill me or let me die, I'm certain he tried to make it look like the bookcase fell on me by accident; I mean, that's the first thing Dr. Richardson thought, so it's not a stretch the police might have ruled that way too. I don't even want to imagine what he had in store for Sammy."

I tried to push the thought of another rape out of my mind, but it was obvious that would've been only the beginning. Despite what Saunders said, I was certain he hadn't meant to let us live. They had been out to kill, and had almost gotten away with it.

I spent the next three days in the hospital, and, just as Apollo said, Tallulah and the Babcocks were the last to leave. Tallulah because she kept wanting to leave and would get all worked up, which worsened her chest pains, and the doctors would insist she needed rest, and she would comply; but in a matter of hours, the whole cycle would start up again.

I couldn't understand it, she's always been such an easygoing lady, and this behavior seemed way out of character; but I guess some people just can't stand hospitals. She kept complaining the place stunk of illness, sorrow and rot.

I asked Apollo if he'd told Lupe about the attacks and he said no, if she knew anything was wrong she'd come up right away. That would put her right in Anna's crosshairs, he said, and he wasn't about to do that to his mother. I agreed, we were already balls deep in this, no need to involve Lupe, Mike Monroe, or anyone else. Instead, he said he told her the "investigation" was taking longer than anyone had expected.

I wish I could say that during my hospital stay everything magically resolved itself. That the police in Osprey Cove caught Anna, Saunders and the unknown third person red-handed, and that they were all going to spend the rest of their lives in prison. I wish I could say that Apollo, Mark and Sammy, who weren't hospital bound, had gone back to Jenny's house, opened the boxes and seen that Sammy and I had received an inheritance so substantial that we'd both be set for life and then some, and that this whole tale ended with us watching the sunset on a Hawaiian beach with Mai-Tais in our hands. But no, life is not like a Hollywood movie, and bad situations do not end all wrapped up in a neat little bow.

The truth is, I couldn't even blame the Osprey Cove Police, they worked out of a rec center and had the fabulous amount of five full-time officers, plus a number of reserves for the ten-thousand or so sickeningly rich people that swelled the town in summer; so yeah, to say they lacked the manpower to send out a massive search in the style of *The Fugitive* is an understatement, not to mention the fact that one of their own was an alleged suspect at best.

I suspected that some of the staff were also scared of Saunders, and that those who weren't respected him as their senior, maybe even admired him. Besides, this was a tiny town, so how many major crimes could there be? The Osprey Cove Police force did not have the experience to handle something like this.

When Jenny died, the only police officer who believed there was something fishy about it was Babcock, not because he had razor sharp detecting skills honed by years of investigating an endless parade of murders like detectives on TV, but because he was her friend, and had had some privileged information. And let's not forget how easy it had been for one detective to cover up a multiple homicide in Peaceville, a town with a much bigger population and adjacent to a state capital.

I could almost bet that Saunders had somehow, and, unbeknownst to Babcock, gained some clout, especially with the younger officers, who probably didn't even know he'd been questioned in the "accidental" death of one of Osprey Cove's residents almost twenty years before.

Mark and Apollo had both called in sick at work come Monday morning, and the guys and Sammy had chosen to stay at a motel in Portland, which was not too far away and big enough to hide in. We thought it would be safest to find lodgings away from Osprey Cove and Brunswick, in the hopes that Anna and Saunders would not follow them there. Like before, they had vanished completely.

I told Apollo to keep Mark out of Sammy's room, but he'd just smiled and said sure thing, though he didn't look like he'd taken me seriously. Abby was staying with her friend Jane, and assured me she'd keep an eye on the Saunders house.

The police told us Saunders's vacation had started two days before, and that there was no reason for him to be seen anywhere. They had tried to contact him, but since he'd said he was going on a Caribbean cruise, hadn't been able to reach him.

Caribbean cruise, my ass. Saunders was still in Osprey Cove and well hidden. This had been planned from the start. We were the only people to claim to have seen him since a co-worker drove him to Portland International Jetport this past Thursday, one day before Mark and I had picked Sammy up at Logan Airport.

What was really puzzling was how they knew we were coming. Did Anna know Sammy had made it to Boston? Was there someone feeding Saunders information? Babcock had mentioned that there were people in town who would love to look into Saunders, so was there someone talking to him on the sly? It was like these guys knew what we were going to do even before we planned anything.

I put down the book I'd been trying to read for the past hour, and sighed. Someone had to have seen Saunders walking around town when we bumped into him. Maybe the whole town knew something was up and was keeping quiet? It had only been a couple of weeks since Babcock, the oldest officer on the Osprey Cove PD, had retired, so it is possible that Saunders had been honing relationships and contacts under the table for years. Maybe Babcock's friends weren't as reliable as he thought.

Tallulah poked her head in, and, when I smiled, she came and sat down by the bed. She'd spent most of her hospital stay sitting with me and we'd talked about everything. We'd talked about Sammy and Mark, Apollo's childhood, Anthropology, books, movies, music, you name it.

Once I even got up the courage to ask her why she hated hospitals so much. She'd looked at her hands and then told me how, when she was just about to graduate university in England, she and her family had been in a tragic train accident. She told me that the only people in her cabin that had survived had been herself and her younger brother Nick ("he was Apollo's dad, Jack, and back then only he'd been in Year Nine, which is like your eighth grade").

Her parents were dead and she'd spent weeks in the hospital recovering from the injuries she'd sustained in the accident. After that, she'd had to finish school quickly and get a job and pull her brother through.

"I felt like Susan Pevensie at the end of *The Last Battle*, only, through no lack of belief from me, I'd been left out of Narnia, and with a thirteen-year-old to boot. We made it out all right, but hospitals always take me back to that time, so I try to stay away as much as possible."

As the sun set on Tuesday, our third day in the hospital, Tallulah told me that Mark and Apollo had called in sick again, and that they'd tried to get back into Jenny's house, but had found it completely locked and shuttered. I supposed that Jenny didn't want anyone going in. I wondered whether Anna and Saunders had tried to enter the house. The guys had reported that there had been no sign of them around town or anywhere, and that Sammy had almost gotten herself arrested when she'd pressured the Osprey Cove Police to look into Saunders.

"I suppose it's as you think, Jack," Tallulah said, "perhaps he does have the town wrapped around his little finger. It's a scary thought, that means that he's got eyes and ears and there's no one we can trust."

"Yeah, that's what I was afraid of. From what Babcock says, everyone on the force who was around when Jenny was alive, is either dead or moved away."

"I suppose we shall have to press on by ourselves from now on. We can't let those two win."

We talked into the evening and I told her about how Anna had wrecked my life. I was poor and had sunk most of my money into a house, which, if the hauntings didn't stop, was unlivable and unsellable. My house wasn't my own, I said, and all because of Anna. Because of her, I owed so much to everyone and they weren't debts that could be paid back in coin. Anna's actions had consequences, and I was going to be the one who got to live with them.

"Oh Jack, I believe we are all here to learn something, and everything good and bad that happens to us, teaches us. When my parents died, I learned I had the strength to pull myself together and make something very good out of my life. I dug myself out of that hole, and I'm sure you can dig yourself out of this one, regardless of what Anna does."

"But still, because of me and her, you all are now in danger. I think it would've been better if I'd never bought that house and stayed a loner in my Roslindale cubby-hole."

"But, you aren't a very good loner, Jack. Look at how many people have stepped up to help you."

"Yeah, and how many have ended up in the hospital because of me. That's not a good sign."

"Hmmm, perhaps," she shrugged, "you can choose to believe that you're some sort of jinx and that you are the cause of a lot of these troubles, or, you can choose to believe that the situation is as it is, regardless of what you've done, and you are the risen hero who has the power to change it."

I shrugged and looked down at my hands, mumbling that by no stretch of the imagination was I a hero. Tallulah took my fingers in hers and smiled,

"I rather think you are. I think that, however bleak the circumstances, we are all going to pull through and be better than before. The pieces are falling into place, so that we will be victorious in the end, and justice will be done, wrongs will be righted, and lessons will be learned."

"I'm scared that someone won't come out of this alive, and it'll be all my fault. If I die, fine, but I dragged you all into this, and if you die, well, that'll be on me."

"First, my darling, you didn't drag anyone, we all jumped at the chance to help you; second, if any of us dies (may God forbid), it'll be because it was meant to happen, not because you had anything to do with it."

She leaned closer as if to tell me a secret.

"Have I ever told you that Pompeii is one of my favorite places in the world? I dreamed last night that we were all flying over Pompeii on a hot-air balloon and there was a rainbow over Vesuvius. We were happy and safe and sound. So you see, everything's going to be all right."

"That's a lot like how *The Last Battle* ends, everyone happy and safe and sound in eternal life; you know, after they *all* die."

"Oh Jack, you can be such a Dismal Desmond sometimes. Everything will turn out for the best, you'll see."

171

CHAPTER SEVENTEEN

The Good, the Bad and the Dead

The house loomed over us, darker and gloomier than it had been before, in spite of the bright summer sunshine. It seemed to create a vacuum that sucked in all the light around it, and this feeling of gloom seeped out onto the street. Even the branches on the thick trees that lined the sidewalks and surrounded the houses hung low, like mourners bowing their heads as a hearse passed by. Jenny's front yard was treeless, and now, with this deep sense of death, the house seemed barren and lifeless. Yet, I knew that there was something going on inside, I could feel it.

Apollo, Mark, Sammy and I stood at the edge of the path that led to the front door, almost like D'Artagnan and The Three Musketeers. I had been released from the hospital on Wednesday morning and had talked the others into going straight to the house. Abigail was sitting with her parents, and the doctors had insisted that Tallulah spent one more night in the hospital. So it was up to the four of us, and I had the feeling that this would be the final showdown. Even the house itself seemed to augur it.

Theoretically, one would say that the odds were in our favor, we stood four against two, yet I was all but useless with a walking cast and a stapled up arm, Sammy was a walking bruise and one-armed, Apollo's chest was no laughing matter (I could tell by the way he hunched over ever so slightly that the wound hurt him) and Mark, big, tough-looking bear that he was, winced whenever so much as a butterfly brushed his bandaged shoulder. We were one sorry-looking bunch, and there was no telling what kind of violence and horror awaited us inside.

"I really think she's in there," Sammy whispered beside me, "I can feel it, something's going down, and it's about to start."

"Agreed," Apollo nodded.

"Are we sure we want to do this?" Mark asked.

"It's now or never," I said, "we might not get another chance, and she won't stop until we're dead."

Mark sighed and straightened up. We stepped forward; and I imagined we were in one of those movies where the good guys all walk abreast in slow motion, ready to do or die against their foes. I felt ridiculous and, unable to stop myself, began to laugh. It was the crazy hysterical 'heeheehee' that comes out of me when I'm scared out of my wits. Apollo chuckled beside me, trying to hold back the laughter, and Mark was trying his hardest not to follow suit. Only Sammy was dead serious and turned to look at us like we were crazy.

"What's so funny?" She stopped and faced us, her hand on her hip like the schoolmarm that she is, "What's so funny?"

"Nothing," the word was barely out of my mouth when I couldn't stand it anymore and bellowed with laughter.

She looked at me with fire in her eyes, waiting for me to answer, her foot tapping the ground. Mark and Apollo burst out in their boisterous laughter. Sammy looked bitter.

"It's just that," I went on as the laughter died down and all that was left was deep, dull pain in my chest, "we look ridiculous, walking like we were the Earp brothers on our way to the O.K. Corral. I know it's no time for laughing, but I just can't help it."

Mark and Apollo gradually stopped laughing too, and Sammy just stood there, breathing fast and shaky, tears springing to her eyes. She passed her forearm over them and sighed, her lips quivering. Silence had closed in around us and as I looked at the guys, I saw fear settling in their eyes too; while we laughed under stress, Sammy cried. Suddenly, she burst into small, panicked sobs, her hand covering her mouth. Mark made a move to put his arm around her, but Apollo was faster and hugged her. She cried hysterically, her tears wetting his shirt, while I encircled her, my hand on her shoulder, and Mark awkwardly tried to embrace her without touching sensitive areas, thus settling on running his hand through her hair.

"We can't die here," she sobbed, "I don't want to live without you guys, I love you all so much and I'm so scared. We can't die here."

As she lifted her face, Mark, broke up the group hug and put his finger under her chin, gently directing her towards him. Then, he took her face in both his hands and kissed her on the lips. I was fuming, and was about to break it up when Apollo stopped me.

Mark slowly backed away and, still holding her astonished and somewhat pleased face, said, "Everything's going to be all right, you'll see, no one's going to die here."

"Yeah," Apollo chipped in, smiling (I really felt like breaking his teeth), "we're not even sure they're in there, for all we know the house is empty and it's just dread we feel. Don't worry Sammy, when we face them, we'll fight back."

Sam looked from Mark to Apollo and then to me. She took a deep breath and rubbed her nose.

"Okay," her voice sounded a little brighter, "let's do this."

She straightened her back and, like a knight, walked towards the door.

Apollo was right, there was no one inside, and everything was in its place. The debris had been cleaned up and the stairs looked brand new. Mark looked around for a door into the hidden passageway, but couldn't find one. I supposed that we weren't meant to go down there again, at least not for now. We separated and made sure the first floor was empty, opening rooms and closets, and shouting "clear!" like on TV.

We met up in front of the staircase and Mark placed a tentative foot on the stairs. He claimed they were sturdy and, for the first time in almost twenty years, a living human being made his way up. Sammy followed, (Apollo, always the gentleman, had let her pass with an 'after you, milady' gesture that had made my blood boil).

"I hope he farts," I mumbled as I climbed after Sammy, while Apollo sniggered behind me. I turned and looked daggers at him.

"Dude, really, just let it go," he whispered as he stepped up beside me, the stairs being wide enough for both of us, "he's always liked her, and she'll be going back to California soon. They can take care of themselves. The worst that could happen is that they have a fling and go their separate ways. How's that so bad?"

"He could break her heart," I grumbled.

"Or, she could break his," he shrugged, and I hated that he was the voice of reason, "we can't control it, so just let it happen. They're big kids, they can look after their own hearts."

I pursed my lips, and growled something that may have sounded like "I guess you're right."

It's true, Johnny-Boy, you've never been jealous before, so why start now? Because I know what a heartbreaker and Casanova he is, I answered Grandpa's voice, but felt no comfort in the certainty of my answer. Truth was, Mark didn't normally look for serious relationships, unlike Apollo and me, who were secretly hoping the next girl was the one. He's always been open about that, both to us, himself, and his female companions; and, like Sammy had said, she didn't need to be with a man, so maybe a fling between them was not such a horrible thing. Who knows? They might even go from casual to serious forever, and my best friend might someday become my brother.   *Now you're getting ahead of yourself, Johnny-Boy, just let them be. They can decide on their own.*

We caught up with them on the landing and looked around. The hallway wound in a squared spiral around the stairs, like four mezzanine floors with waist-high, thick, wooden railings. There were closed doors on each side of the square. The winding hallway around the stairs was not wide, since barely two of us were able to walk abreast; but the stairway landing was far wider, almost like a reception parlor to the upstairs, where several people could be milling or sitting on the sheet-covered chairs against the wall at any given time. The walls on the mezzanine floors were all built-in bookshelves that covered every inch, and each shelf was bursting with books. Apollo and I looked at each other and smiled.

We walked around, trying every door, but they were all locked; I supposed because there was nothing to see. I'd begun to understand the workings of this house, Jenny and her magic slowly guided us to what was important, making sure we weren't distracted along the way. This was how she communicated with us, what wasn't relevant could not be opened or disturbed. I think Sammy and the guys had gotten the drift of that too, because no one looked surprised when Apollo tried one of the doors on the mezzanine hallway directly across the landing, and opened it.

I peeked in and saw that it was only a small, narrow set of stairs; they reminded me of the carpeted steps that had led up to Sammy's old studio apartment in Oregon. This must be the stairs that Pluto had mentioned led up to the widow's walk.

A cold draft blew in from above and sent chills up my spine, as if this breeze carried a dark omen on its back. There was danger in that draft and I'm certain we all felt it, because Sammy assumed her knight pose, Mark clenched his fists, and Apollo looked like a tiger about to pounce. He told us to wait here, and his voice took on such a low growl that nobody contested his command.

Apollo slowly climbed up the stairs and paused less than halfway up, his long body presumably affording him a view of what was at the top without needing to get all the way up.

"It's Anna! Run!" He roared.

Then Apollo came toppling down. I barely managed to push myself against the bookcase next to the door, when Apollo and Anna rolled into the hall. I heard his head bang on the wooden floor and his body went limp.

"You bitch!" Mark lunged at her.

I really wished he hadn't done that, because I had picked up my cane like a bat and was about to hit her over the head with it. My swing just skimmed the top of his hair as he tackled her. My cane went boom on the threshold, inches away from Sam's head as David Saunders slammed her against the wall. Where the fuck had he come from?

He took her head in both his hands and was about to smash it into the bookshelves, when I swung again and hit him on the shoulder. He cried out and turned around to see where the blow had come from. I moved to swing, but someone grabbed the cane from behind me. My body was already in motion, and I stumbled and tripped over Apollo, who lay still with his eyes closed. The cane was wrenched from my hands and pain shot through my broken ankle as I landed. I screamed.

Sam had managed to push Saunders away and was running towards the stairs. She was fast and got to the landing quickly, but instead of running down the stairs, like I'd hoped she would, ran straight across to where the hall veered. She turned, and, with her right leg in front and shoulder-width apart, her good arm up in a fist by her face, bounced lightly on her heels.

Saunders had run after her. He lunged towards her and she threw kick after kick after kick, alternating her legs and forcing Saunders to retreat. He tried to catch her legs and back away from her, but she was relentless in her barrage of kicks which landed with big, loud thuds on his sides, ribs, kidneys, liver, thighs, arms and shoulders. He managed to put some distance between them. While he tried to get his bearings, Sammy took one step towards him, and with her back leg spin-kicked him right in the head. The force sent him flying and down the big, hard, wooden staircase. I heard a loud whack at the foot of the stairs as Sam stood at the top, back straight, legs apart, hand still in a fist and looking down.

Meanwhile, as I tried to crawl away from Apollo's body and get up, someone hit me between the shoulders. I turned around, gasping for air from the pain, and saw a man almost identical to David Saunders holding my cane above his head. Perhaps it was his cold, unfeeling grin and dead eyes—but I knew I was looking right at David Murphy.

"Two Davids!" I gasped. He smiled and brought the dragon head down on me. I lifted my arms to brace for the blow, but it never came. Instead, I heard the distinct ping of metal on metal and looked up to see Jenny's black cane hovering above me, the two dragons going to head to head.

A deep, rumbling sound came from the walls, like a wolf's growl, and David Murphy looked surprised and confused as he stepped back. Jenny's cane pointed itself forward and, like an arrow, thrust itself, dragon first, into Murphy's chest. Murphy groaned, dropped my cane, and fell to his knees, gasping. Sammy weaved her head under my left arm, wrapped her good arm around me and helped me up. She backed us away from Murphy towards the landing.

"We need space, little bro, and we need to stay on our feet," she whispered as we neared the staircase.

Across the mezzanine, Mark was still wrestling with Anna. She had produced a knife and was trying to stab him. Mark held her wrist with both his arms, impeding the knife. Anna was screaming and laughing wildly as she hit his injured shoulder with her other fist. I saw the pain in Mark's face, but he didn't let go.

As we reached the landing, both canes flew and stopped in front of us. I took my cane and tried to stand, but got such a sharp pain in my ankle that my leg gave away and I fell to my knees. I was out of the fight and all I could do was watch while the people I loved most in the world fought for their lives. For all I knew, Apollo was already dead; his body was strewn across the hallway, his legs still on the small, narrow steps. Murphy was sitting against the wall beside him, clutching his chest and gasping for air. Sam grabbed Jenny's cane and ran around to where Mark and Anna were fighting. Just as she was passing by the stairs, a hand reached out through the railing and grabbed her ankle. She fell with a hard thud and, kicking her legs like crazy, released herself from the hand. Saunders was climbing up the stairs.

Fuck the pain, I thought, as I hopped on my good foot to edge of the landing. Saunders was just about to reach the final step, when he looked up and saw me standing above him, Mike's cane on my shoulder like a bat. I swung and hit him on the head, blood spurting out as he tumbled down again. I lost my balance and nearly fell after him. I was grabbed by the nape of my shirt and hurled back, into the wall. It hurt like hell and I was winded, but slid down safe onto the landing. I'd hit the wall a good five feet above the floor. There was no one near me.

Mark rolled onto his back and Anna was on top of him, trying to stab him. Sammy, already up and running fast as lighting and stealthy as a ninja, got to them quickly and, without stopping, threw a frontal kick and hit Anna right in the face, like a soccer player shooting a goal. Anna's head whipped and she landed on her back, her arms flailing. She dropped the knife, and Mark tried to get to it, but Murphy recovered enough to throw himself across Apollo's body and grabbed it first. Mark shuffled back and Sammy pulled him up. They ran towards the landing, and I warned them that Anna and Murphy had both recovered. Anna was running after them, while Murphy ran through the other hallway.

They surrounded us quickly, Murphy at the top of the landing, brandishing the knife. He was smiling and giggling.

"Hey baby, just like old times, right?" Murphy called out to Anna.

"Sure thing, sugar, too bad David's not up here," Anna smirked, blood spurting out her nose and mouth; she had a patched eye, likely from her fight with Sammy in Sacramento.

"Yeah, my cousin's missing all the fun!"

Sam and Mark were standing in front of me. I gave Mark my cane but remained on my knees, I couldn't stand up, the pain in my ankle had gotten even worse and the foot was throbbing. Sammy was looking at Anna, and Mark was facing Murphy.

"Stay on your feet, Mark, whatever else happens, you've got to stay on your feet," Sam whispered.

Mark nodded, not taking his eyes off Murphy.

"So you thought I was gonna miss out on all the fun, huh, Cuz?" Saunders voice came from behind Murphy.

He climbed the top step, holding on to the railing. He was bloodied and limping, but his face was full of a dark, cold mirth that would've stopped a rabid dog in its tracks.

He limped next to Murphy, so that the three of them were facing us, with their backs to the railing. Saunders reached behind him and took out a gun. Sam gasped and Mark's hands trembled, as he held the cane in front of him, like a protective bar.

"You know, guns are no fun," Saunders laughed and set the gun on the floor in front of him, "they kill too fast, I prefer a slow death."

He reached behind again and took out a switchblade.

This was fucked, we were fucked.

Anna and the Davids took a step forward, and Sam and Mark braced themselves.

"Why?" Sam looked steadily at Anna, "Why do you do this? Why do you kill?"

"Why not?" Anna shrugged.

Suddenly, there was a thud, and Saunders fell face down on top of the gun, not moving. Murphy turned around only to see Apollo's sneaker as he kicked Murphy in the jaw. Murphy fell on his side, while Anna lunged at Apollo. He received her with a well placed sidekick that sent her flying against the wall.

Apollo was a giant and now, he looked even bigger; his face showing the steady, easy-going calmness he was known for, but he wasn't smiling and in his eyes there was a cool and collected anger. I'd remembered how Tallulah had told me that Apollo had a dangerous, angry beast inside him that had only shown itself once before, and that if I ever saw it, I should stay away. Apollo called it his Hydra, and he could tame it, she'd said, but never truly kill it.

I now understood what she'd meant; Apollo, cheerful and laid-back as he was, had a temper which rarely stirred, but was quick to rise and quick to quell. I'd only seen a fraction of it once or twice and never directed towards me; it showed in his face, and his voice took on a slithery-like quality that spewed poisonous words, but had never gotten violent. He would say it was just the Hydra rearing its head; but now, the beast was fully awakened, and Anna and the Davids were about to feel its full force.

Sammy moved towards Anna; Mark tried to stop her, and, by his expression, I knew he'd recognized this beast. Sam didn't care (I don't think she'd ever seen Apollo even remotely miffed), and placed herself between Anna and Apollo.

Anna was getting up, and as she tried to throw herself at Sam, my sister received her with a good kick. Anna tried to get up and Sam kicked her again. Meanwhile, Apollo was fighting Murphy much in the same manner, Murphy tried to stab Apollo, but Apollo kicked the raised arm and the knife was hurled between the railing bars and down to the first floor. Then Murphy tried to tackle and punch, but Apollo kicked him hard and sent him flying.

I don't know anything about martial arts, but even I could tell that Apollo, with his height and long legs, had the advantage. Murphy didn't even get close to him before a well-placed kick to his head, ribs, or stomach, knocked him down. It was amazing how both of them, Anna and Murphy, kept trying to get up, albeit slower each time. They really wanted this kill.

"Shit!" Mark said, and I followed his gaze.

Saunders had woken up and was picking up the gun. There was no way either of us could get to him first without risking injuries from our comrades but, when Saunders raised it and aimed at Apollo, Mark lunged and knocked down our giant friend. Saunders looked at me directly, smirked, and shifted his aim to Sammy. *Hell no!* I hurled myself forward and tackled Sam. Saunders fired, and the bullet grazed my shoulder as she and I went down. It lodged itself in the wall. Anna laughed and coughed hysterically as Saunders fired another shot. I heard a ping and Murphy screamed.

"What the fuck?" Saunders exclaimed. My cane hovered between us and the gun, spinning like an electric fan.

Jenny's cane was floating by the guys and spinning in the same manner. Murphy grabbed his bleeding leg and all sorts of obscenities gushed from his mouth. Saunders fired again, I heard the same ping, and, this time, Anna grabbed her arm and screamed. The spinning canes were deflecting the bullets and ricocheting them into our enemies! Saunders fired off a third shot and, this time, the gun miraculously (or magically) backfired as blood exploded from his hand. He grabbed it and clutched it to his chest.

I was still on top of Sam and she was not moving. I was afraid I'd killed her or knocked her unconscious, but her voice was muffled as she said,

"Jacky, look!"

I followed her gaze; there was a strange light trickling out from the bullet-hole in the wall. The hole grew bigger and soon the trickle became a cascade. As the light landed on the floor, it steamed upwards, and shapes formed. Little by little I recognized Paul, then Beth, Jenny, Jeff and finally, little Tommy. They looked transparent and flimsy, but I noticed that Beth and Paul each had one very real object in their hands: the rusty axes! Until now, I'd assumed they had lain under the furniture in the Funhouse.

Jenny placed herself above us, while Jeff did the same over the guys, and the words "keep you safe" rang throughout the house. Sammy was squirming to get out from under me, so I rolled onto my side. Mark had gotten off Apollo, but both were still lying on their stomachs. Anna began to scream hysterically as Beth moved towards her, ax raised above her head. She ran towards the opposite hallway, and Beth hurled the ax. I closed my eyes and only heard Anna's footsteps stop, and a thud on the floor. Murphy was trying to slither away, but Paul came slowly towards him. I felt a tap on my shoulder and saw little Tommy in my face. He looked into my eyes, then covered his own with his hands.

"Shut your eyes, Sammy," I whispered.

"Way ahead of ya, little brother," she answered.

Murphy's scream ended abruptly.

Saunders was still clutching his hand and had backed up against the railing. I felt Jenny's presence leave us as she moved towards him. She stood in front of him and raised her arm. At the same time, Saunders was lifted off the ground, he floated for a moment, and was thrust clear across to the opposite hallway and into the open door as Jenny pushed her arm forward.

Jeff did the same with Anna's and Murphy's bodies and the ghosts floated towards the door.

Apollo and Mark stood up, while Sammy raised herself onto her knees. Mark held her by the waist and lifted her up. Apollo draped my arm across his shoulders and pulled me up,

"I can't walk," I said, as Mark turned and draped my other arm around him, wincing a little as my forearm touched his injured shoulder.

His T-shirt sleeve was wet, and I noticed a thin string of blood oozing down his arm. Apollo's shirt was also sodden and sticking to his chest, and I assumed the gash had probably reopened when everybody had trampled over his unconscious body. Tommy was waiting in front of the open door and we slowly made our way towards him. Sammy held her broken arm tightly to her chest, even with the sling, and was slightly hunched. She limped a little and I noticed her sandaled feet were all torn up and bloody. She stepped in front of us into the narrow hallway; Mark let go of me and I held on to the railing.

Tommy came to us and took Sammy's hand. He led her to the open door and up the stairs.

It was difficult, we could only climb in single file, and I had to crawl up the narrow, steep stairs. The steps led to a small studio surrounded by windows. The view was breathtaking, you could see all of Osprey Cove. The guys held me up between them again and we limped toward a sliding door that led to the widow's walk.

I was surprised the sun was still shining brightly, it had seemed like the fight had lasted hours, but now I realized it had only taken a few minutes. The family was lined up on the walk, pointing down at the cliffs below. We came up beside them and looked. Three mangled bodies lay flattened on the rocks below. They had landed just shy of the pebble beach and onto the rocks that jutted out from the cliffs which hid the tunnel entrance from view.

"This is how you died, isn't it?" I said to Jenny, and she nodded.

Images flashed in my mind. David Saunders was walking up the stairs with a limp Jenny, in boots and snowflake sweater, swung over his shoulder. The hallways were covered with plastic, wooden planks, ladders and all manner of building material, that Saunders had to move and slide things around in order to make his way to the studio stairs. There, Jenny began to stir.

All I could see were these images, it was like a watching a movie surrounded by IMAX screens; and I knew that Jenny was showing me the last moments of her life. I wanted to ask her to stop, but it was too late. In my mind, she woke up just before Saunders flung her over the railing, and managed one long final scream. Her scream morphed into my sister's voice, Apollo and Mark's fingers were digging into my shoulders, and I realized they were seeing this too. Meanwhile, the images kept coming; David Murphy and Anna finding Jenny's body on the beach, both Davids placing her at the foot of the stairs, as Anna looked on, satisfied. Anna, pretending to cry and calling the police, while Murphy quietly slipped away.

Sam was crying openly and freely now, wailing like a banshee, instead of the quick, short sobs from before. Mark's hand covered his eyes and his shoulders were shaking, while Apollo's tears streamed down his face as he quietly looked at the floor. I felt like something stuck in my lungs and as I grunted to release it, tears gushed in thick streams from my eyes.

Jenny put her ghostly arms around me and I felt the same dewy sensation on my skin. Tommy let go of Sam's hand and embraced her legs, while Beth, passing through me (it was a strange, warm feeling, like having your soul embraced), floated to Apollo and wiped the tears from his face. Jeff and Paul had hovered to Mark and were quietly consoling him.

The ghosts then lined up on the widow's walk, directly above the fallen bodies. They'd stirred a warm, comforting breeze inside me, and my tears, anger, despair and sadness subsided. Apollo took a deep breath and passed his forearm over his eyes, Mark looked up and Sammy rubbed her nose.

Tommy still clung to Sammy's legs. He let go and joined his family. The family linked hands and together lifted their arms up, like a heavy metal band about to take the final bow. Almost immediately, and to my horror, a wave rose up from the ocean, so high that its crest reached the widow's walk and looked like it would engulf us all. I caught a look at a mildewed and rackety old boat riding the big wave, 'Malarkey' written on its side.

The wave reached its apex, paused, and, when the family lowered their arms, crashed down, without wetting the walk's railing. I heard a splintering of wood as the little boat crashed onto the rocks. When the water pulled back, the rocks were washed clean. The bodies, the axes, the gun, and the knife, all were gone.

The ghosts turned to us, then smiled and faded into the sunshine.

We stood for a moment in silence, basking in the heat and sun of the beautiful summer day. I hadn't realized the house had been cold until we'd come out here. Apollo smiled and closed his eyes as a soft breeze ruffled his hair. Mark was looking at Sammy and she was smiling at him. I breathed and told myself that whatever happened, or didn't happen, would be all right.

"I hate to be a joy-kill," I said when I realized that blood was dripping from my bandaged forearm onto the wooden railing, "but I think we need to go to the hospital. My ankle really hurts, I think my shoulder might need stitches and the wound on my arm reopened."

"Yeah," Mark placed his hand on his wound, "but how the fuck are we going to explain all this in the ER? I'm pretty sure they'll call the cops."

"You won't have to explain anything to anyone," a strange voice said behind us.

Abigail Babcock stood on the threshold of the sliding door with an unknown man beside her. She was panting and holding both the canes in her hands.

The man looked straight at us and said,

"I'm Rick Larson, Jenny's lawyer. Well, I'm your lawyer now. Is everyone all right?"

We nodded, and he continued, "Pluto just filled me in and this is how it's gonna go. Saunders is supposed to be on a Caribbean cruise and he simply won't return when he's supposed to. If the Osprey Cove Police want to search for him, that's their problem. Anna has not been seen in town since the death of her aunt, and I doubt anyone will be missing her. The Jenkins murders will remain unsolved in the eyes of the Peaceville police, and the official ruling on Jenny's death as accidental will stand."

We all looked at him wide-eyed, Sammy even had her mouth open. This man had *presence*. He was bug-eyed and chinless, and as skinny as Pluto was fat; but his stance and his voice made him seem impressive.

"Right now, you are all going to squeeze yourselves in my car and I am going to drive you down to the Osprey Cove Physicians. Doctors Susan and Michael Lansbury will attend to your medical needs. They, the Babcocks and myself are the only people still in Osprey Cove that knew and loved the Jenkinses, and we will help you in every way we can. None of us have ever believed Jenny had an accident."

"But," Sammy whispered, raising her hand like a schoolgirl, "what if the bodies wash up ashore? What about the other guy? Murphy, right? (She turned to us) It was him, right? He was the one that helped Anna murder in Peaceville, and I bet he's the one that tried to kill Tallulah. He's the only one that could've done it."

"Yeah, and we all told the Osprey Cove and Brunswick cops we saw Saunders," Apollo piped in.

Larson scrunched his face in a pensive expression,

"Hmm, that was just a case of mistaken identity," he said to Apollo, "you saw someone that resembled Saunders and thought it was him. We saw the wave from the gate, and there was something riding it, did any of you see what it was?"

"A boat," I said, "the Malarkey."

Larson grinned and mumbled that he wouldn't put it past them.

"The Malarkey," he explained, "was Jeff Jenkins's boat, which was lost during a violent storm not long after Jenny died. It was presumed sunken."

"And now it might seem, and could be thought, that Anna and an unknown companion were aboard it when it went down and no one knew," Mark spoke up, "although I seriously doubt those bodies will ever turn up again."

"Agreed," Larson looked at him, "now, shall we?"

On the way to the doctors, Larson explained how he had just returned the night before from visiting his grandchildren in Canada, only to learn that the Babcocks were in the hospital. He'd gone to see them that morning—we had probably even passed him as we left—and Pluto had told him everything. He had insisted on coming to the house right away, and Abigail had offered to come along and introduce us.

He said they knew something was amiss because the house seemed unusually dark, and as they'd gotten out of the car, they saw the wave rise up behind the house.

We were ushered into the clinic through a side door, and brought to two adjoining examination rooms. The doctors closed the doors and had already pulled down the shades, probably as soon as Larson had called them on our way to the car.

They were husband and wife, both about Babcock's age and very soft-spoken and kind. Sammy and I were attended by Doctor Susan in one room, while Doctor Michael attended Mark and Apollo in the other.

Doctor Susan told us about how much she'd loved Jenny and Paul, and about how her husband had grown up with them. They'd made her welcome when he'd brought her home the first time, and then, as a new bride, the Jenkinses had cheerfully opened their door to her, and had never closed it. Her eyes welled up when she explained how she and Doctor Michael hadn't been able to perform Jenny's autopsy, as they had been away for Christmas.

"Evidence," she said, voice quivering, "we would've found evidence that it wasn't an accident, I'm sure of it."

"Did you talk to the doctor who did perform it?" Sammy asked.

Doctor Susan shook her head and repeated what Babcock had told me ages ago; the man had died before they could talk, and, soon after that, the investigation had been closed.

"That's the only time I've ever regretted taking a long trip, but you see, my mother was ill—my husband's the Ossie, I'm from Pennsylvania —and it was our last Christmas together, so we stayed away longer. We rushed back when Pluto called. I went to two funerals in a week, my mother's and my best friend's."

She cleaned the bullet wound on my shoulder, and I winced.

"All better now, this is only a minor cut that will need a few stitches, nothing more," she said, and shushed us when we started to describe what had happened.

"All you need to tell me is whether Anna or Saunders are ever coming back."

"No," I looked her in the eye, "they are never coming back."

She breathed and looked relieved; her elderly, sunken eyes lit up a little and she looked ten years younger.

"Don't worry, this town won't miss Saunders much, he was more feared than respected; and if anyone from outside gets curious, they're probably going to find a lot of shady dealings on his part, starting with how most of the older residents have suddenly moved out of their family's houses, or died under suspicious circumstances. You know about the old Chief of Police and his Alzheimer's? Well, the new Chief practically wees in his pants whenever he sees Saunders. Yeah," she smiled, "this town is better off without him."

CHAPTER EIGHTEEN

The Neat Little Bow

It's been almost two months now since the standoff between The Good, The Bad and The Dead, and Sammy is still here, though she's set to leave next week. The principal at her school called a few days after The Showdown to let her know that the School Board had chosen someone else for the position she'd been a candidate for. As always, she took it in stride, and I was more angered than she.

"It's okay, Jacky-Boo," she'd said when I'd expressed my frustration, "I would've had a lot more administrative responsibilities and frankly, I don't think I really want that just now."

The hauntings at the Funhouse have stopped and the pungent scent of rust is gone. It smells like a home now; it's My House; although I've sometimes seen little Tommy playing in my office or running in the yard. I'm not scared anymore, and I even enjoy his presence.

Apollo and Mark went back to work that same week, their excuse: car accident. Apollo's boss had called him in to reprimand him about his absence and all Apollo had had to do was show his bandaged and bruised chest for the man to back off. Tallulah returned to a much concerned Lupe, who nearly bit our heads off for not keeping her in the loop. The Babcocks were home, recovering; and Mike Monroe had his father's cane back.

Rick Larson had gone over the new will—a new door had mysteriously appeared under the stairs, and the tunnel was still as hidden as ever, only now everyone knew about it—and, since Jenny had signed and dated the will before she died, it was deemed legally valid.

Our casts have come off and Sammy's bruises have healed. Her lips were scarred, but not destroyed, and Doctor Susan said the scar would fade in time. Sam shrugged her shoulders and smiled. My arm would have a permanent scar, as would Apollo's chest and Mark's shoulder, but they were battle scars, so we were cool with that. My sternum healed and the doctors said my lungs have recovered entirely, although I still feel out of breath when I walk up the street that leads towards The Falcon Grove Cemetery; Mr. Wheatcroft's grave is the first one by the gate, his epitaph proudly displays his greatest accomplishment, the book   *Innocent, Evil*. Jenny is not buried there; as Babcock said, she was cremated, and no one knows what Anna did with her ashes.

Now about the will; Sammy's box was full of gold bars. No kidding! There was even a certificate of ownership titled to John Hiram Jenkins, our ancestor who'd gone to the Klondike Gold Rush. Amelia was right, his life read like a movie and Jenny had found mountains of information on him from journals, diaries, newspapers and letters he'd sent to his sisters, but more about that later.

My box was full of securities, dating as far back as John Hiram. The man had been a business genius and invested in The New York Gas Light Company, which later bought the Edison Illuminating Company and became Con Edison, one of the largest investor-owned companies in the country. He'd also invested in the Coca-Cola Company and his children had purchased World War II War Bonds, and all those titles and certificates were in that box. Larson is helping me claim them, and I've wondered why Jenny never claimed them for herself.

Larson told me that she'd only approached him about changing her will the year she died, so it's possible she only found out after the Peaceville murders. He thinks that was the reason Anna killed her. That Jenny had discovered the inheritance and Anna wanted it all.

I didn't want to get my hopes up and Larson had said it would take some time to figure everything out. Luckily, all of Jenny's ancestors, including John Hiram, had left wills, and the house and its belongings had been legally passed down from one direct heir to another. Sam and I were the only ones who had received John Hiram's inheritance without being direct descendants. We were, however, his sister's direct descendants and Jenny's heirs, so Larson said the courts should not have any objections. Still, Sammy and I weren't financially out of the woods yet.

"Ay Yack," Lupe had said when I'd told her my concerns, "eet ees going to be okay, joo'll see. *Dios aprieta, pero no ahorca* —emm, how joo say?—God squeezes, but does not choke." She'd come up to Osprey Cove to look at the tunnel, and said she thought the tunnel was built at the same time as the house, probably as a sort of cellar or storage, perhaps for seafood; but she couldn't be sure.

Sam and I have been staying at Jenny's house for the last couple of weeks, going over everything and working directly with Larson on the inheritance claim. The house still looks as if time has stopped and nothing is deteriorated, but now, everything can be moved, the TV plays the current programming and we had to open a new electric contract.

I think Jenny still works her magic on it, Sammy has heard her singing in the backyard, and I've seen her sitting on one of the living room chairs on occasion. I suppose that even if a ghost's unfinished business is done, they can still come back and visit.

Anna Jenkins left many unanswered questions behind. Why did she kill? How did she meet the Davids, and at what point did they realize they all loved to kill? I mean, it's gotta be some kind of macabre game that fate played, right? Three murderous kids, all from the same area, two cousins even...how the hell did they even get together? Where did they hide? How many more people have died at their hands? How did they all manage to get away with murder so easily?

"That's something we'll never know, Jack," Tallulah had said, as we'd all sat in Lupe's living room, relating everything.

Sammy thought Anna might have met David Saunders through David Murphy, and that they just kept leaving trails of fear behind.

We did find out that Kevin Murphy, the doctor who had performed Jenny's autopsy, was David Murphy's much older brother; and we suspect David Saunders was Detective William Sanders's son. He and Murphy were related, they said so, and we know Murphy's mother was the detective's sister. It's possible that by adding one letter to his last name, Saunders gave himself a whole new identity.

I can't imagine what the Murphy and Sanders households must have been like. Were they all living in fear? Did they all wonder when they would die at the hands of their kids? Was there some sort of mental disease in the family?

"Does it matter?" Apollo had asked me, "Who cares? They're dead, and only they know the answer to those questions. Why bother with them? Let go, Jack, it's all behind us."

Jenny had done very extensive research on her family and, like the librarian she was, had kept everything perfectly well organized. There were letters, journals, diaries, newspapers, you name it, she'd found it.

Apparently, people like Anna ran in the family. Her ancestor, Mary Anne Jenkins had been widowed three times and all three husbands had died under suspicious circumstances, but Mary Anne had never been arrested or tried for any crimes. She too had died suspiciously; her body had been found floating on Peregrine Falcon Beach. The town had not been too concerned about looking into her death—although her daughter Annette had been questioned—and it seemed like she hadn't been badly missed.

Annette had married a rich young man from Chicago, and Jenny had found out that the man had died in his sleep, not long after the wedding. They didn't have children, and, although Annette had inherited everything, she never remarried. She'd been regarded as a pariah in her husband's society, and the in-laws had never allowed her to leave the family estate. She'd died two years after her husband, at the age of twenty-four. Apparently, she'd fallen asleep with a candle lit, the room had caught fire, and no one had been able to rescue her. The fire had been contained to her side of the estate, and no other person had been hurt.

John Hiram Jenkins had left Osprey Cove and sought his own fortune after a fallout with Mary Anne, who had schemed and connived to separate him from his other sister, Samantha Maria, recently married and moved away. He'd made his way west with nothing but the clothes on his back. When the Klondike Gold Rush began, John Hiram and his close friend, Patrick Monroe, packed their belongings and headed to the Yukon.

As John Hiram described it, they struck gold almost by accident, when Patrick Monroe claimed he had dreamed that two fire-breathing lizards had shown him a piece of land next to a stream, whose currents were forked by a rock shaped like the head of a bear.

When they had come upon this parcel, they'd pooled their money and bought the claim, which turned out to be replete with gold. To commemorate the findings, they'd had two canes custom made, one of black wood and the other of red wood, both with winding dragons.

I showed Jenny's cane and John Hiram's journal to Mike Monroe. He laughed and said his father had always talked about gold running in the family. His grandfather had been rich once, but they had lost most of their fortune during the Great Depression. Here was proof, I'd said to him, his grandfather hadn't been lying.

"I suppose my ancestah wasn't as savvy as yours, kid. I'm happy for ya, and I'm glad it's ovah. Have ya noticed how the sun shines on the street an' ovah yer house now? That's all because of ya, kid. Thank you. An' don' be a strangeah."

We'd been having dinner once a week and he'd often come over for a beer on my deck. He's come up to Osprey Cove for a few days since we've been staying here.

Anyway, when John Hiram returned he'd found his sister Mary Anne dead and no record of his other sister's whereabouts. He discovered the murderous Mary Anne had falsified a death certificate under his name in order to keep the house, which had been abandoned since her death.

He'd come back a rich man and through some legal proceedings had managed to reclaim the estate. He had never been able to find Samantha Maria—our direct ancestor—so the family was irrevocably sundered, until Jenny began her investigation in the '90s.

I think that was probably when she found the tunnel, which had been lost and forgotten since John Hiram's time. He may have been the last person to know about it, and I think that's where he had hidden Sammy's gold and the papers belonging to him. That's why nobody knew about it. I believe Jenny found the World War II bonds somewhere else in the house and later hid them all together.

Our parents returned to Maryland, and Sammy and I had spent a good five hours on the phone with them. When we told them everything that happened, Mom cried and Dad berated us for not telling him the extent of Sam's attack. Apparently, she'd made it seem like a burglar had broken in and had been scared off when he'd seen her. We asked them if they knew about the relatives and Mom "kinda remembered receiving a strange message on the answering machine many years ago," but she'd thought it was just advertising. Besides, she'd said, Grandpa was the only one interested in the family tree. He had just nodded and shrugged when he'd heard the message. Since Grandpa had never brought it up again, she'd put it out of her mind.

Mark and Sammy are not in a romantic relationship; but I see the looks, and the smiles, and I believe that maybe someday, the memory of that one kiss will change Sammy's mind and heart and they'll end up together. In my opinion, any relationship they might have will probably go down like the Hindenburg, but, like Apollo says, that's all up to them.

Tallulah once told me that I should be grateful for all the good and all the bad that happened in my life. That I should thank the people that brought light and love into it, as well as those that brought darkness and pain. I'd scoffed at the thought then, but now, I think she might be right.

Anna Jenkins wreaked havoc on this earth, but her evil and darkness brought me close to people like never before. When I'd once been the Lonely Man in the Last Homely House, I was now like the Great Gatsby, the host of a never-ending party. People passed through my houses every day; Apollo, Mark, Tallulah, Lupe, Mike Monroe, the Babcocks, Rick

Larson, Drs. Lansbury and even the ghosts of Jenny and Tommy. Even Fugly Gabby visited last week.

Now that everything's been wrapped up in a neat little bow, this story does not end with us sipping Mai-Tais in Hawaii. Instead, Sam, Apollo, Mark and I are sitting side by side on the widow's walk, our feet up on the railing, sipping Spotted Harrier Lager straight from the bottles.

THE END

Made in the USA
Columbia, SC
20 August 2019